Praise for Bonnie Bluh

The Old Speak Out

"Thrilling, just shimmering with life and hope. I feel as if I had travelled all those miles with Bonnie Bluh, and wish I had. So many vivid, life-affirming portraits! And her own arguments and conclusions are so mind-opening and important. Bonnie Bluh writes with clarity, conviction and compassion."
  —*Elizabeth Forsythe Hailey*
    author of "A Woman of Independent Means"

"This extraordinary confrontation between one gutsy woman and a lot of other people amounts to so much more than a series of interviews. It's the reader's introduction to his country, his society, and to himself. ...The depth of feeling in every page was evidenced by the trouble I had putting the book down and the trepidation with which I picked it up again. This isn't a one-gulp read...rewarding beyond anything else of this nature I've read in years."
  —*Jan De Vries, The Philadelphia Bulletin*

"Ms. Bluh's moving series of interviews with men and women, aged 65 to 106 gives us a closer relationship with the elderly."
  —*Elsie Robinson, Houston Chronicle*

Banana

"Joanna Banana's high velocity monologue is raucous, dirty-truthful and chortlingly funny. She's the lady inside all of us, waiting to get out and take our piece of the action."
  —*Elizabeth Pomada, San Francisco Chronicle*

"This is a novel with a raised consciousness, a mature, intelligent novel of real talent and excitement."
  —*Publishers Weekly*

'What makes *Banana* exceptional and fascinating is its inventiveness, its verve, originality, its sometimes sheer madness, its rage. Preposterousness and eccentricity woven into the mundane, the result as colorful and variegated as a Peruvian scarf..the most scintillating dialogue I've come across in a long time."
  —*Linda Schor, Ms. Magazine*

"A 'torrent of consciousness' sweeping before it all the modern jargon and confused issues of today...includes a cast of sixteen people. This reviewer groaned when she saw them listed on the jacket, but couldn't lay the book down after starting, having practically to prop her eyes open with fingers, to finish reading at 3 am."
  —*Budicki, Voice News*

Woman to Woman

"Rarely has the print media lent itself to such a high level of consciousness raising...*Woman to Woman* may be the first book on honest politics."
  —*Kit Kennedy, Majority Report*

"It is a beautiful, intense, informative, and moving story."
  —*Women's Guide to Books*

"Interesting and enlightening...By its warm, personal and probing nature, *Woman to Woman* does much to reaffirm the existence of an international sisterhood of women."
  —*Karen Lindsey, Boston Herald American*

"...reactions of one committed American feminist to her sisters abroad."
  —*Mary Pradt Ziegler, Library Journal*

"There isn't one page of this book that any female cannot see as part of her own life. It touches the soul."
  —*Regina Axelrod, Ph.D.*
  Chair, Political Science Dept. Adelphi

Books by Bonnie Bluh
Woman to Woman
Banana
The Old Speak Out

Plays
And Never To Touch
N, My Name is Nicki
The Day God Died

Coming in 1999
Strangers In A Strange Land

THE
ELEANOR
ROOSEVELT
GIRLS

Bonnie Bluh

LYRE BIRD BOOKS
a paperback original

This is a work of fiction. The characters and events are all fictional.

Book and cover design by Craig Lowy Design.

Library of Congress Cataloging-in-Publication Data

Bluh, Bonnie.

The Eleanor Roosevelt Girls / Bonnie Bluh

ISBN 0-9664820-1-8

Library of Congress Catalog Card Number 98-066696

Printed in the United States of America

THANK YOU

For a studio deep in the woods where I wrote much of this book, I wish to thank the Virginia Center for the Creative Arts.

To Olga Cabral, lovely poet and friend, gone but never forgotten, for her encouragement and invaluable suggestions.

To Sabina Nordoff, kindred spirit, forever inspiring.

To Mort Cohen for his music, his friendship and his loving support.

To Craig Lowy for his friendship, his designs, his wonderfully inventive ideas and his unfailing good humor.

To my family for always being there – Craig, Kenn, Brian, Karen –and especially, my mother.

For
the original
Eleanor Roosevelt Girls

And for
Shawn-Alexandra
and
Mariah

❧

the new generation

THE
ELEANOR
ROOSEVELT
GIRLS

What one has to do
usually can be done.

MALLORY 1937

Looking back it's clear my life began when I was seven, the
year my family moved from the Bronx to Sunnyside, land of bigots
and Jew haters, land of bars and ugly squat three story buildings.
And land of Mallory.
Mrs. Brady stands in front of the blackboard, her arm around a
girl. –Class, I want you to welcome our new student, Mallory
Grossman.– Mallory squints at us, a look that says don't start up
with me. Don't even try. A Jewish star hangs from her neck. I'm so
happy I could scream. I am no longer the only Jew in class. During
recess I rush to her. She eyes me suspiciously. I'm Jewish too I say.
Then from nowhere a smile that guarantees my undying love.
Everything about Mallory is special; her name, her curly black
hair, her enormous brown eyes, the way she talks. She's the smartest
kid in class, the most beautiful, the best in sports. And she's my best
friend.
It is 1937. The Nazi party is growing in Germany. The German
Bund is growing in America. Both hate Jews. And in Sunnyside
Mallory and I become the only Jewish girls in a Jewish gang. The
boys make us the lookout for the kids from St. Theresa's whose main
hobby is beating us up. Mallory has other plans. We're going to fight
just like the boys. I can't I say. She gives me her *look* and tells me to
hit them in the bread basket. To pinch and bite and pull their hair.
And kick. Don't forget kicking. But the best place to get boys is

between their legs. You just grab their pecker and pull. It kills them.
Girls you sock in the arms.

Bread basket? Pecker?

—I used to hit them in their chest but my aunt Ceil said I
shouldn't do it. She says it could stunt their boobies growth.—

—Boobies?—

She points to her nonexistent breasts and yells. —Don't you
know anything! Boobies. Here.— She takes a deep breath, all the time
looking at me as if I were hopeless. Which I probably am.

Mallory knows everything. She's been reading since she's four.
She tells me the reason the Catholic kids beat us up is because they
think we killed Jesus. Which is a lie. It was the Romans and she can
prove it. She takes a book off the library shelf and reads it to me. The
librarian stands over us, telling us we don't belong in the adult
library, that the children's library is downstairs. Mallory hates being
told what to do. She continues reading. The librarian's soft voice
takes on a menacing tone. I shrink. Mallory stares. —This is a public
library and we don't have to leave unless we want to.—

When we do leave Mallory gives the librarian her famous *drop
dead* look followed by her loud laugh. Mallory always has to have
the last word.

In the five and dime she buys broken pieces of chocolate which
she shares with me. We go to the Bliss Street theater because we
know the ticket taker, Mr. Jeremy, will let us in for free. We sit
through the double feature twice. The third time round my mother is
standing in the aisle next to the matron in white motioning me with
that *wait til you get home* look. I leave. Mallory stays. Nobody cares
if Mallory comes home or not.

Mallory lives in a house with her grandparents and her mother.
Her father died when she was six. I never go there. She says it's
because her grandmother is very sick but I think it's because Mallory's
mother doesn't like me. When Mallory and her mother walk on
Greenpoint Avenue Mallory smiles at me while her mother grabs her
arm and pulls her, looking straight ahead as if I were invisible.

Mallory is always getting in trouble. Once the monitor watched us while Mallory was taken by Mrs. Brady to the principal's office. Her mother was summoned. Mallory was absent for days after that. When she returned her arms were bruised, her face swollen. —I had a fight with a kid,— she told us. Annie asked who. Mallory tightened her mouth and said nothing. After school I asked her why she had to go to the principal's office.

—I was caught playing with myself.—

My face was on fire. I looked down at the sidewalk. *Dirty Jew* was written in white chalk. I began erasing with the soles of my shoes. Mallory erased with me.

—My aunt Ceil says I shouldn't feel bad because it's natural but I should do it in private.—

—Did you really have a fight with a kid?—

She stared at me. —You calling me a liar?—

I stared back. If you stare hard enough it stops tears from falling. Neither of us is crying.

Mallory's hidden tears are suddenly replaced with joy when I tell her my birthday is next week. —Julia, we're the same sign.—

—What's a sign?—

—Astrological. We're Aries. Aries are strong and wonderful.— She grabbed both my hands and we turned and turned. —We're strong and wonderful.—

—I'm going to have a party Mallory and you're invited.—

—I'm not having one. My grandma's sick. She's not supposed to have any excitement.—

—What's wrong with her?—

—I don't know. They won't tell me.—

—Mallory, where do you play with yourself?—

—Boy are you dumb.—

Mallory oh Mallory. Lying under the stairs, touching one another, rubbing each other until that lovely warmth and quiver envelops our bodies. Oh the sweetness of it. The innocence.

Walking into the five and dime, buying broken pieces of chocolate, holding hands, feeling the wetness between my legs, looking over at Mallory, my mouth full of chocolate. The prettiest girl, the smartest, the most unafraid. My friend. Always my friend.

Til death do us part.

1994

Here is Mallory's new machine message.

–This is Mallory Grossman. I can't pick up now. (laughter) Actually I won't be able to pick up later either. Where I'm going there aren't any telephones or computers that say have a nice day. (more laughter) Where I'm going we are all angels peeing on the dopes below. (now she's singing) So when you hear it thunder don't run under a tree. There'll be peeing from heaven, it's me...me...me.–

This is her note.

Julia, I know this is going to come as a shock. I wanted to tell you but couldn't. I leave you everything, my furniture, my jewelry, my tchotchkas. Don't go to antique dealers or second hand stores. They'll only rip you off. What you don't sell throw out unless Sandy wants it. Which I doubt. Think of it Julia. No more diets. No more sleepless nights. No more worrying about cancer or strokes or heart attacks. No more body pains from exercising. No more spending hours choosing the right clothes. What a joke! People stopped noticing me years ago. No more worrying about cholesterol. My last meal will be full of fat and sugar and booze and wine. I'm going to spend a fortune on that meal and then walk into that beautiful Montauk sea until it swallows me.

No funeral Julia. What's the point of burying an empty box. I want a party in Montauk. I'm leaving a list of people for you to invite. If Montauk turns out to be too complicated, would you have it in your apartment? Mine as you know is a mess.

There it is Julia. The pittance of old age. I ran out of youth. I ran out of health. I ran out of work or should that be pushed. It seems I ran out of everything including lovers. And friends. Except for you Julia. You were always the best friend I ever had. Buy champagne and please put out a glass for me like we did for Elijah on Passover and don't be surprised if it's empty at the end of the evening. You know me Julia. Forever the lush.

I love you. Mallory.

You love me? You love me! You don't know the meaning of the word. Where do you get off leaving me instructions? A party! Shopping for food. Being pleasant to people I can't stand. And your guest list Mallory. The Eleanor Roosevelt Girls. How do you expect me to find them? I haven't seen them in twenty seven years. I doubt if I'd know them if I fell over them. Howard! I wouldn't give that bastard the right time. And Ron! That shit. And who are these people whose names I do not know? Also, would you tell me how you could even think of inviting Ilya?

Of course I could ignore your last wishes and your guest list. You'd never know. I could take the money and give it to some charity. Or keep it. I think I will.

You want a party. Make it yourself.

MALLORY BECOMES AN ORPHAN 1938

Mallory didn't come to my birthday party. Her mother died the day I turned eight. She was out of school for a week. Everybody knew her mother had died but nobody knew what to say. Your mother dying was the worst thing that could happen to you. During recess a group of girls surrounded Mallory, all of us tongue tied, our arms dangling at our sides. Then Annie started crying and Cleo and Margaret. Suddenly we were all crying. All except Mallory. How brave I thought. How very brave.

We walked home together. —I'm an orphan,— she said. —I'm the only orphan I've ever known. I don't know where I'm going to live. I might move, Julia.—

—Don't say that. I'll die if you move.—

—My grandpa wants me to keep living with him but everybody says he's too old. Besides he's got his hands full taking care of my grandma. And my aunts are all too young. Did you know that Millie is twelve. She's only four years older than me. But Ceil is twenty five so she could be my guardian. That would be great. Of course they could put me in an orphanage.—

—Don't say that.—

—My mother didn't love me.—

—She did too. All mothers love their children.—

—Yours doesn't. She's mean to you. She says awful things.—

I clench my fists, staring hard.

—My mother used to love me before my father died. She was so nice and then she changed. Remember when I was caught playing with myself. She could have said I don't believe you to that awful principal but she didn't. And when we got home she gave me the worst beating. She never ever hit me before. My grandpa came in and said Sylvia, what are you doing to the child. Are you crazy or what! And she said what about me. Doesn't anybody care about me. Then my grandpa took me out for an ice cream soda and he explained how hard her life was since my father died and how much she loved him. When we got home she went right to me and put her arms around me. She said she was sorry, she didn't know what had gotten into her. But I didn't cry. Not one tear. And I didn't cry at her funeral either. Everybody kept watching, waiting for me to cry but I didn't.—

MALLORY'S FLEA MARKET 1994

Mallory's apartment. She's kept everything she ever had and if that isn't bad enough she prowled the streets looking for treasures. Once she found a ring that was worth thousands of dollars. You've got to look she tells me over and over again. The trouble with you Julia is you don't look.

I'm looking Mallory. I'm looking. At pins and rings and watches and necklaces, at dishes and glasses, candle holders, napkin holders, old magazines, old programs from theaters, concert halls, operas; first edition books, paperback books, tattered books. The walls are lined with paintings and posters. Her shelves hold silver, gold, brass, pottery, little containers. Porcelain figurines, dogs, cats, all kinds of animals. Dolls from every nation tumble from her bedroom closet.

I open a drawer. There's a Mickey Mouse watch, a Dick Tracy watch, an Orphan Annie Ovaltine mug, games we used to play. A Shirley Temple doll sits on top of the dresser. Another doll leans against her. I touch the doll and hear *mama mama*. If I give her some water she'll probably pee all over Shirley.

What am I going to do with all this crap I ask the room. The wallpapered flowers nod. Why ask us?

MALLORY IS ADOPTED 1939

Mallory moved in with her five aunts a month after her mother died. Her aunt Ceil became her legal guardian. When Mallory was nine Ceil made her a birthday party. All her aunts were there; Millie, now 13, Tessie 15, Esther 19, Ruth 22 and Ceil 26. One was more glamorous than the other, even 13 year old Millie.

I'd never seen such wonderful food. Cold cuts and even ham which Jews don't usually eat and a paté. I never ate that before. Potato salad and cole slaw and all kinds of pickles and olives.

Mallory's birthday cake was made with real whipped cream, not that sweet sugary stuff that looks like it. Her aunts gave her the most beautiful red coat with a fur collar. And a skirt and blouse and pearls. Her friends gave her books and games, all except Cynthia whose father was a clothing manufacturer. Cynthia brought a paisley skirt and a blouse with a lace collar. Lynn brought *Roget's Thesaurus*. None of us knew what a thesaurus was except for Lynn and Mallory who screamed with delight.

At Mallory's ninth birthday I realized that everybody knows more than me. My mother's daily *stupid* is true. I am stupid.

THE ELEANOR ROOSEVELT GIRLS 1942

When we're eleven Mallory and I are separated. She goes into the Rapids, a special program where they put bright kids like Cynthia and Lynn. I stay behind with the rest of the dopes. The following year Mallory decides to form a club so we can be friends forever. It's then that we discover Lynn isn't twelve like the rest of us but ten. She's been skipping classes all along and will graduate high school before she's fifteen. We're all impressed.

Mallory, a great admirer of Eleanor Roosevelt insists our club should be named the Eleanor Roosevelt Girls. Lynn says she likes it. I say nothing. Cleo wants us to be called the Amelia Earhart Club.

Annie chimes in. —Why don't we call ourselves the Blissettes?—

—The Blissettes?—

—Don't you get it? The subway station is Bliss Street and the *ette* is like the *ette* in the Rockettes.—

—How about the Girls of Sunnyside?—

—Margaret, we are going to name our club after someone who will inspire us.—

—My mother says Eleanor Roosevelt is a communist.—

—What's a communist?— Margaret asks.

–A communist is a person who's against America.–

Margaret looks at Cleo. –Is that true?–

Cleo nods.

–That's awful,– Annie says.

–She can't be against America. She's President Roosevelt's wife.–

–They only call her a communist because she speaks up for poor people and workers so they can have a better life,– Lynn says.

–She has to. Don't you know she was forced to do good deeds when he got polio?–

–What!– Mallory screams. –She was fighting for social change long before he got polio, even before she married him.–

–So! Amelia Earhart gave up social work to become a pilot.–

–I knew that Cleo.–

–Oh you know everything Mallory and what you don't know Lynn knows.–

–This is getting silly,– I say.

–You can't compare them. Eleanor Roosevelt is a suffragette.–

–What's that?– Annie asks.

–A suffragette fights for women's rights.–

–We have rights, don't we?–

Mallory gives Margaret one of her famous looks and groans.

–Just because you like her Mallory doesn't mean she's the best.–

–I'll bet you didn't know that Eleanor Roosevelt and Amelia Earhart were friends.–

Cleo's face turns beet red. –I'll bet you didn't know that I did know.–

–And did you know that Eleanor Roosevelt flew with her and they were both wearing evening gowns?–

–So what?–

–She served hot dogs to the King and Queen of England. Isn't that great!–

Mallory stares at me, shakes her head in disbelief.

–I have it,– Annie says.

–We don't want the Blissettes.–

–The Sunnyside Starlets?–

–She only fights for women because the President tells her to.–

–That's not true Cleo. She was a suffragette before she met Roosevelt. She even gave a speech to the Democratic convention before he was nominated. Do you want to know what she said? She said that if women ever expected equality they'd have to work with men, not for them.–

–Listen Mallory, Eleanor Roosevelt isn't the only one who fights for women...–

–She's a great woman Cleo. Why can't you admit it?–

–Ok Lynn, she's great. But Amelia Earhart is a hero. She's the only woman who flew across the Atlantic so I vote for Amelia Earhart.–

–Me too,– Margaret says.

–I'm for Eleanor Roosevelt,– Lynn says.

–That's two for each. Julia?–

–Eleanor Roosevelt. She's for women and so am I.–

–Oh sure. Why don't you admit it? If Mallory wanted to call our club the Silly Willies you'd vote for it.–

–And how about Margaret, Cleo? She always agrees with you.–

–Well it looks like Annie has the final vote,– Lynn says.

–Not if she votes for Amelia Earhart. Then it would be a tie.–

–Couldn't we flip a coin?–

–No Annie, we can't. Now think. Why do we have a club?–

–I don't know.–

–Yes you do. It's because we're friends. Now do you want to know what Eleanor had to say about friendship when she was fourteen? She said that the greatest women are those who are loyal and honest and believe in friendship to the end.–

–Mallory, you made that up.–

–Cleo, I did not.–

We are now officially the Eleanor Roosevelt Girls. We meet once a week, usually at Lynn's. We love her mother, her Scottish brogue, her wonderful refreshments. There's loose tea made in a teapot, scones with jam and butter. Our parents have tea that comes in bags. We've never had scones before or cloth napkins unless it's a holiday. We never met a Scottish Jew before. We didn't even know there were such people.

Sometimes we meet at Mallory's, sometimes at Annie's. Nobody wants to go to Cleo's where her father sits around in an undershirt refusing to leave. Margaret has eight brothers and sisters so that's out. We have a meeting at my apartment. My mother and father take the opportunity to tell my friends what a disappointment I am, how stupid and sloppy. Sloppy is a big crime in my home. I sit saying nothing. Nobody suggests coming there again.

We're all starting puberty. Well some of us got there early. We're all starting to sprout breasts, everybody except me. I know because at one meeting we took off our blouses and compared them. Mine were humiliatingly flat. We're just starting to notice boys, everyone except Margaret who's going to be a nun. We're just starting to have that dreamy eyed look. All except me. Mine as my mother says is just plain stupid. All of us have our period except for Cleo and Margaret. Even ten and a half year old Lynn who teases them. —Maybe it's because you're such good friends that neither one of you will get it without the other.—

We're all going to have great careers and get married and have children except for Margaret. The dreamy eyed look we get over boys Margaret gets when she talks about being a nun. She breathes double time just at the thought of it.

—Did you know pigeons are also called nuns?—

—Mallory, did you just make that up?—

—Look it up if you don't believe me.—

While Lynn gets her dictionary Annie says she could never be a nun. —I want to be a teacher but my mother says good Catholic girls stay home and take care of their children. I was thinking of going to Hunter College although I'd love Vassar but my parents could never afford that. Anyhow it wouldn't be right to take up space in college when I'm not planning to use the education. That's what my brothers say.–

–Your brothers! Your mother! It's your life, not theirs and you know what, you're right Mallory. Pigeons are called nuns.–

–Maybe I agree with my family and I never heard a pigeon called a nun.–

–Well I know what I'm going to be. A pilot.–

Lynn laughs. –Like Amelia Earhart?–

–That isn't the only reason I wanted our club to be named after her.–

–Have you ever been in a plane?–

–No Mallory but so what.–

–So nothing. I just asked.–

–You never told me you wanted to be a pilot.–

–I never told anyone before, Margaret.–

–Cleo, your parents would never approve. They'd have a conniption fit.–

–I've made up my mind. I'm going to leave home right after I graduate from high school.–

–But how will you pay for your rent or food or...–

–I'll think of something. How about you Julia?–

–I don't know.–

–Of course you know. You're going to be a famous writer and I'm going to be the most fabulous fashion designer in the entire world and Lynn's going to be a great dancer.–

–My mother says I went on point before I could walk. I was four when I had my first dance class. Our teacher smelled like fresh lilacs. She handed us these long chiffon scarves. Mine was red like fire. Be free she said, let the mood take you and there we were a bunch of kids running around the room our scarves flying in the air and in that moment I knew I would devote the rest of my life to dancing.–

Lynn's mother is divorced. Mallory's parents are dead. We've never met Margaret's parents so we know nothing about them. The rest of us have parents who fight except for Annie's. I even saw them kiss once. When I ask my mother why she and my father never kiss she gives me a lecture on germs. You don't eat off somebody else's plate and you don't kiss them on the mouth unless you want to get their germs.

Mine is a germfree home.

GOD'S LIGHTHOUSE AND SANDY 1994

I leave Mallory's apartment and walk along Hudson Street. The air is cool and sweet. City trees are turning gold and orange, red and rust. Suddenly I'm glad to be alive. Then I think of Mallory. Stupid I say out loud, stupid. My mother's words are coming from my mouth.

In front of God's Lighthouse people are lining up for the free breakfast. I'm embarrassed walking past them. Ashamed. I am alive. I eat. I have a place to sleep.

Not long ago Mallory and I walked past a homeless woman. That could be me I told Mallory.

–Don't be silly Julia. That will never be you.–

–How do you know? Remember that woman I told you about, the woman in the East Village? She never thought she'd be begging. She had an apartment, a job, health insurance, the works. And what happens? She gets a heart attack. She has a bypass. She's sick longer than expected. She's fired. Her insurance is dropped. She can't pay her rent. It couldn't happen? It does happen.–

–Then you'd go on welfare.–

–I'd die first.–

–No you wouldn't.–

–Are you telling me you'd go on welfare?–

–Yes. I would.–

–You're full of shit Mallory.–

–I certainly wouldn't kill myself. I wouldn't give up one sunset. I wouldn't give up one day of my life.–

I'm at the corner holding back my tears when I hear, –Julia, Julia. It's Sandy.–

Sandy! I haven't seen her in years. We move toward one another, then stop.

–I just came from mother's thinking I could take care of her belongings. The super said you have the only set of keys. Lucky I saw you.–

–Lucky you recognized me.–

–You haven't changed that much.–

–I don't think I would have known you.–

–Don't tell me. I know. I got fat. Julia, I'd like to have a set of keys so I can get started sorting things out.–

–It's ok Sandy. Mallory asked me to do it.–

–When did she do that?–

–She left me a note.–

–I know this is going to sound stupid but what did she die of? Was it the cancer?–

–No.–

–Then what?–

–She...she...–

–What? She what?–

–She took her life.–

–I don't believe you.–

–Look Sandy, you can come by anytime and take whatever you want.–

–Thanks Julia. That's very generous of you.–

–Sandy, I know you're upset.–

–Upset! Why would I be upset. I read about my mother's death in the obituary page. Do you know what that feels like? No, how could you? She left you a note. I don't suppose there was a note for me.–

I say nothing.

–So much for mother love.–

–You know she loved you.–

–If it isn't too much trouble, would you mind telling me about the funeral arrangements? The newspaper didn't say.–

–She doesn't want a funeral. She wants a party in Montauk.–

–Did you happen to notice if I was mentioned in her note?–

–Yes, of course.–

–You're a liar just like her. I suppose she told you I hardly ever saw her. I didn't but it wasn't my fault. She didn't want to see me.–

–That's not true and you know it.–

–You're so like her it's pathetic. But then the two of you were always so tight. I can imagine what she said about me. Then again she never did have a good word for anyone except you so why should I complain. Well tight friend, why did she kill herself?–

–I don't know.–

–Really! I guess that means you didn't know her as well as you thought. Daddy always thought you were lovers.–

–Why are you so angry with me? I know you feel terrible and I'm sorry I...–

–Terrible? You think I feel terrible? What I feel is relief. No more expectations, no more wanting what I never had and never would have. She didn't like me but I'm sure you know that.–

–Sandy, we used to be so close. We were...–

–You never even called.–

–How could I call? I don't know your married name.–

–You could have contacted my father. There's plenty of things you could have done if you'd wanted to.–

–Sandy, do you think we could go somewhere and talk?–

–I'd appreciate a copy of her will. I'm sure you have that too or perhaps you could tell me her lawyer's name?–

–I don't know who her lawyer is.–

–And the will?–

–Sure,– I say wondering how I'll find it in all that mess.

–As for the party, here is my card. Call me if it isn't too much trouble. I'll even bake a cake.–

–Sandy, don't be like that.–

She hails a cab, gets in quickly without looking at me.

On Jane Street I burst out crying.

A DREAM AND AN INTERRUPTION 1994

Mallory and I are running through the streets of Sunnyside. Golden lights of winter make patterns on the brick walls. Look she says. I lived here. You know about my aunts don't you? Why is she telling me what I already know. She pulls me into the White Castle. Sit she says. Sit.

I don't eat hamburgers anymore Mallory. You know that.

So what? They're free. Hamburger please she tells the white uniformed counter man. She takes the burger and walks outside.

Is it good? I ask. What does it taste like?

Come off it Julia. You've eaten plenty of hamburgers in your day.

My day? What does that mean, my day?

It was the name of Eleanor Roosevelt's column. Don't you remember? *My Day*.

Who said that? I turn.

Annie? Is that you Annie?

I saw you coming down the street and I said that's a Julia walk if ever I saw one. Would you have recognized me?

Sure I say but it's a lie. She's gotten matronly. She's become an old lady. All that grey hair.

Mallory I say. It's Annie. But Mallory has vanished along with her hamburger.

Do you still live in Sunnyside, Annie?

Of course.

It's such an ugly place.

Maybe I like ugly. Did you ever think of that?

A loud banging stops my dream before it's finished, before I know how it ends. There's a note under my door.

Julia, we've been trying to reach you by phone. We were, as you can imagine, quite upset over Mallory's death. We want to do a feature story about her since she was the editor of *Elegante* the last five years. Would you write it? You were, after all, her best friend and a writer we all respect. Please call as soon as possible.
All the best, Nina Black.

I rip up the note and go back to bed.
My message comes over my machine, then David's voice.
—Mom, it's David. I just heard. Why didn't you call?—
I pick up the receiver. —How are you David?—
—The question is how are you?—
—I'm ok.—
—You don't sound ok.—
—You woke me up.—
—Woke you up! It's two in the afternoon. Why are you sleeping at two in the afternoon?—
—David, I'm hanging up.—
—When am I going to see you?—
—I don't know.—
—How about tomorrow? Is tomorrow alright?—
—Sure.—
—How about tonight?—
—Whatever you want.—
—Meet me at Gus's eight o'clock. Alright?—
—Yeah. Alright.—

DAVID 1994

I loved him on sight. He had to be pulled from me. His father said he looked like he'd been in an alley fight but to me he looked beautiful. And still does.

I talk about Mallory, her note, the note from Nina Black, meeting Sandy unexpectedly. —Imagine Sandy telling me that Mallory never had a good word to say about anyone.—

—Well, she was rather critical.—

—She was wonderful.—

—From what you say, Sandy didn't think she was wonderful. You yourself said...—

—Don't throw what I said in my face. In what way wasn't she wonderful?—

—She gave Sandy up. That's a hard thing for a kid to live with.—

—She did not give her up.—

—That's your opinion.—

—It is not my opinion. It's a fact. And what about your brother. Did I give him up?—

—In a way, yes.—

—Why? Because I didn't applaud his joining *Jews for Jesus?*—

—You said some pretty nasty things.—

—While he was all sweetness and light.—

—Just because you don't approve of somebody's life style doesn't mean...—

—Listen, I am not going to sit here and get indigestion over your lousy brother and your distorted view of Mallory.—

—Oh so now it's my distorted view.—

—The truth is you never liked her.—

—She was cold mom. Nobody entered her life.—

—I entered her life. If I knew you were going to pull this crap I'd never have agreed to have dinner with you. I feel bad enough.—

—You asked me in what way wasn't she wonderful. I gave you my honest opinion, something you taught me and now...—

–You are insulting my best friend, my dead best friend. I don't need that kind of honesty. I could say plenty about your ex–wife but do I? No. Because you wouldn't appreciate my honesty any more than I appreciate yours.–
 –I thought you liked her.–
 –I did.– I take a sip of wine.
–Why are we arguing? This is so silly.–
My eyes fill with tears. –It's true. You never did like Mallory.–
–You're wrong. It's just that I never understood how the two of you were friends.–
 –Really! Sandy said we were two of a kind.–
We sit silently while our food is placed before us.
 –Have you told grandma?–
 –Not yet. She's going to be shocked.–
 –I'm sure she will.–
 –What's happening with you David?–
 –The same old story. Work work and more work.–
 –Are you writing at all?–
 –I'm too busy earning a living.–
 –Even if you write an hour a day...–
 –Julia, it's not as important to me as it is to you. There are other things in life.–
 –Like what?–
 –Like living Julia.–
Without warning all my stored tears pour out. –There's a hole in my heart.–
 –She had cancer mom.–
 –She was cured.–
 –You don't know that for sure.–
 –I said she was cured.–
 –When is the funeral?–
 –There isn't going to be any. She wants a party in Montauk.–
 –Sounds good to me.–
 –Her list is ridiculous. I don't know half the people. And the

Eleanor Roosevelt Girls. That was our club when we were kids. How am I going to find them? I don't even know their last names.–

–How come?–

–How come? Because they're women. They took their husband's names like dopes. We were all dopes then.–

–You didn't take dad's name.–

–Well you know me. Riding ahead of the pack, my banner waving high in the breeze. A lot of good that did me.–

LYNN GETS SOUL KISSED 1943

Cynthia, who is Lynn's best friend joins the Eleanor Roosevelt Girls. Tall and beautiful like Lynn she is a teen model. Our discussions about ourselves our dreams our futures changes overnight. Suddenly it's boys boys boys. Who is cute, who is disgusting. How far will we go. I have the worst crush on Junior who lives on the next block. Sometimes, like a sleuth from a mystery novel I follow him. Sometimes I sit on a stoop waiting for him to pass by. I'm always prepared with my most bored look in case he looks over at me. None of us has ever kissed a boy until today when Lynn tells us she has. Leave it to eleven year old Lynn to be the first.

We're all talking at once when Cynthia's mother pokes her head in the door. –I don't mean to interrupt. I just want you girls to know that refreshments were laid out by the maid.–

Laid out. The maid!

Cynthia is the only one who lives in a house and has a maid who lives there too.

The door closes. We jump on Lynn. –What was it like?–

–It depends on who kisses whom. Boys don't know how to kiss. They spit all over you.–

Annie squeals. –You mean you did it with a girl?–

–Not a girl stupid. A man.–

–She's making it all up,– Cleo says.

–Who was it?– Annie asks.

Lynn's neck grows at least five inches. –My ballet teacher's husband. Well I think he's her husband.–

Cleo. –Your ballet teacher's husband! How disgusting.–

–What happened?– we ask. –Tell us.–

She looks from one to the other. Her eyes land on Margaret. –Well, only if you insist.–

We all yell we insist except for Margaret and Cleo.

–He rubbed his mouth against mine and then he sucked my lips.–

–He sucked your lips?–

–Precisely.–

–And then?– Annie asks.

–Then he put his hands on my breasts. Well actually he rubbed his hands on them.–

–Was he mad when he discovered you don't have any?– Mallory teases.

–She's flat as a pancake.–

–I am not flat. Julia's flat.–

–Thanks Lynn.–

–Don't mention it Julia.–

–Lynn get on with it. What was it like?–

–Great Mallory. It was great.–

Margaret gasps. –You're awful. You really are.–

Lynn dances around the room. She's on point, she does her turns. Every movement is graceful and then suddenly her dancing becomes wild and dramatic. –That's Katherine Dunham. I saw her at the Martin Beck on Sunday. She is a primitive genius.– She turns to Margaret. –My nipples got hard like rocks. It was quite interesting.–

–Didn't you say anything?– Annie asks.

–First I gave him my famous icy stare and then I said I am not interested in men. That's why I'm studying dance with your wife. I am going to devote my life to dancing. And he said how admirable and put my nipple in his mouth.–

    –You let him?– Annie gasps.

    –What could I do? I couldn't scream. My teacher was in the next room.–

    Margaret grabs her coat. –If that's what...if that's what...– She opens the door and slams it shut.

    Mallory. –I don't think Margaret is coming back.–

    Cynthia. –Who wants a nun in the group anyhow.–

    Cleo.   –You know how this kind of talk upsets her.–

    Cynthia. –I don't know why. Kissing and petting is perfectly natural.–

    Annie.   –It may be natural but it's not what decent girls do and boys who do it to you will never marry you.–

    Mallory. –Marry! Who wants to marry. I'm with Lynn. I'm never going to marry.

    Annie.   –Don't you want to have children?–

    Mallory. –No. I don't even like children.–

    Me.   –How old is he Lynn?–

    Lynn.   –Probably twenty five or thirty.–

    Cynthia. –Did you let him go all the way?–

    I'm just about to ask what all the way is when Lynn yells, –Do you think I'm crazy?–

    Cleo stands at the door, her coat and muffler in hand. –Lynn, everytime you open your mouth a lie comes out. You lie all the time just so you can get attention. Honestly, I pity you.–

    Annie moves out of her chair as the door closes. –I have to go too.–

    –What do you mean go? We haven't had refreshments yet.–

    –Sorry Cynthia.–

    –What's wrong with Annie?–

    –I think she's uncomfortable when we talk about sex.–

    –Well it doesn't matter. Everyone likes Annie. But Cleo and Margaret, why are they in our club? They're so...–

    –Repressed.– Leave it to Lynn to find the perfect word.

–Yes, repressed. They're different from us.–

–This is your first meeting Cynthia and you're already criticizing our members. How would you like it if you left and we criticized you?–

–This is my home. Remember.–

–What's your point Cynthia? Do you want to vote them out?–

–I couldn't do that. That would be mean.–

–What you're saying is mean.–

–Julia, you're taking it all wrong. All I meant was...–

–It doesn't matter. They're going to leave on their own.–

–You think so Lynn?–

–Definitely.–

Mallory turns to her. –Now that the repressed ones are gone tell us the truth, the whole truth and nothing but the truth without your pirouettes and dramatic pauses.–

–Julia won't like it.–

–Are you serious? Julia knows more than all of us put together.– She puts her arm around me.

Now I won't be able to ask what all the way means.

Lynn looks at me, dying to see my reaction no doubt. I am determined to look stone faced no matter what. –He didn't just suck my lips, he put his tongue in my mouth. I swear he was down to my tonsils. And wait til you hear this...–

Don't let me gasp or yell or do anything stupid.

–...He didn't just rub my breasts, he sucked my nipples. Julia, that was the weirdest feeling.–

I'm going to pass out.

–What do you mean weird? Was it good weird or bad weird?–

–Great weird Mallory, great. Of course it will never happen again. I could lose my scholarship. What if my teacher found out? They're married, well I think they're married. Besides I don't ever want to fall in love or have babies. Once a dancer has babies she's finished.–

–Well I think men stink.–

–Didn't I tell you Julia wouldn't like it?–

Mallory hugs me. –I agree with Julia. I think they stink too.–

–Well I don't. My father is a lot nicer to me than my mother. It depends on the man. Don't you agree Lynn?–

–Absolutely Cyn. Absolutely.–

Margaret and Cleo leave as predicted. Claire, who was in Annie's class became our newest member. She was short and fat with deep dimples in her cheeks like her four other sisters. They lived behind the laundry their parents owned and operated. Claire's parents were always working. When we went there our snacks were whatever we could find in the refrigerator. Chunks of salami, sour pickles, herring, farmers cheese. The food was strictly delicatessen and we all loved it. And Claire with her deep dimples and great smile.

ANNIE FINDS ME 1994

–Annie. Oh Annie. It's so wonderful to hear your voice. How long has it been?–

–Too long Julia.–

–How did you get my number?–

–You're in the book.–

–Have you been in New York all this time?–

–Yes. You?–

–No. I guess you heard.–

–How could I not. It was in the *New York Times*, on every newscast. I was devastated. How are you doing Julia?–

Her words bring on a flood of tears. My voice is immediately nasal. –I'm doing lousy.–

–I can imagine.–

–Do you know she left me a note with instructions.–

—That sounds like Mallory.—

—She wants a party and I have to locate all the Eleanor Roosevelt Girls. Would you believe?—

—Well you know where you are and you know where I am and I know where Lynn is and Lynn knows where Cynthia is. That's about half of us. Are you free tonight?—

—Sure. Since I turned sixty I'm always free.—

—You're sixty! Funny. I'm sixty four.—

We sit in a Japanese restaurant drinking sake, waiting for our food to come. She isn't matronly. She doesn't look anything like the woman in my dream. She's thin. Her hair is white and gorgeous. Her skin is young and lovely. She could be fifty.

—I had a dream about you.—

She laughs. —Was it a wet dream?—

—Annie! What would Tim say?—

—Tim! I divorced him twenty years ago. Are you married?—

—Not anymore.—

—What do you do Julia?—

—I've published four books.—

—You're a publisher. Great.—

—I'm not a publisher. Four of my books were published.—

—Well, you always were a writer.—

—But you didn't know about my books.—

—Don't take it so personally. I'm not a reader. I never was unless they're mystery stories. If you were a mystery writer I'd know all about you. Anyhow, weren't you a playwright? I still remember when they did your play in P.S. 150. How old were you? Seven?—

—I don't remember you in the second grade.—

—I was the kid who wet her pants.—

—And I was the child prodigy who couldn't make the Rapids. What do you do Annie besides not read?—

She bursts out laughing. —Character.—

—Well. What?—

–I'm a detective. One of New York's finest.–

–No kidding. I am impressed which is more than you were when you heard about me.–

–I am impressed. I'll even buy your books. Ok? Now tell me about Mallory. What happened? Was she sick? The media didn't say.–

–She committed suicide.– The burning behind my eyes releases itself. I motion to the waiter, point to the sake. –I talked about killing myself and she talked about sunsets and gargoyles. I wouldn't give up one sunset she said. She sucked me in with her lies. She always could. I never knew the woman. Never. For all I know she's alive somewhere looking at some fucking sunset.–

–She's dead Julia.–

–Why? Because the *New York Times* said so. You're the detective. How can you be sure someone's dead if you don't have a body?–

–The ocean's a big place.–

–I'm so glad you told me. I would never have known.– I down my second sake.

–God, you're angry.–

–You bet I'm angry.–

–At Mallory or just in general?–

–At everything, every damned thing in this rotten world.–

–What's new. It's never been great.–

–You've changed Annie.–

–So have you. When the hell did you get so bitter?–

–Is Lynn in New York?–

–No. She's in Philadelphia teaching dance.–

–Doesn't she dance anymore?–

–She's over sixty like the rest of us.–

–No. She's younger.–

–She's sixty two.–

–How did glamorous Lynn ever get to be sixty two? What does she look like? No, don't tell me. I don't want to know.–

–She's still beautiful.–

–She's probably had a facelift.–

–She hasn't.–

–Mallory did. She didn't like the results.–

–If you get into that shit you have to pay the consequences.–

–I thought she looked good.–

–What's looking good. Looking younger? Is that it?–

–You look good Annie.–

–Because I'm happy. I enjoy life despite this uncaring violent world.–

–Did Lynn ever marry?–

–No. She was true to her word.–

–I have two sons.–

–Well well. Surprise.–

–Does Cynthia still live on the west coast?–

–Yes.–

–And nothing ever happened.–

–Nothing.–

–It really is amazing when you think of it.–

–You'd be shocked at how many unsolved crimes there are. It happens more than people know.–

–One of our shining hours.–

–It's hard to believe we were so naive.–

–And got away with it. Do you think Cynthia will come to Mallory's life celebration?–

–I don't see why not.–

–That leaves Bettina, Cleo, Margaret and of course Claire.–

–Well we could always call the Pope for Margaret.– We laugh. –Don't worry. I'm not a detective for nothing. If anyone can find them I can. Are you with anyone Julia?–

–No. You?–

–Yes. I'm with Tommie.–

–Is he nice?–

–Yes. She's great.–

IN THE OLD DAYS WE KEPT OUR MOUTHS SHUT 1943

When I'm thirteen I learn that people who like you are going to like you no matter what. And if they don't, you can stand on your head and they still won't. But I'm only thirteen and I want the entire world to love me.

Cynthia's mother stands at the door flashing her plastic smile. She has a real smile but it's never for me. I've brought her sick daughter's homework so she won't fall behind in school. This was given to me by Lynn, Cynthia's best friend, who can't find the time to bring it herself. I've walked out of my way in the freezing cold and I'm about to subject myself to Cynthia's germs but none of this impresses Cynthia's mother. She doesn't even say thank you, just a frozen why don't you go up to Cynthia's room and give it to her. I run up the steps to the second floor planning to surprise Cynthia. I quietly open the door to her bedroom. She is lying on the bed, her father bent over her. I tiptoe in. There's a giggle in my throat. I am invisible. I'm just about to yell surprise but the word stops midway in my throat. I don't believe what I'm seeing. Cynthia's father is fondling Cynthia's bare breasts. Cynthia, suddenly aware of my presence quickly covers herself up. Her eyes fill with tears, then close. The tears are dew drops in the corner of her eyes. Her father looks at me defiantly. I drop Cynthia's homework on the bed and run out of the room.

I am thirteen. I know how babies are born. God comes to you when you're sleeping and blesses you. But Cynthia's father had his hands on her breasts. What does that mean?

She has breasts I tell Mallory. Big ones. So Mallory says, not everyone is flat like you. But her father had his hands on her breasts. Mallory looks at me squinty eyed. —Don't be silly. He's her father. Why would he do that?—

—I don't know but he did.—

—You're sure.—

—Yes I'm sure. I'm more than sure. I'm positive.—

–That's so weird.–

–What's weird?– Ceil stands next to us. –Well what's weird?–

–Tell her Julia.–

We sit and talk for a long time. Ceil decides it's best we don't say anything because if we do it will be a terrible embarrassment for Cynthia and think of her mother. –The poor woman probably doesn't know what's happening. Why harm her?–

–But it's wrong.–

–Julia, sweetheart, maybe he was rubbing her chest with Vicks.–

–It was her breasts. I know what I saw.–

–Well let's wait. If Cynthia says something...–

–But Ceil what if he goes all the way.–

What the heck does all the way mean I want to ask. Instead I say –Right. He wouldn't do that.–

I'm upset. Ceil calls my mother and asks if I can have dinner there. I'm sure she'll say no the way she always does but this time she says yes. For the first time I have wine with dinner and roast beef bought at Fruchter's. With gravy on white bread with the crusts cut off. We never have white bread at my house. There's canned peas and carrots, canned creamed corn. For dessert we have apple pie from the Bliss Street Bakery. All Mallory's aunts talk at once. One is more interesting than the other.

After dinner Mallory asks Ceil if we can go window shopping on Greenpoint Avenue. Only for an hour Ceil says. I don't tell her I'm not allowed to go out after dark. Window shopping on Greenpoint Avenue. I'm so excited I have difficulty breathing the cold night air. Everything is so incredibly beautiful. Everything is lit up, the stores, the street lamps that shine on the snow, the car headlights that grow as they come toward us.

Mallory and I stand at Silver's windows. I love the mannequins' painted faces, their painted hair, their pencil thin eyebrows and tiny red lips, their small rounded breasts without nipples. Cynthia has enormous nipples. I look at the display of clothing. –Isn't it beautiful Mallory? Isn't it just beautiful?–

–Beautiful? Sunnyside is in the dark ages. You should see the windows at Saks Fifth Avenue or Bendels or B. Altmans. Stunning, absolutely stunning.– Only Lynn and Mallory say words like stunning. She turns to the window. –See this black suit. If they'd used a simple gold choker instead of those chunky pearls and took off those ridiculous cuffs...–

Mallory knows everything about clothing. Nobody in Sunnyside dresses like Mallory, not even Cynthia or Lynn. Ceil, who's a salesgirl at Saks Fifth Avenue, chooses all her clothing from the designer copy department. A man looks at Mallory as he walks by. She doesn't notice. Everybody looks at Mallory. She's that beautiful.

–You could be a salesgirl like Ceil.–

–A salesgirl! Don't be ridiculous. Maybe I'll design clothes. Then again I might be a writer or an actress. And you Julia, everybody knows you're going to be a famous writer like George Eliot.–

–Oh, I don't know.–

–But you write all the time.–

I shrug.

–Well, you'd better know. You can't get what you want if you don't know what it is you want.–

I want to be most of the things Mallory wants to be but I can't say it. Mallory walks like she owns the street. I move gingerly as if the sidewalk is doing me a favor letting me be there. And if I feel like that on Greenpoint Avenue how am I going to feel on glamorous Fifth Avenue where I've been only once? Mallory lives in an apartment with five gorgeous aunts eating exotic foods, even out of cans. There are no cans in my home. Mallory drinks wine with dinner. We have soda and only when we have company. Mallory's in the Rapids with the bright students. I'm Julia the dreamer, inventing stories and never getting anything in school above a C. Mallory's home is full of interesting discussions. Mine is full of fights.

We stop in front of the Sunnyside Theater. Joel McCrea looks at us from his shiny photograph. Mallory moans. –Isn't he gorgeous? I was sick when he married Frances Dee. I even dreamed of him once and when I woke up my bed was wet. Millie had a fit. She screamed so everyone on the block could hear. –Mallory wet the bed. Mallory wet the bed.– Ceil asked what the fuss was about and when 'the girls' told her she was furious with them. Then she took me aside and asked what happened and when I told her she put her arm around me. You had an orgasm darling. And then she explained what it was. –It's fantastic Julia, just fantastic.–

Everyone looks at Mallory. Nobody sees me. No wonder. Mallory wears clothes seen only in fashion magazines. I have ugly ones picked out by my mother. Mallory sleeps peacefully in her own bedroom next to Joel McCrea. I sleep in a room with my brother. The thin wall next to my bed connects with my parent's wall. They're always yelling. I'd love to wet the bed like Mallory and have an orgasm, whatever that is, but I know if I did I'd never hear the end of it.

It's 1943. Boys are fighting in a war against Germany. And on August 13th Eleanor Roosevelt writes in her column *My Day* that the Jews in Europe have suffered as no other group and hopes we can do something to save them, to find them homes.

Mallory and I talk about this. What does it mean?

A Movie Star Joins the Eleanor Roosevelt Girls 1944

Cynthia comes to the weekly meetings as if nothing happened. At fourteen she's five foot nine, pencil thin and striking. She's a model in her father's dress manufacturing loft and is the envy of the entire club. Except me.

Lynn continues her dance classes. Mallory works in Silver's on Greenpoint Avenue. Claire helps out in her family laundry. Annie and I baby sit.

Bettina Lacy is our latest member. Born in Muncie, Indiana, her family moved to Hollywood when Bettina was offered a movie contract. All our lives pale next to hers. She's our age but has bleached blond hair which she curls every night. She wears makeup, mascara on her blond lashes. She lives with her mother and father in a two family house. On Sundays they eat dinner in a diner in Brooklyn. I have never even been to a diner. Afterwards they go to one of the beautiful Brooklyn movie houses with chandeliers and stage shows.

The first time we meet at her house we are greeted by her parents. Her mother is fat and dumpy, her father young and gorgeous. They tell us they're going to the Merry-Go-Round Bar on Queens Boulevard, then in unison say, don't do anything we wouldn't do. Bettina's father opens the door with one hand, grabs her mother's behind with the other. He winks at us. Bettina's mother's laughter moves from one side of the door to the other.

At that meeting I notice for the first time how close Cynthia, Mallory and Lynn have become. The three tallest, the three prettiest, the three smartest. Obviously Mallory was unaffected by what I saw at Cynthia's. Annie and Claire have been close since Claire joined the club. Nobody chooses me or Bettina. But Bettina has an excuse. She just joined.

Bettina and I walk to school together. We do our homework together. We have afternoon snacks together, always at her house. Her mother gets a kick out of me. –So you're Jewish,– she says. –I would never have guessed it. Where did you get your red hair?–

Like I'm the only Jew with red hair.

Bettina spends all her spare time reading movie magazines, cutting out pictures of her favorite movie stars. She pastes them on her bedroom wall. Deanna Durbin, Linda Darnell, Judy Garland, the Lane sisters. –I know them all,– she tells me. When I ask why she stopped acting in movies she says she reached that awkward age and her mother thought it best she quit for a while. It never dawns on me that everyone else who reached that awkward age is still in Hollywood. But Bettina hasn't really quit. She's been accepted by the Performing Arts High School. –One year to go,– she says.

Then what. I won't have a friend in the world.

LAKE OSCAWANA, THE SUMMER OF '44

I am going to the country because Bettina refuses to go unless I go. Bettina has lounging pajamas. My mother buys me lounging pajamas. Bettina has a pink bathing suit with white trimming. My mother buys me a blue bathing suit with white trimming. I am going to spend two whole weeks away from my fighting parents, my nerd brother and the Eleanor Roosevelt Girls who ignore me anyhow.

Lake Oscawana is beautiful. We sleep to the lap lapping of the water. We roast marshmallows and hot dogs in the fireplace. We go to the clubhouse and dance with boys. We swim and dream. My two weeks up, Bettina informs her mother that if I go back to Sunnyside she's going with me. I end up spending the entire summer there.

Sitting in a row boat in the middle of the lake Bettina explains the reason I'm staying is Jerry.

Jerry!

—He can't keep his hands off me.—

—Who's Jerry?—

—The man my mother lives with.—

—Lives with? Aren't they married?—

Her laugh is what she calls her Hollywood laugh. Right on cue. You have to be able to do it she confides or you won't get work. Laugh when they tell you, cry in seconds. That's the way it is. —My father left us when I was two. I don't even know what he looks like. You know Jerry is twenty years younger than my mother.—

—He is?—

—Yes. He's thirty five.—

—Your mother's fifty five?—

—Yes.—

—She was over forty when she had you?—

—Yop. She looks great for her age, don't you think. Nobody ever guesses it. Promise you won't tell anybody what I'm about to tell you. Cross your heart and hope to die.—

—Jews don't cross their hearts.—

–So what. Do it. My mother locks me in my room at night.–

–Why?–

–Otherwise he tries to come in.–

–What if you have to go to the bathroom?–

–She leaves a commode for me.–

–How awful. Why does she stay with him?–

–He pays the bills Julia. You can't live unless somebody pays the bills. That's basic.–

–Can't your mother work?–

–Doing what? She's never worked. She can't even type.–

At Lake Oscawana I discover boys like me. At first I think they're just being nice because of Bettina who's almost as beautiful as Mallory but in a showy way. But no. They like me for me. You're so cute Matt tells me.

Well cute isn't as good as beautiful but it's better than nothing.

–Of course you're cute,– Bettina's mother tells me. –With that curly red hair and those freckles. But if I was your mother I'd put you on a diet.–

–Really!–

She tells me I'm fat. –Bettina is five foot six and she only weighs one hundred and five. How tall are you?–

–I don't know exactly. I'm still growing.–

She puts Bettina and me back to back, then pushes my head down. –You're short aren't you. I'd say you're five foot two.–

–No, I'm taller than that. My mother is five three and I'm taller than her.–

–Maybe you're five three. What do you weigh?– I shrug. She puts me on the bathroom scale. –One hundred and thirteen. Oh my. You have to lose at least ten pounds.–

–Really!–

She laughs. –Yes really. Oh Julia, you are so naive for your age.–

–I am!–

–Yes. Now I don't want you to take this the wrong way but do not, under any circumstances, let the Jewish boys go all the way.–

Jewish?

–I am really very open minded but Jewish boys are Jewish boys and you know what that means. They think they can get away with murder and we mustn't let them.–

Later on I ask Bettina, what murder, what going all the way. –What is your mother talking about?–

–What she's saying is that it's ok to pet but it's not a good idea to let them go all the way.–

–What's all the way?–

–You don't know. You really don't know?– Bettina's laugh is not her Hollywood laugh. It's loud and real. Phyllis Lacy enters. –What are you two laughing about? Bettina tell me. I want to laugh too.–

–She doesn't know what all the way means.–

–Don't be silly Bettina. Of course she does.–

–Well ask her then, go ahead, ask her.–

–I do too know.–

–You do not Julia. Admit it.–

That night Phyllis Lacy sits with me and explains intercourse. My face is on fire. No wonder my mother is so mean to my father. Who wants to do that? I thank her for her disgusting report leaving out the word disgusting but that's not the end of it. Phyllis Lacy now sits on the sofa facing us, her lips smiling, her legs apart. Under her skirt is nothing but flesh. I can see everything. The more I try not to look the more she spreads her legs. I hate her. I hate Bettina. I even hate Lake Oscawana.

I am trapped. If I stay I have Phyllis Lacy to contend with. If I leave I have hot sweaty New York, no place to go, nothing to do, my battling parents and my brother who now masturbates under the cover knowing I hear everything in the next bed.

A SOHO PARTY 1994

I am standing in the middle of an enormous Soho loft filled with
large paintings done by the owner, the party giver. His lover I am
told is a male stripper. Everybody is designer jeaned, well almost
everybody. Everybody is young and good looking. What am I doing
here standing around in Mallory's clothes. Why aren't I home
among my old photographs and shitty memories, gorging myself on
the broken chocolate of my childhood.

David who invited me shows me around the loft. –Not bad huh.
Let me introduce you to Theo.– He leads me to a tall dark man who's
deep in conversation with a man and woman, waits for an opening.

–Theo, remember I told you about Julia.–

–Julia. Oh right. And what do you do Julia?–

–Julia's a writer, remember?–

–Oh right. Sorry. Early senility. So David, are you still painting
scenery?–

–I do graphics Theo.–

–Right. Well, help yourself to some food,– he says moving on,
the woman trailing behind. The man smiles.

–Hello. I'm Richard.–

–I'm Julia and this is...–

–David. I'm David.–

–Have you known Theo a long time?–

–Not really. I work with one of his friends. You?–

–No.– He looks over at me.

–Never saw him before.–

–Can I get you some wine Julia?–

–That would be nice.– He walks toward the bar, turns around.
–What color?–

–Red.–

David grins. –I know when I'm not wanted.–

–Oh sure.–

–He didn't ask me what I wanted.–

–David, he's not much older than you.–

–So.–

–It's Merlot,– Richard says handing her the wine. –I hope that's alright.–

–It's fine.–

–Excuse me,– David says. –I think I see a friend of mine.–

–I hope I didn't chase him away.–

–Don't be silly.–

–Did you come together?–

–I came alone.–

–I'm glad.–

A woman rushes over. –Richard. Am I glad to see you.–

–Doris, this is Julia.–

–Richard, I have to talk to you. I tried getting you on the phone but all I got was your damned machine. Are you avoiding me?– She pulls him to the other side of the room. David is next to me. –That was fast. What happened?–

–Doris needs to speak to him, whoever Doris is. Everybody is so damned young here.–

–Let's dance. Comeon Julia.–

We move to the loud music. I watch David klutz along. Once I thought I'd have a daughter. She was going to be a dancer. Well, once I thought I'd be famous, happy, loved, that time would never move. And I'm not famous or happy or loved and the daughters never came, just two sons, one who loves me I think and one who once did but not anymore. Richard smiles at me across the room, his head cocked as if he's intently listening to Doris. David and I leave the dance floor for a drink.

–I wonder who started the glass clicking.–

–It was a Scandinavian.–

–No it wasn't. It was a Russian.–

–Really! Are you sure?–

I laugh. –I don't know.–

–It's good to see you laugh.–

–Thanks for inviting me David. I forget everything when I dance.–

–Then you should dance more often.–

–Yeah. Like the clubs are filled with women my age.–

–Stop harping on your age. You dance like a kid.–

–I wish. He's really adorable.–

–Who?–

–Richard.–

–So go for it.–

–I can just see myself calling you three years from now. Hi David. It's me. Remember that cute guy, that young cute guy, the one you said I should go for. Well surprise I did and I now have AIDS.–

–Use protection.–

–Would you go with someone my age?–

–Mom, I'm me.–

–Right. Let's dance.–

–I can't. I have a deadline. Why don't you stay?–

–Can't you stay a little longer?–

–I promised the job for Monday.–

We're half out the door when Richard comes toward us. –You're not leaving so soon.–

–I told her to stay.–

–I wish you would Julia, I mean if it's alright with David.–

David has an amused look on his face. –It's fine with me. We're not going the same way anyhow. She loves to dance.– He looks at Richard. –You do dance don't you?–

–Of course.–

–Great. See you around Julia.–

–Cute David.–

–I'm always cute, you know that.– He closes the door behind him.

–You're sure you didn't come with him?–

–Positive.–

–Then let's dance.–

The clock on the wall says 1:30. The loft thins out. –I didn't realize it was so late.–

–As they say time flies when you're having a good time. I hope you had a good time.–

–I did. You're a good dancer.–

–Thanks.–

–And for your information time flies whether you're having a good time or not.–

–Does it? I never noticed.–

–That's because you're young.–

–I'm not as young as you think.–

–Maybe you are. Anyhow young or old, everybody's trapped in time.–

–Are your next words going to be, you'll find out.– He laughs.

–Something like that and therein lies the tragedy.–

–Why would that be a tragedy?–

–Because when you're thirty you're trapped in a thirty year old's time and when you finally grow old enough to see it's too late.–

He grins at me. –Now that sounds like a tragedy. Can I give you a lift? My car's parked just around the corner.–

–That would be great.–

–I have a better idea. How would you like to go for a drive?–

–Where?–

–Where we can see the stars. Do you have any ideas?–

–I like the stars in Montauk.–

–Montauk! We wouldn't get there for hours. Everything would be closed.–

–The sky wouldn't be closed, the sea wouldn't be closed, the sand wouldn't be closed.–

–Do you drive Julia?–

–Yes.–

–Good. Give me five minutes. I'm going to get us some warm

sweaters and some food.–

–Where?–

–I live up the block.– He unlocks the car, ushers me in. –I'll be right back and by the way I haven't seen thirty for years.–

–I wasn't talking about you.–

–Really! You could have fooled me.–

I watch him through the driver's mirror.

Cute ass. And he's bright.

I sit in the locked car waiting for him to return.

MONTAUK 1994

He brought scotch, wine, cheese, fruit and bread, a few cans of sardines. In case I hadn't eaten. I hadn't and neither had he. He brought a blanket so we could picnic by the sea. He brought warm sweaters for the two of us.

We listened to tapes as we drove on the Long Island Expressway. Keeping awake music he called it. He said he preferred classical music but it made him sleepy when he was driving. Soon after that he asked if I would mind taking over the wheel. He fell asleep almost immediately. I played the same tape over and over again because I didn't want to fiddle with the tape deck. I parked the car on Ditch Plain Road. He was in a tight sleep and didn't hear me turn off the engine or the silencing of the music. I opened a window, breathed in the damp night air, then closed it. I took one of the sweaters from the back seat, looked at him. He was amazingly good looking.

I walked along the sea wall. Remembering. Mallory 1983. I'd sublet a small house in Montauk that winter so I could finish my novel. I'd been writing long hours except for walks on the dunes when suddenly the words stopped. I called Mallory, asked her to come for the weekend.

The day she arrived was dark and rainy. We talked and talked, watching the rain beat against the windows. At sundown the rain stopped. A double rainbow came out of the sea, green and purple, red and orange. We went outside. Golden lights settled on houses, the sky was inked in shades of blue. We ran along the sea until we were out of breath. Then plopped on the wet sand watching the sandpipers do their nervous little dance, the seagulls dipping and diving for food. Clouds swooped down swallowing most of the rainbow. Mallory and I looked at one another happily. She took my hand, kissed it and said with such tenderness I love you Julia.

I sit on the sand watching the sea breathe. Why did I suggest Montauk? What was I thinking? Mallory died here. It was a night like this. Beautiful and still. She called Montauk her spiritual home. Maybe that's where you're meant to die, in your spiritual home. Oh look she said our first time here. She'd picked up a beautiful rock with an orange circle inside. Take it Julia. It will be your life rock and bring you marvelous luck. Her voice so vivid I could feel her standing over me but when I looked up it was Richard. He asked why I didn't wake him.

—You were sleeping so peacefully. No, that's a lie. I wanted to be alone.—

—Are you alright?—

—What?— I say and burst out crying. He put his hand on my shoulder.

Mallory, I'll never see you again, never be able to talk with you, never hear you say I love you Julia. There's a hole in my heart that will never heal.

We sit on the sand eating food, watching the stars fade. We finish a bottle of wine, then walk along the sea's edge. He tells me he's glad I went to Ditch Plain Road, that he always stays at the East Deck when he comes to Montauk, that he rented a room before we left New York in case we were too tired to drive back.

—You rented a room at 1:30 in the morning?—

—The owner is a friend of mine. He never goes to bed before three.—

What am I doing with this man?

I sit on the edge of the bed trying to get the TV to work. Richard checks the plug, tells me it's broken. Besides he doubts if anything is on at this hour. I know I say and lay down, close my eyes.

Oh to be held, to be loved, to mean something to somebody. I open my eyes, look at Richard only to see he's looking at me.

Why is he here? What does he want?

—My best friend died here.—

—No kidding! What happened?—

—She walked into the sea.—

—Why? Do you know why?—

—That's the mystery of it. Why?—

—Did they ever recover the body?—

—No.—

—Then how can you be sure?—

—She left me a note.—

—At least you got a note.—

—What are you talking about?—

—I haven't the vaguest idea of what happened to my friend.—

—Are you just going to leave it there?—

—It's embarrassing to talk about it. I was dumped.—

—Dumped?—

—Yes dumped. I waited at the airport with two tickets to Brazil in my hand and she never showed. I figured something happened so I called but the number she gave me wasn't hers.—

—How long did you know her?—

—A month more or less.—

—And you never called her? How come?—

—She asked me not to call unless it was an emergency. She called me. She called me every day, sometimes twice a day.—

—But you knew her name and where she lived.—

—Her number was unlisted, her address was not her address.—

—She was probably married.—

—She wasn't.—

—How do you know?—

—I just do.—

—You thought I was with David.—

—Because you were so familiar with one another. Look, maybe I didn't know her but I knew a lot about her.—

—You had mutual friends.—

—No.—

—You hired a detective.— I'm trying not to laugh.

—She was famous. Everybody knew about her.—

—This is getting very interesting. Is she an actress? No. A painter? A writer? A TV personality? Wait. I've got it. Hillary Rodham Clinton. Sorry. You said she wasn't married.—

—I'm glad you think it's funny.—

—Were you in love with her?—

—You're really enjoying this, aren't you?—

—I'm a writer. Writers have to know everything, that's what makes us writers.—

—What do you write?—

—Novels, plays. What do you do?—

—I'm a lawyer.—

—What kind?—

—I try to keep the poor from being evicted.—

—That's noble. I'm impressed.—

—I don't know if it's noble but it's certainly necessary. What's your last name Julia?—

—Jaffe. What's yours?—

—Kaplan.—

—Jewish?—

—All the way. You?—

—Me too.—

—You're very beautiful. You have a lovely profile but I guess you've heard that before.—

—I'm not going to bed with you if that's what this is all about.—

—Are you seeing anybody?—

–No. Were you in love with her?–

–Right now my feelings of rejection far outweigh any feelings I may have had.–

–How long ago did this happen?–

–Last Sunday.–

–And in less than a week you find my profile lovely?–

–Your profile would be lovely whether I loved her or not.–

–I'm sixty four.–

–You're incredible looking.–

–Do you know who Zazu Pitts is?–

–Why? Is it important that I know? She's obviously from your time. Does that mean I get rejected for not living long enough? You remind me of the woman who stood me up. She must have been around your age.–

–Don't you ever go with women your own age?–

–My ex-wife was only eleven years older than me. So, who is this Zazu Potts?–

–Pitts. She was an actress in the thirties. A comedian.–

–Like you. I'm sure you write comedy.–

–My writing weighs a ton.–

–I'll have to read it.–

–Look, I'm tired.–

–Why don't you use the bathroom first unless you plan to take a two hour bath. My wife used to take two hour baths.–

–I'd like to soak for a half hour so you go first. Who was she anyhow, this famous older woman?–

–It doesn't matter.–

–Was she famous like a Jacqueline Onassis or a Helen Gurley Brown?–

–You're on the right track. She was editor–in–chief of a well known magazine and that's all I'm going to tell you.– He goes into the bathroom just as his words seep in. My heart races. –Open up Richard.– I bang on the door. –Open up.–

He opens the door. –What's up?–

–Like you don't know. You're beautiful, you have a great profile. You don't know who I am.–

He looks bewildered.

–You knew damned well who I was. That's why you hung around me all night, that's why you agreed to come to Montauk. Why are we here Richard? I want to know why we're here.–

–What's going on Julia?–

–You didn't know I was Mallory's best friend. You didn't know she died?–

He sits on the edge of the bed. –She what?–

–Died. She's the friend lying on the bottom of the ocean.–

–Oh my god.–

–You expect me to believe you didn't know? You didn't read about it in the *New York Times*. You didn't hear it on TV?–

He looks at me numbly. –She's dead?–

–I saw Mallory the night before. We talked about a lot of things but she never mentioned you or any trip. Why is that?–

–I don't know.–

–You don't know.–

I rush into the bathroom, turn on the bath water so I don't have to hear his explanation. I sit on the edge of the tub staring at the water. When I come out he's gone along with his car. The morning sun makes golden patterns on the faded bronze carpeting. There's the chipped dresser, the ugly print of a boat about to capsize in the swelling sea. Who chose such a print? What were they thinking?

I draw the blinds and fall into a deep sleep. Mallory and I are walking along Greenpoint Avenue, two girls, young pretty hopeful, our whole lives ahead of us. When I awaken Richard is on the other bed watching himself in the dresser mirror. I sit up. We are both watching each other's reflection.

–She's dead,– he whispers. His face crumbles, tears fall from his eyes. Am I supposed to reach out, put my arms around him, say soothing words? He looks up, wipes his tears. Our reflections are sparring with one another. He moves next to me.

–Can't we hold each other, comfort each other? Nothing more,
nothing more.–

Oh to lose myself in that lie, to put my body next to his, to hurl
myself into the universe and join Mallory. Never to return.

I HAVE DINNER WITH ANNIE AND HER MOTHER 1994

Annie invites me to have dinner with her. I'm just starting to tell
her about Richard when a woman comes out of the kitchen, then in a
mad rush is next to me hugging me.

–Julia. Isn't this grand?–

–Mrs. Riley! Annie didn't tell me you'd be here.–

–Wild horses wouldn't keep me away. The minute Annie said
Julia is coming for dinner I said if she's coming so am I.–

–You look wonderful, just wonderful.–

–Don't tell me I haven't changed because I have changed. And
you Julia...let me get a good look at you.– She studies me carefully.
–Thin as ever but to tell the truth I don't think I'd know it was you if
I saw you on the street. Would you know me?–

–Yes, yes I would. I can't tell you how happy I am to see you.–

–Me too. You're a sight for sore eyes.–

–Just seeing you makes me feel happy.–

–Then let's dance. You were always a good dancer, wasn't she
Annie?–

She loops her arm through mine as we prance around the room.
–Enough, enough,– she says plopping herself into a chair. –Oh I
used to love dancing, folk dancing and square dancing and ballroom
dancing. Vincent was a good dancer, wasn't he Annie? The best. Oh
well, water under the bridge... We cooked a great meal for you.
Corned beef and cabbage and potatoes. I remember how you used to
love that. I hope you still do.–

–Oh I do,– I lie.

–Good. I was afraid you were going to be one of those vegetarians.–

–I love corned beef,– I say with false enthusiasm.

Annie looks at me. She knows.

–Where's the whiskey Annie?– She watches Annie take the bottle from a cabinet. –Irish whiskey's the best. You do drink.–

–Oh yes.–

–Thanks be to god. I hate all those goody two shoes that have recently come out of the woodwork, no butter, no fat, no whiskey, no meat. Organic this and organic that. I say as long as you're alive you should eat whatever you want and to hell with the consequences. My Vincent was seventy eight when he died and he enjoyed every minute, didn't he Annie? Do you remember him Julia?–

–Of course I do.–

She raises her glass. –Let's drink to life. You Jews have a toast for that, don't you. What is it now?–

–L'chayim.–

–That's it. L'chayim. So Julia, l'chayim.– She pours more in our glasses. –Never dilute good whiskey... I was very sad when I heard about Mallory. It's a terrible sin to take your life.–

–Mom!–

–Well it is. They say you go to hell.–

–Mom, Mallory was Jewish.–

–Don't they go to hell too? You believe in hell don't you Julia?–

–Yes but it's here on earth.–

Her look is one of disbelief. –Really! Well I happen to know that Jews do believe in hell. That's what my Jewish friends say. Well, I'd better check on the food.– She goes into the kitchen.

–That's my mother. If she says Jews believe in hell, then they believe in it.–

–Annie, I'd like to tell you about Richard before she comes back.–

–Look, you don't have to eat the corned beef.–

–Am I talking to the wall?–

–You're a vegetarian, am I right? Tell her.–

–I can't. She went through all that trouble preparing the meal.–

–Too bad our dog died. You could have slipped the meat under the table.–

–Annie, why are you shutting me up?–

–I don't want to discuss anything personal in front of my mother. Later. Ok?–

–How do you know it's personal?–

–You wouldn't be so riled up if it weren't.–

–Annie, please don't say anything about my being...–

Mrs. Riley enters the room. –Don't say anything about what?–

Annie gives me a *see what I mean* look. –Nothing mom.–

She shakes her head and sighs. –Secrets, secrets, that's my Annie.– She takes my arm. –Let's eat.–

During dinner Mrs. Riley talks about Annie's three sons. –She did a good job raising them, I'll hand her that. They're grand, just grand.–

–My only claim to fame.–

–There's nothing wrong with raising three wonderful boys. Annie tells me you have two sons. I always say sons are the best.–

–I wanted daughters.–

–That's because you don't have them. If you did you'd be singing a different tune.–

–Did I tell you Julia writes books?–

Her eyes light up. –Are they romantic novels?–

–Hardly. I write about strong women who not only don't get the men in the end but don't want them.–

–Why not? What's wrong with men? I wouldn't mind finding one myself, even at my age.–

–Really!–

–Yes, really.–

–Mom, are you kidding?–

–If I could find another Vincent I'd jump at the chance. Tell me Julia, how is your mother doing?–

–She's fine.–

–Is she now. I'm glad. And how old is she?–

–Eighty five.–

–I'm going to be ninety on my next birthday, god willing.–

–Really!–

–When was the last time you saw me Julia? Was it Annie's wedding?–

–It was Anthony's christening.–

–Anthony's christening. That was some party we had, wasn't it Annie? I could dance up a storm in those days.–

–That was thirty two years ago mom.–

–Thirty two years! Imagine. I was still a young woman.–

Annie laughs. –You were fifty eight mom.–

–When you're ninety, fifty eight is young.–

–It's hard to believe you're ninety.–

–My bones know I'm ninety believe me. And don't tell me I'm wonderful for my age or any of the stupid things people say.–

Annie pours wine into our glasses. –She's gotten tough in her old age.–

–Might as well. I haven't a thing to gain by being nice. Everybody expects old women to be cranky and miserable so here I am, not disappointing a soul. Annie tells me your mother moved to Manhattan.–

–She lives on the upper eastside.–

–Good for her. I never moved.–

–She hates Sunnyside but she's too stubborn to move.–

–I'm too old to move.–

–I've told you a hundred times that Tommie and I would do all the work. You wouldn't have to lift a finger.–

–I'm fine where I am.–

–Because you're near the church. My mother still goes to church every day. It could be a blizzard but she goes.–

–It wouldn't hurt you to go yourself.–

–The day the church accepts me the way I am is the day I'll return.–

–She always has something to say about the church as if it were the church's fault that the world has gone crazy.–

–I'm talking about me mom.–

–The problems of the world are a lot bigger than you Annie. Don't you agree Julia?–

–Why ask her? Ask me.–

–Why should I ask you when you've jammed the answer down my throat a thousand times. I tell you there's nothing wrong with the church. It's the people. That's what's wrong. In my day people had respect for one another.–

–Oh sure mom. That's why the kids from our church used to beat up the Jewish kids. You can ask Julia about that one.–

–Oh please. Don't talk to me about the few riff raffs. You can't blame all Catholics because of a few rotten kids.–

–Mom, why can't you admit that it was the church that taught us that the Jews crucified Christ which is what motivated the Catholic kids to beat up the Jewish kids in the first place. And how about Father Coughlin? Didn't you listen to him every Sunday night on the radio while he talked or should I say screamed about the Jews taking over the world?–

–You'd say anything to get my goat. The truth is we got along with one another in the old days. I lived next door to a Jewish family and we never said a cross word. Everything was different then. You never heard about drugs or muggings. You could go on the subway at all hours of the night and not be afraid. Today they mug you in broad daylight. They're that brazen.–

–Who's that brazen mom?–

–You know who I mean. At least the Jews brought up their children to be respectful. And it's not just the subways. You can't walk on the street anymore without fearing for your life. And the police, they used to be our friends. We knew every one of them by name. Now where are they? You never see them on the streets. Where did they all go? You should know the answer to that one Annie.–

–We were in a recession mom.–

–I'm sick of that excuse. I tell you it was different in my day. People had respect.–

–It was the same then. The big difference in the good old days was silence. You didn't air your dirty laundry in public. How about Mrs. Farrel?–

–Mrs. Farrel would have tried the patience of a saint.–

–Which gave her husband the right to beat her up.–

–Nobody saw anything. It was all rumors.–

–The Farrel children saw. Let me tell you something mom. In your day there was wife beating and child beating and incest and rape. Men did the same things they do today only then they got away with it.–

–Oh men. Of course men.–

–Yes mom. Men.–

–All men beat their wives and rape, is that right?–

–No, all men don't but all batterers and rapists are men.–

–Don't make women out to be saints. They do plenty. It's a miracle your sons turned out as well as they did considering how you hate men.–

–I don't hate men. I just hate their behavior.–

–Tim was an angel but you divorced him just the same.–

–You're right. He was lovely but I'm a lesbian mom. I know you don't approve but that's what I am.–

–I don't care what you are as long as you don't go blabbing it to the world.–

–The world? I can't even say anything to the family. I can't take Tommie to family functions as my mate or to your church for that matter.–

–You can take her as your friend.–

–But she's more than my friend.–

–If you ask me it was better before when we did sweep everything under the carpet. I think it's disgusting how everybody talks about everything. What kind of an example are we setting for the children? What's on television today is disgusting. The talk shows are a disgrace.–

–Well you've done a good job of sweeping Tommie and me under the carpet.–

–I keep telling you. It's nobody's business but your own.–

–And I keep telling you it's not for them. It's for me. It's important for me to say who I am.–

–Say it then. I mean it Annie, if it will stop this endless fighting, say it.–

We sit awkwardly staring at our plates as if something magical will rise from them. Good girl that I am I say, the meal was delicious, instead of defending Annie.

–Yes it was if I have to say so myself. Stop brooding Annie and get the coffee and cake. I baked your favorite Julia. At least it was your favorite in the bad old days. I hope you still like chocolate.–

–I'm addicted to it.–

–Thanks be to god for little favors.–

I watch Annie leave the room. Mrs. Riley sighs deeply, her eyes rheumy. –Annie and me, we fight all the time. Still she's the child I count on and trust. She thinks I don't approve of her life. It's not that I disapprove. It's just that I don't understand. Two women together. What do they do? I like Tommie, she knows that. She's a good girl, very kind. Still my Vincent would turn over in his grave if he knew.–

We drive Mrs. Riley to Sunnyside. At her door she kisses me. –I always liked you the best. There was just something about you.–

I ask Annie to drive slowly through the neighborhood. We go down 44th Street where I lived, then 42nd Street where I lived the year I married Howard.

Greenpoint Avenue had changed. Silver's was no longer there. Or Fay's or Miles Shoe store where I worked part time. The Bliss Street Theater was now a Pentecostal Church. The curtain store, the corner candy store, the five and dime where they sold broken chunks of chocolate and Tangee lipsticks. All gone. The White Castle that fried skinny hamburgers and onions was still on the same corner. St.

Theresa's Church was there. So was the Sunnyside Jewish Center where the Catholic kids came to break our stained glass windows. The Merry-Go-Round Bar that revolved slowly while we sipped rye and ginger ale remained. And all the mean little three story tenements, one apartment in the front, one in the rear. We crossed the 59th Street Bridge in silence.

Drinking cappuccino at Cafe Reggio on MacDougal Street Annie talked about her mother. —She'd like me to be married like my sister Katlin and the funny thing is Katlin doesn't give a damn about her. Or my brother Matthew who treats his wife like shit. My mother sees it and makes excuses. You have to look away sometimes she tells me. As for Tony and Terrance, they do us a favor by showing up at Christmas.—

—Why go on and on Annie? She's old. She's not going to change.—

—You think I'm wrong?—

—What's the point?—

—And she's always throwing her wonderful marriage in my face.—

—Your father did love her.—

—Yes but would he have loved her if she hadn't looked away? She did everything to please him. His word was law. She was the perfect wife and she taught her daughters well. We did the housework, we helped with the meals and the cleaning up. We even shined our brothers' shoes. When my father said anything nasty to her she'd smile and say ah Vincent, ah Vincent. I was sucked into that loving home.—

I tell her about Richard, ask her if she doesn't think it weird.

—Weird,— she answers. —Weird is going on a three hour trip in the middle of the night with a man you just met.—

—No. Weird is his telling me he didn't know Mallory had died. Weird is planning a trip to Brazil the day she picked to kill herself.—

—Was she depressed?—

—Everybody's depressed but they don't walk into the ocean on

the day they're going away with their lover.–
  –They might. People do strange things.–
  –Like you. Suddenly becoming a lesbian.–
  –I thought everyone knew I had a crush on Claire.–
  –So! We all had schoolgirl crushes.–
  –Some of us knew it was more than a crush.–
  –Then why didn't you act on it?–
  –Have you forgotten? We of the good girl generation never
made waves.–
  –And now is different?–
  –Of course now is different.–

  How did we get from there to here? Annie's mother is right.
Then people cared. You could walk anywhere without fearing for
your life. Who am I kidding? Hate groups galloped through the
streets. Some hated Blacks, others Jews, others found their own
groups to hate. But the streets were basically safe. There were gangsters who had guns but they weren't children. So why did two of my
junior high classmates get the electric chair for murder?
  Still things were better. We danced to live bands or canned music
in the park. We played stickball on the street. We tapdanced and
roller skated. We laughed a lot. But if laughter was so prevalent why
did I hide in movie theaters and libraries?
  Mallory's gone where there are no memories. She's not going to
spend money on an analyst trying to remember all that she worked
so hard to forget. Mallory soars in the Escape Speed where memories
vanish, where feeling becomes nonfeeling, where there's no pain, no
joy no sadness no fury no hurt. No tension or anger. No love pangs
for someone who doesn't pang for you, never panged for you and
never will. She's where there are no regrets over what you did or
worse what you wanted to do but didn't because you might be
wrong. Like having an affair with a man thirty years younger than
you.
  In the Escape Speed there are no headaches or bellyaches or

libraries or movie theaters to hide in. You don't need to hide. Or feel. You can't feel when you're speeding through the universe at 25,000 miles an hour. How can you feel when the Escape Speed folds you in its center dancing to music past time.

AT LAKE OSCAWANA, MY FIRST KISS 1944

His mouth grabs mine. A foul smell gushes forward. Finally my mouth is released. Is this what I've been dreaming about? Without warning another kiss. This time he thrusts his tongue down my throat. A horrible odor is making its way down my body. Now I'll never get rid of the smell. I push him away. He likes it. Playing hard to get he says as he grabs me, pinning my arms down. His sweaty hands grope for my breasts. His bulging pants press against me. I hold my breath so I won't gag.

I want to tell Mallory but Mallory isn't here and Bettina isn't Mallory. She'll laugh her Hollywood laugh and say oh Julia. Whenever I say something and she doesn't want to respond or can't, she says oh Julia.

Bettina, your mother says the Jewish boys are ruining the wall behind the sofa. She says they rub their greasy Jewish heads on the wall. I'm Jewish.

Oh Julia.

Bettina, your mother says my mother hasn't got any taste, that her clothes are ridiculous.

Oh Julia.

Bettina, please ask your mother to stop calling me fat. I've lost five pounds.

Oh Julia.

Bettina, you've got to talk to your mother about the way she sits. It's obscene.

Finally in desperation I tell her. She explains if I don't pet they won't want to date me. —Like my mother says let them go just so far but not all the way. You know, don't let them put their pecker in your vagina. You can let them rub it against you but that's all.—

—Do you let them do that?—

—Sure.—

—Who?—

—No one you're going with.—

There's no one to talk to, not even when I return to Sunnyside. My mother would kill me if she suspected I knew anything about sex. I don't have one friend. The bright girls are with the bright girls. Annie's with Claire, Claire is with Annie. I hate Bettina. Besides what movies? None of us has ever seen her in a movie. I go to Mallory's apartment. She looks great, tells me she can't talk, that she's late for work.

—I'll walk to Silver's with you.—

—Silver's. That antiquated shop. I'm working for Irving Marko. If you want you can walk me to the subway.—

—You work for Cynthia's father? After what I told you?—

—What you said was absurd. He's a pussycat, a real sweetheart. He would never do anything like that.—

—He did. I saw him.—

—Julia, there's no way I'm going to allow your sick imagination ruin my life. I am going to be a designer and this is my break.—

—You're designing clothes! You're not even fifteen and he's letting you design clothes.—

—I'm not exactly designing them but he does listen to my ideas.—

—Exactly what are you doing, Mallory? Substituting for Cynthia?—

—You are disgusting Julia, really disgusting and you have the nerve to call yourself my friend.—

—Your friend! We haven't been friends for eons Mallory, not since you were accepted at Hunter High. You've gotten too big for me Mallory.—

—You're jealous.—

–That's not true.–

–Oh it's true all right.–

–How about loyalty Mallory or isn't that word in your thesaurus?–

–Goodbye and goodluck Julia.–

She walks away. I scream you stink Mallory as she runs for the subway. Tears flow down my eyes. Why did I have to open my big mouth? Why couldn't I have said, designing clothes. That's great. Now we're finished as friends for sure.

The Eleanor Roosevelt Girls now meet every other week. Mallory ignores me. As far as she's concerned I'm not there. Nobody likes me except Bettina and I can't stand her. I live in the library. I read or write my stories there. My mother knows where I am. Blood is in her eyes when she finds me. If it's me. Sometimes she calls to the wrong girl. Even my mother doesn't recognize me. Once she brought the wrong girl home for dinner. The wrong girl is fat and dumpy. I'm small and thin. The wrong girl has squinty eyes, a pudgy nose.

Nothing like me. Not a bit like me.

CYNTHIA 1994

Mallory found a rug in the basement of her apartment house. She couldn't believe her luck. –Isn't this exquisite. Imagine someone throwing this away. It looks like it belongs in the Metropolitan Museum, don't you think?–

Her treasured rug rests beneath her dining room table on top of the Persian carpet she found on the street which rests on top of the Swedish one she paid $10 for at her favorite thrift shop.

–If you look you find,– she tells me.

And what did Mallory find before her walk into the ocean? Did she find the rocks she loved, then throw them in the sea knowing this time she wouldn't be taking any home. Were the stars bright? Did she bray at the moon as we once did? Did she pop the champagne cork, watch it spray, drink from one of her favorite crystals? Once she said that life was the best gift.

No Mallory, I say standing on her three carpet mountain. Life is shit. You always get what you don't want.

Ridiculous she answers. You are so negative it would be pathetic if it weren't so funny.

Oh sure Mallory sure. So how come the lover of life walked into the ocean leaving her collection to the negative one? Answer that Mallory.

Dead people don't have to answer the living.

She walks out of the ocean, seaweed mingling with her hair. She is a creature of the sea, a character in a B movie. When she laughs a fountain springs from her mouth.

My laugh is mortal laugh, spittle, fillings showing.

That was a spiteful act Mallory, a very hostile thing to do, the ultimate fuck you act.

You always did take everything personally.

Why did you do it? Just tell me that.

My knees hurt.

Your knees hurt? That's your answer? Your knees hurt?

Did you ever watch old people walk, the way their knees bend. They do it because of the pain. I don't want to walk like that, that's a loser's walk, an old person's walk.

You killed yourself so you wouldn't have to walk with your knees bent?

Every day a new pain, every day something else goes, something is taken away until we're not even a shadow of what we once were. Dead people never age.

She runs on the sand laughing her spraying fountain laugh.

Mallory, you wrote you ran out of lovers. What about Richard?

Julia, let's not waste time on what was. You want my advice. Lose your past, invent another one, the one you were entitled to but never had. Sunnyside was shit. It was always shit. You can't avoid facts.

Another voice joins Mallory's. You can't avoid facts.

My eyes fly open. I know that voice. My body jerks itself into a sitting position. I stare at the woman on the screen. I know that face.

–Regardless of what our male expert says it is a fact that one out of every four girls will be molested by the time they're eighteen and those are the reported cases. Who knows how many more there are.–

Cynthia. Cynthia Marko.

June Lawrence, the show's host runs among her audience looking for the raised hand. A woman speaks. –We're told that most sex offenders were also abused as children but how can we know who they are? Are there any signs to look for?–

–Unfortunately no. Molesters don't look any different from any body else.–

Another audience member. –If that's the case, what can we as mothers do?–

–Teach your children that their bodies are sacred, that they should say no to any touch that doesn't feel right.–

–That's ridiculous Walter. How can a child tell the difference between a touch that's alright and one that isn't. Molestation starts very simply, a touch here, a touch there.–

–Are you suggesting that we shouldn't teach our children the difference...–

–No. I'm simply stating that a three year old child does not know the difference.–

–When a stranger comes up to them and touches them, they don't know the difference? Really Dr. Marko.–

–But the strangers Walter are often trusted family members or family friends. Now how can you say to a child you mustn't let your father touch you?–

–Cynthia, there are touches and there are touches.–

–From personal experience I know that those touches start off very innocently and lovingly, at least to the child and by the time they move into dangerous territory the girl is not only thoroughly confused but too frightened to say anything, not to mention the guilt she lives with.–

A male member of the audience takes the microphone. –Where is the mother while all this is going on? Isn't it her responsibility to stop the abuse of her children?–

–No, it's men who have to stop it.–

Walter jumps in. –He's got a point. You can't ignore the mother's complicity in all this.–

–Her complicity?–

–I don't see how she can morally avoid responsibility. She's there, she must know something.–

–I don't think the word moral is apropos but I'll ignore it. Let's assume as you say she has some responsibility. Does that exonerate the father, does that get him off the hook?–

–Of course not but if we take Nazi Germany as an example, were the people who stood by and did nothing as responsible as those who committed the heinous acts? No. But they certainly had some responsibility, wouldn't you agree?–

–We're not talking about Nazi Germany Walter.–

–That's true. We're talking about responsibility, the responsibility of the bystander. In this case, the mother.–

–Why are you so focused on the mother?–

–Because she's the logical one to bring this abuse to the authorities.–

–Do you know how often those charges are dismissed?–

–You are giving a false picture. They are not dismissed. The perpetrators are not sent to jail if they agree to go for rehabilitation.–

–Which is rarely successful. You know Walter it constantly amazes me to see how assiduously men protect men. I think it's high time that men like you started taking responsibility for the behavior of your violent brothers and stop pointing the finger elsewhere.–

There is wild applause.

Now the audience jumps in. I was. He did. My mother knew. He beat her, threatened if she told, I didn't realize, I cried, tried to kill myself. The shock, the shock.

Cynthia. Cynthia Marko.

ANOTHER TONGUE ASSAULT 1945

Pigeon Galamonts raise their legs, wave their feet and open their mouth for mating.

I'm fifteen. A boy named Bill asks me to go out on New Year's Eve. I don't want to but say yes. I don't even like him. He has pimples on his face and pimply faced boys are not popular. I don't act stupid around boys so I'm not popular either. He probably asked me because he couldn't get anyone else to go out with him.

We go to a Chinese restaurant, we go to Radio City Music Hall. At midnight we stand in Times Square and scream with the other screamers. *Happy New Year.* My parents are allowing me to come home at one in the morning. Unheard of. My curfew has always been eleven o'clock. They like Bill. He's shy, he's studious, his father owns the neighborhood drugstore.

We walk in the hallway of my ugly squat apartment house. Without a word he pushes me against the wall. I say cut it out. On the out he has his tongue in my mouth. I want to scream but if I do everyone will know I'm with a boy whose tongue is waving in my mouth. I move to get away. His tongue plunges deeper. He pins me against the wall. His penis is like a rock. He rubs his body against mine. His hand goes down my dress. He's pulling hard on my nipple. What if my parents come down the stairs and find me there? They'll blame me.

The front door opens. Bill jumps away from me, almost losing his hand down my dress. It's the couple upstairs, the one whose baby drops her bottles on the floor in the middle of the night. They're tipsy and laugh knowingly when they see us. I say nothing. My eyes tear as I watch them weave up the stairs. Bill waits. I start to leave when he grabs my hands, holding them behind my back with one hand and pulling one breast out of my dress with the other. His mouth is on my nipple. My knee connects with his penis. He screams. I adopt Bettina's laugh and saunter up the stairs.

My parents are asleep but not my brother who's yanking away at his penis. Julia he says knowing I know. So how was pimple Bill? He uncovers himself and continues masturbating. I turn to the wall fully dressed. I will not cry. I will sleep in my clothes. I will not show any emotion.

I've sworn off boys for life. They're disgusting. They smell, they have tongues and appendages they can't control. White spit always stays on the sides of their mouth.

On Saturday nights when other girls are dating I'm sitting in the bathroom writing. Sometimes I actually write in the bedroom but that's only when my brother is with a friend or sitting in the living room listening to the radio. Why aren't you going with boys my mother asks. You don't want to be an old maid, do you?

I'm only fifteen mom.

So she says. So. You'd be surprised how fast time flies.

ILYA 1994

Mallory's list is ridiculous. Friends and enemies are intertwined. Ilya, who left her for a woman half her age when she was in her fifties. Ilya, who thinks he's a feminist because he shops and cooks, washes and cleans. Everything but his own body. Ilya, who looks good at sixty two but smells like leftover food. Once when Mallory and I talked about people we would kill if we could get away with it, Ilya was at the top of Mallory's list.

He calls. My god. Can't believe. Why? So beautiful. So talented. Did you tell her that when you dumped her stays on the tip of my tongue.

–Come over for dinner Julia. I need to talk. Just give me an hour to shop.–

Ilya enjoys preparing dinner while his guests are there. Tonight it's just me. He pours the wine. We drink. He peels shrimp while the rice simmers. The salad stuff is waiting on the sidelines to be washed and broken into smaller pieces.

–Where's Rachel?–

–She's at her Theosophist meeting.–

–Why didn't you go?–

–It's absolute nonsense.–

He looks at me, a shrimp in his hand. –Why Julia? You knew her better than anyone. Why would she take her life when she had so much going for her?–

–Like what?–

–What do you mean, what? Brains, talent, personality, beauty.–

–Right Ilya. Old brains, old talent, old beauty. Nobody wanted it.–

–That's nonsensical. I'm the same age and people want my work.–

–You're not a woman.–

–You work. Don't you work?–

–Sure I work but nobody wants that either.–

–Because you've become an angry woman.–

–But angry men are alright. That's perfectly acceptable.–

–Jesus Julia, you're giving me indigestion before I eat.–

–Your plays are full of woman hatred but they're produced.–

–Woman hatred! That's not true. All I'm doing is showing things the way they are. My work mirrors the misogynist society.–

–Take your mirror and shove it. We don't need to see that shit on stage or anywhere else for that matter.–

–You're judging my play and I know for a fact you haven't seen it.–

–Ilya, if I went and I'm not going to, I'd storm the stage and kick the shit out of the man.—

—He's an actor Julia an actor and it's a play. And if you went you'd see that women are the worst offenders.—

—Of what?—

—Can we talk about something else?—

—Of what?—

—When she's beaten it's women who cheer the loudest.—

—Well, there's nothing like self hatred to spur you on.—

—Did anyone ever tell you that talking to you gives one vertigo?—

—As a matter of fact, yes. Men who go from A to Z without any detours invariably get dizzy.—

—I'm glad to hear that. I was beginning to think it was just me.—

—It doesn't bother you to have an A to Z mind.—

—That's called logic Julia. More wine?—

I watch my glass being filled.

—Cheers Julia.— He clinks glasses with me and laughs. —Despite your miserable disposition you look beautiful.— He puts down his glass and gives me a bear hug. Leave it to Ilya to freely show affection.

—Whatever happened to what's her face, the one before Rachel, the twenty seven year old you left Mallory for?—

—Take a breath for christsake.—

—Selma. Was that her name? Selma.—

—Thelma.—

—It's so hard to keep track.—

—Jesus!—

—And then you left Thelma for Rachel who was even younger. Tell me Ilya, if older women are so beautiful and appealing and intelligent, why aren't you with them?—

He heats up the butter, washes each leaf separately, turns to the frying pan and puts in the garlic tossing it in the oil, then the shrimp. He pours more wine in both glasses.

—You told Mallory she was old. You actually said that to her.

After eight years, you shit.–

–Apparently she didn't think I was a shit or she wouldn't have invited me to celebrate her life.–

–She also invited Nina Black who took her job from her.–

–Julia, if it will make you happy, I regret breaking off with Mallory. It was a big mistake. Satisfied now?–

–No.–

–You think you knew her but you didn't. She was a very difficult woman. She couldn't stand being close to anyone including you although knowing you you'll never believe that. She's dead Julia. I'm going to miss her the rest of my life. You're going to miss her but all the regrets and all the recriminations are not going to bring her back.–

–You had no right inviting her to be with you on your birthday. The relationship had ended and you made her believe...–

–I made her believe nothing.–

He puts the food on the table, pours more wine. I take a bite of the shrimp, mutter *liar* under my breath. I eat some rice. –You certainly can cook Ilya. I'll hand you that. This is delicious.–

–Thanks,– he says grudgingly. No doubt he heard my liar.

–The wine's good too.– I look at the label, then at Ilya. –We're old Ilya. We've gotten old. You hang on to your lost youth by fucking younger women. But you're still old.–

–I don't think of myself as old.–

–Neither do I but so what. We are old. We don't look young anymore. Ten years from now you're going to find it harder to get a young woman. Then what will you do?–

–Ten years from now I might be dead.–

–Why did you do it Ilya? She was so damned vulnerable. She'd lost her job, she...–

–It was mutual Julia. As a matter of fact Mallory was the one who initiated the sex.–

–Come off it Ilya. You'd fuck anyone with moveable parts.–

–I never fucked you.–

–Because I see through all your counter culture bullshit. I see through those gentle parts. I see straight through to that selfish core that says me me me. I want. I'll get.–

–You're drunk Julia.–

–Damn straight I'm drunk.–

–We all say me me me including you you, yes you. As for fucking when did you become the virgin of the year?–

I grab my coat and rush to the door.

–Julia, comeon.– He's standing next to me pulling me inside.

–She's dead. I'm never going to see her again.–

He puts his arm around me. –I know. I know. Sit down Julia. Here, have some more wine.–

–Finally I tell you off and I can't even tell Mallory how great I was.–

He bursts out laughing, gives me a long hug.

–You're such a shit Ilya.–

–You're probably right.–

–So, how do you like that woman who chopped off her husband's prick?–

RICHARD 1994

Bald eagles circle in the air, swoop, dive down and finally lock their claws in ecstasy when they mate.

I've circled, I've swooped, I've dived, locked claws and other parts. I've even mated a few times.

But ecstasy!

I've laughed and cried, groaned and yelled. I've twisted and turned, the back of my head almost went bald doing that one. I've bumped noses, got cramps in my legs, gyrated while my mind was on other things. I've held my breath, held in pain, words, burps, farts. I've pretended it wasn't him, pretended it wasn't me. I've sometimes been surprised, even delighted.

But ecstasy! Never.

Richard calls. –Can't we see each other as friends?–

–We could if we were friends but we're not friends.–

–Why? I never hurt Mallory. If she were alive, she'd tell you herself.–

–But she isn't Richard.–

–Do you like Stravinsky?–

–I'm hanging up.–

–I got tickets for the New York Philharmonic, an all Stravinsky program this Saturday. I'll meet you at the fountain quarter to eight.–

I don't hang up. He does.

DANCING AT THE U.S.O. 1945

President Roosevelt will die in a week. Eleanor Roosevelt's column *My Day* will not appear from April 12th to the 19th. The war will be ending soon. All of this is unknown to us as we dance to live music at the U.S.O. We don't know about the six million Jews who were murdered in concentration camps. We don't know that the U.S. is about to drop nuclear bombs on Japan. We don't know that the world we once knew will be gone forever. The war is something that's happening there, where boys go to fight and sometimes die.

Every Friday night I go to the U.S.O. to dance with these GIs, to cheer them up before they're shipped out. This is my war effort. I lie about my age. If my parents knew they'd kill me. I tell them I'm with Bettina. At the U.S.O. I meet Cleo. Cleo's parents think she's with Margaret.

I dance almost all the dances with Private First Class Chet Rich who was wounded in the Battle of the Bulge. He's twenty two, from Muncie, Indiana. Bettina lived in Muncie before she moved to

Hollywood. I convince her to come the following week. She dances with Chet, tells me she thinks he's real cute, that they're going to start dating. He tells me she's not his type.

The following Friday there's no Bettina. Chet invites me for an ice cream soda. I sip my soda while he tells me about himself, how he worked in a factory, about his best buddy who turned out to be a Jew. He'd never met one before, was looking for his horns. Horns? Sure he says, didn't you know some Jews have them. Where do they have them I ask. He laughs. Only kidding. I used to think that.

I'm wondering if I should punch him or just call him a stupid jerk and leave. He tells me I'm pretty. –How could you think Bettina is pretty. You are the pretty one.–

Now's my chance. –You think so?–

–You bet. Julia, I'm not going to lie to you. Now promise me not to get mad. I have a girlfriend in Muncie and it was sort of expected that when the war ended we'd marry but after meeting you...Julia, I just can't stop thinking of you.–

–I'm fifteen.–

–You are,– he gulps. –Gosh, you're so mature.–

–And guess what?–

–What?–

–I'm Jewish.–

–You are?–

–Yop. 100% Jewish but I don't have horns. Sometimes they run out of them, especially when a lot of Jewish babies are born at the same time. So some of us don't get them. I hope you're not disappointed.–

–Geeze Julia, I know Jews don't have horns. It was a joke. Besides, how was I supposed to know you're Jewish. You sure don't look it.–

–You're a jerk.–

–What?–

–A stupid ignorant jerk.–

I storm out of the ice cream parlor before I finish my soda.

KURT 1946

After the war we hear names of places we never heard before. Auschwitz, Birkenau, Bergen Belsen, Sobibor, Treblinka, Buchenwald, camps expressly set up to rid Europe of its Jews. We see movies of weightless dead bodies thrown into open graves. We see emaciated survivors, their faces expressionless. Their rescuers, American, British and Russian soldiers weep while the half live concentration camp survivors remain dry eyed. Some are greatly agitated, their stick like bodies moving moving, their words incomprehensible. Three quarters of European Jewry dead. How many Gypsies nobody knows. How could it have happened? Why didn't somebody tell us?

My scrapbook of movie stars is replaced with photographs of the death camps. I write stories as if I were there. I invent another family. We are dragged out of our homes, thrown into open trucks, then cattle cars. I have a little sister I take care of. My parents huddle around us trying to find words of comfort but there are no words. The cattle car screams through the night. People wail and moan in the cramped space, gulping whatever air they can.

Now I am in a death camp. I am flung into an open grave, my body on top of another body, another body on top of mine. I can't breathe but how can the dead breathe? At other times I am a survivor wandering naked through the rubble. But where is my sister? Where are my parents? Is there nobody left but me?

My father comes home one night and tells us that the Red Cross notified him that his aunt's daughter's son is in a refugee camp. Will my father vouch for him so he can come to the States? How did he know about me, my father asks nobody in particular. Are there others? My father numb with shock. What did you say, my mother wants to know. I said yes. What else could I say? But where will we put him she answers and what about money? We barely manage. Where, my father screams, where? We're talking about a life. If they find ten more I'll vouch for them if I have to put my own life in hock.

My mother's nostrils flair, her mouth turns down. Charity she says begins at home.

After dinner she goes into the bedroom. If looks could kill my father would be lying dead on the kitchen floor. He sits with me telling me his father had six brothers and sisters in Czechoslovakia. My father never met them, had never been in contact with them. What if they're all dead? Had I known he says. If only I'd known. For the first time I see my father cry.

We worry how we'll communicate with our newly arrived relative. We're surprised at his good English. He was in his last year of college, a language major, when the war against the Jews broke out. That's what he calls it, the war against the Jews. We've agreed not to mention the war unless he brings it up. He doesn't. All through that first dinner every time I look at Kurt I find him looking at me. My mother's eagle eye catches this. She shakes her head disapprovingly. My father, an only child, is too overcome with emotion to notice anything. His first cousin's son, the only relative he has now that his parents are dead. Anything I can do he tells Kurt. Anything.

Kurt finds a job in a haberdashery store. At night he goes to college. He moves to a walkup apartment in Yorkville. A mensch my father says. He doesn't sponge off anyone.

It's on the sixth floor, a floor through with tiny dark rooms. The living room has a painted stained window that faces a brick wall. We sit on a sofa eating tuna fish sandwiches and drinking coke with lemon in it. He tells me next time we'll go out and eat in one of the wonderful Hungarian restaurants in the neighborhood. He asks me what I'm doing with my life. I love Kurt. He actually thinks I have a life.

My parents don't know I'm here. Kurt may be a mensch but my mother doesn't like him. Why my father asks, what have you got against him? She answers, –He's different.–

Different is up there with germs.

Kurt is always cold. He says he can't get enough warmth, that the war altered his metabolism. I wear a thin blouse while he wears a

heavy sweater and jacket. His hands are always like ice. He tells me
that Americans are always warm. —To be an American is to be safe
and warm. Look at you Julia. No troubles, no problems.—
    —That's not true. I have plenty of problems.—
    —Oh poor baby,— he teases.
    —Don't treat me like a child. I am not a child. I know your life
was horrible even though you refuse to talk about it. I'm not stupid
you know. Oh never mind.—
    —Good. We never mind.—
    —Just answer one thing. Why do you always look at me the way
you do?—
    —I look. I look!—
    —Yes you look.—
    —We don't talk about it ok.—
    —No we don't talk about it. We don't talk about your family, we
don't talk about the war, we don't even talk about your life now. All
we can talk about is how lucky I am to be an American.—
    —We talk about your writing, don't we?—
    —But never about you.—
    —I tell you about school, no?—
    —You're an enigma.—
    —I am sorry. What is enigma?— He laughs. —Is a bad word, am I
right?—
    —It's a puzzle, a mystery. You are a mystery.—
    —A mystery is very romantic no.—
    —No.—
    —You want me to talk. Ok. I was not in a camp.—
    —Where were you?—
    —Underground with the resistance. I was a partisan. Everyone
thinks I am Aryan so I get false papers, many false papers. I speak
four languages so I am very useful.—
    —I'm glad your life wasn't as horrible as I imagined it to be. You
could have been in a concentration camp.—
    —What do you know about it?—

–I've seen pictures.–

–Oh pictures. Very good.–

–Don't make fun of me.–

–I don't make fun.–

–What I mean is you couldn't be so normal if you were in one of those places.–

–Julia, look at me. I ask you to look at me. I am normal looking no? I do all normal things. I go to school, I work, I have apartment. If you see me you say there goes normal person, just like other normal persons. But I am not. You are warm, I am cold. You have these big feelings. I have none. All things to do with feelings are finished for me, they are gone. The only time I feel is when I look at you.–

I grab him, kiss him. He pushes me away. –Don't do that. What is wrong with you?–

–But you said the only time you feel is when you look at me.–

–Because you look like my sister.–

I am trying not to cry. –Your sister!–

–Yes, my sister so when I see you I pretend it is she, that she is still alive. Even your name. She too was Julia.–

–What happened to her?–

–She died in Sobibor.–

–I'm sorry. I thought...– I run into the bathroom, lock the door. I expect him to knock but he doesn't. When I come out he is on the bed staring up at the ceiling. –You are beautiful just like my sister,– he says without looking at me.

–So are you.–

He smiles. –I am beautiful!–

–Yes.–

–But not nice person.–

–Yes you are.–

He looks at me. –You don't know. It is best you don't know. If you knew you would run for your life.–

–I'm not running.–

—You're not afraid to be alone with me?—

—No.—

—You have no right to go into a bedroom with a man you don't know. Is this what you do? Where is your head?—

—You sound like my mother. She says men only want one thing.—

—Your mother is right. Go home Julia. Please go home.—

I can't believe I'm taking my clothes off, I can't believe he's watching me. What am I doing? I get into bed with him waiting for him to do something. He covers me, lies there without moving. After a while he gets out of bed and slowly removes his clothes. I see a number tattooed on his arm. But he said he wasn't in a camp.

He gets into bed next to me. His body is icy. He holds me close, strokes my hair. Without warning he begins sobbing. I rock him in my arms while he speaks a language I do not know, cannot know, will never know. And then the word. Julia.

MALLORY RE-ENTERS MY LIFE 1946

I'm sitting in Fruchter's Delicatessen on Queens Boulevard, eating a hot dog with sauerkraut, drinking creme soda, writing a short story about Kurt and me when out of the corner of my eye I see Mallory walk in. I continue eating, my eyes glued to the paper.

—Julia. Hi.—

She stands there, a big grin on her face. —What are you doing?—

—What does it look like?—

—You're not mad at me?—

—Mad. Why? Have you done anything that would make me mad like ignoring me?—

—Julia, don't start that again.— She sits down. —That looks great. I think I'll have one.—

—Mallory, I'm writing.—

–Sorry.– She gets up, looks for another table.

–You might as well sit down. You've ruined my train of thought.–

–What a bad mood you're in.–

–I am not in a bad mood.–

–I guess if I worked for Miles Shoe Store I'd be in a bad mood. Annie told me they asked you to work late one night and you were so angry you mixed up all the shoes in the boxes and they went crazy the next day.–

–Did she tell you I made her help me?– We both laugh.

–Oh Julia, I've really missed you.–

–Why can't you be honest with yourself. You avoid me.–

–That's not true Julia. I'm so busy between working and school I don't have time for anyone.–

–Everyone has time for people they care about. Even I know that.–

The waiter stands over us. Mallory orders a hot dog and a cherry coke. –Julia, I'm going with somebody. That's the main reason I haven't seen you.–

–Well! Congratulations. Who is he?–

–I can't tell you.–

–Why? Is he an ax murderer?–

She chokes on her laughter, reaches for my hand. –I really have missed you. You could always make me laugh.–

–And you've always made me cry.–

She moves her hand away. –Don't say that. It hurts.–

–I'm sorry it hurts but the truth is the truth. I'm no longer the sweet naive Julia you knew. I tell the truth now and to hell with the consequences. If people told the truth there never would have been concentration camps.–

–Concentration camps? I don't understand what that has to do with this conversation.–

–Jews were taken from their homes, put on freight trains. People saw but they never told. They said nothing. Don't you ever think what would have happened if our grandparents hadn't come to America. We would be ashes in the wind. When you interrupted me I was writing about a man whose entire family was cremated.–

–Really! Is he fictitious?–

–He is not. He's my cousin.–

–Is that the man Lynn saw you with?–

–Yes.–

–She said he was simply gorgeous.–

–He is.–

–What's happening between you two?–

–You're not going to tell me who you're with and you expect me to tell you the intimate details of my life. Forget it.–

–Then it is intimate.–

–I said, forget it.–

–Look Julia I can't tell you because he's married.–

–You don't have to tell me. I know who he is.–

–Who told you?–

–What difference does that make?–

–But nobody knows.–

Before I can stop the words they're out. –Cynthia's father.–

She gasps, –Who else knows?–

–You're sleeping with Cynthia's father! I said it as a joke. How could you Mallory after what I told you about him and Cynthia?–

–You're wrong about him Julia. I confronted him and he denied it.–

–Oh sure. Like he's going to admit it. How old is he anyhow?–

–He's only forty three.–

–Only! My father is forty.–

–Your father is different.–

–You're right. He is. He never touched me.–

–No wonder you write. What an imagination. Cynthia and Irving.–

–I didn't imagine it. I saw it and he knows I saw it. Why Mallory?–

—He loves me. You can't believe how wonderful he is. He takes me to the greatest places and he's teaching me the business. I'm actually designing clothes and he's using them. I'm only sixteen and I'm a designer.—

—Would you marry him?—

—Yes, if he wanted me.—

—You'd be Cynthia's stepmother. If that isn't ridiculous. Have you told Ceil?—

—No. Nobody knows but you.—

—If he's so wonderful why are you hiding it? Because it's wrong and you know it.—

—It's not wrong. He's opened the world for me, restaurants I've never eaten in...—

—Here in New York?—

—Sometimes but mostly on the Island. Did you know Long Island has the most beautiful inns with food that's made in heaven and Irving knows every one of them. We go to foreign movies. His mother is Italian. When he makes love he talks to me in Italian. *Te amo mi amore, te amo.* What I feel is so wonderful it can't be wrong.—

—What about Cynthia and her mother? Have you thought about them?—

—You don't even like her mother. You told me so.—

—But she's his wife.—

—So what. She doesn't make him happy. She hates sex. She thinks it's dirty. Do you know she never even took off her nightgown when they did it. He's never seen her with her clothes off. She undresses in the closet.—

—Why are you telling me this?—

—Don't look at me like that Julia. I love him.—

—You wouldn't love him if he were a plumber. You only love him because he's letting you design his clothes. You're smart Mallory. You don't need him.—

—Please don't tell anybody.—

—If you're going to marry him you're going to have to tell people.—

–I'll worry about it then.–

–He's not going to marry you. He's forty three. He's Cynthia's father. He's a creep.–

MALLORY'S APARTMENT 1994

Why did Mallory kill herself? That is the question. I tread carefully over the junk mountain on Mallory's floor. I sleuth between layers of carpeting. I read her note over and over again searching for clues.

There's a photo on Mallory's desk. I don't remember posing for it but I was there. I am the squinty eyed kid next to Mallory. We're seven, before she was orphaned, before I learned to fight the kids from St. Theresa's. Before the Eleanor Roosevelt Girls. We're holding hands, looking at one another. We're so damned young, so sweet.

Mallory and I played a game all our lives. It was called *Who would you really miss if they died?* It was amazing how few names we came up with. Sometimes the names would change. Divorced husbands, ex-lovers, friends who were no longer friends. Some names remained always. Even when Mallory and I separated, even when we were angry with one another she was always on that list of people I'd miss.

A box leaps from her closet and heads straight for my head. There's the start of a lump. Thanks Mallory. I look through letters, love letters, business letters, an angry one from Mallory and one from me dated July 5, 1947.

Dear Mallory:

I know why you're angry but you're wrong. I never told Cynthia. I wouldn't hurt her or you. I wouldn't even hurt Mrs. Marko despite the fact that I can't stand her. I don't know who snitched but it wasn't me. Lynn told me you're marrying Cynthia's father. I'm writing to wish you luck. Well what the hell. I said I'd always tell the truth so here it is. You're not talking to me anyhow. I think you're dumb to marry a man twenty seven years older than you whose morals stink.

Letters are great. Nobody answers you back. You actually get to finish a sentence.

I always thought that when either one of us got married the other one would be there. Obviously you don't want me at your wedding. Obviously you don't want to be friends anymore. Obviously if I were to die tomorrow I wouldn't put a hole in your heart. I think you should know that although you're alive you've already put a hole in mine.

I am your friend always even though I'm not yours.

Love, Julia.

P.S. I happen to know that you invited all the Eleanor Roosevelt Girls except me and Bettina.

A WEDDING PARTY WITHOUT THE BRIDE 1948

Cynthia, as expected, wouldn't go. Lynn refused to go because of Cynthia. Margaret said it was immoral. Annie, Claire and Cleo went. Well they more than went. They were the bridesmaids. Ceil was the Maid of Honor. It was rumored that Mrs. Marko slit her wrists the night before and had to be rushed to the hospital.

I met with Margaret and Bettina at Lynn's apartment. Lynn's mother put out food and drink for the uninvited. Wine, cheese, bread, little cakes. She joined us until her date came, then introduced us and left. We sat sipping wine, not one of us saying a word.

Why had we gotten together? Whose idea was it anyhow?

–I think Cynthia's coming,– Lynn finally said.

–Maybe we should have invited her mother.–

—Julia, you can't be serious.—

—I'm dead serious. I don't think she should be left alone considering what she did last night.—

—What did she do?—

—She slit her wrists Margaret.—

—No!—

—Julia, that is simply untrue. If you knew her you'd know how silly that rumor is. She never even loved him. She told Cynthia she married him because her parents thought he was a good catch. Actually she was in love with another boy who happened not to be Jewish so that was the end of that.—

—Irving's not Jewish. He's Italian.—

—Bettina, he's Italian and he's Jewish like I'm a Scottish Jew. One is a nationality and the other is a religion.—

—Really! I never knew that.—

—If you ask me you're the lucky one Margaret.—

—Julia!—

—Well she is Lynn. If I were Catholic I'd be a nun too. No man, no cooking, no cleaning, no dirty diapers, no stupid job.—

—Julia, one more absurd remark and I'm going to throw you out.—

—You and who else Lynn.—

We were clowning around, throwing each other off balance, rolling on the floor when Cynthia entered.

—Aren't you two a little old for that?—

—Cynthia,— we said in unison.

Lynn rose, put her arms around her. —Sit down. Have some wine.—

—Wine! How festive. Are we celebrating something?—

—Comeon Cyn. You know we're only here to support you.—

—Why? Do I look like I'm falling apart?—

—Is your mother alright?—

—She's fine Margaret, just fine. Of course nobody believes it because of that stupid wrist slashing rumor so now her friends and relatives, the loyal ones who wouldn't go to the wedding are watching her like hawks for fear she'll do something silly like take pills or slit her throat.—

—That poor woman.—

—She's not a poor woman Margaret and she's not going to do anything to hurt herself. To put it bluntly she's just embarrassed. What will the neighbors say. She'll have to move. She never cared for him. I ought to know. He was just her meal ticket. All she ever wanted from him was money so she could buy clothes and jewels and furs to show off to her friends. Of course he left her. What man would stay with a woman like that?—

—Cynthia, she's your mother.—

—Thanks Margaret for reminding me.—

—Well I agree with Margaret. It must be terrible to have your husband leave you for a woman who's not only your daughter's age but your daughter's friend.—

—Right Bettina. And she never lets me forget it. If it weren't for you Cynthia. You invited that whore into the house. You arranged for her to get a job at your father's place. You knew what was going on.— Cynthia pulled off her blouse, pulled down her bra. —There. How do you like that?—

Her breasts were full of bruises and scratch marks. Her back was a railroad track gone wild. —My skin is probably still under those long manicured nails of hers. That poor woman as you put it Margaret.— She took a long sip of wine.

I thought of that other time when her breasts were exposed.

—What are you staring at Julia? If I didn't know better I'd think you were queer.—

Lynn put her arms around her. —Cyn, everybody is here because we love you. Comeon Cyn, we're your friends.—

Enormous tears fell from Cynthia's eyes. —My life is hell. I can't go home. I don't have a home. She says if it weren't for me. I can't even tell you the rest. It's so disgusting it makes me want to puke. I've lost everything, my father, my mother, my friend, my home, my work. I'm through. Finished.–

–Listen to me Cyn. Cyn, stop crying and listen. You can stay here until we sort things out.–

–Your mother won't like it.–

–Don't be silly. It will be fine. We'll go to your place and get your things.–

–I'm locked out. Don't you understand? Locked out. I'm only here tonight because there's no place for me to go.–

At midnight Lynn's mother returns, welcoming Cynthia as Lynn predicted.

My mother is hysterical when I get home. –Where have you been? Do you realize what time it is? Your father is furious.–

–So where is he if he's so furious?–

–Sleeping.–

–How come he always sleeps when he's furious with me?–

–Sit down Julia. I have to talk to you.–

–I'm tired mom. I don't feel like a talk.–

–Julia, Mrs. Marko tried to kill herself tonight. She's in the hospital. They're trying to find Cynthia. Do you know where she is?–

I remember Cynthia's bruised body and say nothing.

–Julia, I'm talking to you. Do you know where she is?–

–Wasn't she at the wedding?–

–No.–

–I wonder how Mallory is doing.–

–Mallory? Mallory is the cause of all this. Julia, listen to me. Mrs. Marko tried to kill herself. She was found naked on Greenpoint Avenue. In this freezing cold weather. She was bleeding from head to foot and screaming about her whore daughter and her whore daughter's friends. She...–

–You expect me to tell you where Cynthia is after hearing that. Even if I knew where she was I wouldn't tell you.–

–Don't you care that she could be dying?–

–I care about Cynthia. I care about Mallory. I care about my friends. I don't care about a woman who calls us whores.–

—Why would she say such a thing? Look at Mallory. She just takes another woman's husband and not any woman but your friend's father, a man old enough to be her own father. It makes me wonder about your Eleanor Roosevelt Girls. How do I know you were at Lynn's. How do I know you weren't with some man?—

—You mean doing dirty things like kissing and petting. Getting his germs.—

—You have some mouth.—

—I have no desire to do dirty things with boys. I don't even like boys and I'm certainly never going to marry one.—

—I'm glad to hear that because if you did I pity the man who would be stupid enough to marry you.—

—What a lovely thing to say to your daughter. Thanks mom.—

—The truth is the truth.—

MALLORY'S WEDDING, SECOND HAND 1948

One week after Mallory's wedding the invited got together with the rest of us to give us a first hand report on Mallory's wedding, her gown, the flowers, the music, the food.

—You never saw so much food in your whole life. I thought the hors d'oeuvres were the meal, we all did didn't we Annie and then somebody said we should go to our tables and they served us an entire meal from soup to nuts. I thought I'd pass out from eating.—

—Are you kidding! You should have seen Claire wolf down the food.—

—Me! How about you Annie. She got drunk. Cleo and I had to practically carry her to the Ladies Room.—

—She puked all over.—

—That was from that stuffed whatever they call it.—

—Stuffed derma.—

—I never had it before. I had three portions and it didn't agree with me.–

–A likely story. You were drunk.–

Lynn made one of her dramatic entrances. She pulled a pack of cigarettes from her coat pocket, lit one, then looked at each of us sighing. –That home is the most depressing place I've ever had the displeasure of visiting. Both are inconsolable. Both blame the other. The minute I entered the foyer I could feel layers of ice covering my body and the longer I stayed the thicker the layers became.–

–How beautiful. Inconsolable. Layers of ice. You should be a writer,– Margaret said.

–So what happened Lynn?–

–Nothing Julia.–

–Nothing,– Cleo said. –Nothing?–

–That's right. Nothing. We just spoke about things in general.–

–What things?–

–Things Annie, you know things. We never mentioned the wedding or the attempted suicide if that's what it was.–

–Well I can tell you that what started out as beautiful turned into a disaster. Poor Mallory.–

–Poor Mallory! Did you take a good look at Irving Marko? He's stunning. And the way he held her when they danced. I've decided to marry an older man just like Irving Marko.–

–When will that be Cleo? You're eighteen and you're still sneaking out on dates.–

–Never mind. I will.–

–Lynn, did you tell Cynthia you're still going to be modeling for Irving?–

–Do you think I'm an insensitive clod?–

–How can you work for him being Cynthia's friend and all?–

–I'm only staying until I find another job. Marko Originals. What a laugh. Do you know what they call originals? Stealing from the top designers, making changes here and there. That's the design Mallory does. She doesn't have an original bone in her entire body but she's great at rearranging what's already there.–

—That's not true.—

—I can't believe you're still defending her. Honestly Julia.—

—Well I for one feel sorry for Mallory.—

—You would Cleo.—

—It was horrible seeing all those policemen coming in in the middle of the reception. We'd just come out of the bathroom after Annie puked.—

—Annie puked?—

—You should have seen her Lynn. Was she ever drunk.—

—I was sick from stuffed whatever.—

—Derma. Stuffed derma. Anyhow, the police spoke to Irving and he turned white and I mean white. Then he said something to Mallory and went out with the police. Everybody was looking at Mallory. Then Ceil came over to her but before she could say anything Mallory ran out of the room.—

—We ran after her. She was getting on her coat and Ceil was trying to convince her not to leave. Where will you go she asked and Mallory said home. Then Ceil said what home are you talking about and Mallory screamed how should I know. Suddenly all her aunts were there. Millie said, will you calm down. Everybody can hear you and Mallory said so let them. What do I care about them? What do I care about anybody? All I know is anytime anything good happens to me it has to be ruined.—

Annie said, —Then Julia, you're not going to believe this...she yelled where's Julia and Ceil said you didn't invite her and she said I did so invite her and Esther said don't you remember...—

—Well go on Annie.—

—I can't. They took her outside so we never did hear the end of the sentence.—

—Until that happened it was a great wedding.—

—That phony suicide was a spiteful act to ruin Mallory's wedding.—

—Are you saying she slit her wrists to make Mallory miserable? Come off it Julia. You're only siding with Mallory because you think

she invited you. Well she didn't. Mallory is nothing more than a con-
niving...–

–How dare you Lynn. How about you, working for Irving?–

–Don't fight. Please don't fight. We're friends.– Tears fell from
Claire's eyes.

Lynn put her arm around her. –I'm sorry. It's just that I hate to
see Julia being taken in. She's so blind when it comes to Mallory.–

–I am not.–

–Ok, you're not. Can we drop it?–

Margaret looked from one to the other. –Is it true Mallory lives
in a penthouse on Fifth Avenue?–

–Yes.–

–Have you seen it Lynn?–

–Yes I have.–

–Does Cynthia know?–

–Of course she knows. She asked me to go and report back to
her.–

–This is awful. This is the worst thing that's ever happened to
the Eleanor Roosevelt Girls.–

1948 TO 1950

Ceil invites me for dinner. To get Mallory and me together no
doubt. She isn't in the living room but knowing Mallory she'll pop
out of a closet or the bathroom and dash toward me, a big smile on
her face.

It doesn't happen.

'The Girls' brag about Mallory's Fifth Avenue penthouse. The
greenhouse with tropical plants, the unparalleled view of Manhattan.
The priceless paintings. A showplace Ruth says. She has a brilliant
interior designer, Millie adds.

After dinner Ceil takes me aside. –What a mess that girl got

herself into. What a horrible mess. Call her Julia. She misses you.–
–Me! Call her! After the way she treated me?–
–Rise above it sweetie. Call.–
I don't.

Annie and I graduate from Newtown High. I find a job as a receptionist in a Fifth Avenue beauty salon. On my lunch hour I write short stories.

Annie is a clerk typist in a law firm, a job she hates.

Lynn moves out when her mother marries the man she's been dating. She joins a modern dance company in New York and earns her living waitressing.

Cynthia is with an off off Broadway theater group. There is no admission but at the end of every performance a hat is passed. We tell Cynthia she's great but how can we know. The plays are amateurish and pointless.

Bettina lives with her mother and her mother's new lover. During the day she studies acting, at night she's a cocktail waitress.

Cleo enters into an arranged marriage. She meets Paniotti for the first time when he gets off the boat. I watch her walk down the aisle, tall, lovely, elegant. Her father holds her arm. I expect to see him in an undershirt but he's managed to dress for the occasion. Her groom is short on looks, short on hair, short on height, short on English and charm and for all I know short on everything else.

The ancient Greek ceremony begins with the chanting of Byzantine hymns by three priests. Cleo and Paniotti repeat their vows three times, exchange rings and flower crowns three times as they walk around the altar through the incense. The ceremony is beautiful.

Annie is engaged to a man who left the Franciscan order when he fell in love with her. Good looking and gentle, he is perfectly suited for Annie. He is now back in school getting his teaching credentials. Annie is a paralegal.

Cynthia graduates from off off Broadway to Broadway. She has a small part in a good play. We all tell her how marvelous she is and she is. Her mother who somehow managed to take her clothes off for strangers on Greenpoint Avenue but not for Irving is once again married. This one looks nothing like Cynthia's father but could pass for his double.

Bettina leaves her mother's home to marry her auto mechanic lover when she discovers she's pregnant. Bettina, her blond hair still freshly curled, her makeup applied perfectly now vomits up her meals to keep her weight down. She dresses herself and her daughter in matching fashion plate clothing to go to the supermarket while her husband wears nothing but jeans that show the slit in his behind every time he bends down. Big bellied, full of beer and dirty jokes he does not approve of married women working. So ends Bettina's acting career. Her mother, now deserted by her latest lover lives alone in Sunnyside, near her daughter. She sits with vacant eyes ignoring Bettina and her little granddaughter. Sometime she fondles her breasts, unaware, without the smile, without the teasing look. Bettina confides that her mother has a masseuse who masturbates her. Mrs. Lacy tells me as I'm leaving one day that Jewish men are the best. They stick with their wives. Apparently their greasy heads are no longer important.

CLAIRE 1950

Two years after Cleo's wedding, Claire married the man her mother chose for her in the hospital before her gall bladder operation went wrong and killed her. Arnie is the man she chose, a good boy according to Claire's mother. You could do worse she told Claire. Claire married him honoring her dead mother's wishes but not her own.

We were all at Claire's wedding except for Margaret who was now a novice and Mallory who hasn't been seen by anyone other than the pigeons who roost on her terraced penthouse. Cleo, who looked like death warmed over came with Paniotti, who stood around awkwardly. In two years she had two children. She suffered constantly from stomach pains.

Claire's mother's prediction that she could do worse was wrong. She couldn't have done worse. The day after Claire's wedding she called Annie at her office. Annie was at a meeting and couldn't be disturbed. She then called Cleo and got Cleo's mother who told her in broken English that Cleo was taken to the hospital that morning. I was half out the door when my phone rang. Claire was so hysterical I called my boss to say I'd be late. I rushed over to her apartment. Her face was swollen from crying. When I asked what happened she said she couldn't tell me. I tried calming her down, made her tea, tried to figure out what was wrong.

–Did you have a fight? Claire, did you and Arnie have a fight?–

–No.– She was crying bitterly.

–Then what?–

–I need a doctor. Not Dr. Steinberg. I won't go to a man.–

–I don't know any woman doctors. I'm sure there are women doctors but I don't know any. I'll bet Lynn does.–

–Don't tell her.–

–Tell her what? I don't know anything.–

Lynn didn't have a woman doctor but was positive Cynthia did. She gave me the number of the theater. –What's wrong Julia? Are you ill?–

–It's nothing serious.–

–I thought Dr. Steinberg was your doctor. Why can't you go to him?–

–I'd rather have a woman.–

–You're not pregnant.–

–No.–

I called the theater. Cynthia was furious. –This better be good. You got me out of rehearsal.–

–I'm very sick. I need your doctor's number.–

–What's wrong?–

–Can't you just give me the number?–

She repeated the number twice, then asked me to call back. –So I don't worry unnecessarily.–

Claire called and was so hysterical the doctor agreed to see her immediately. She begged me to go with her. I agreed only if she would tell me what was so urgent.

–I'm bleeding.–

–So! As far as I know most virgins bleed.–

–You don't understand. He ripped me. He tore my insides. I think he damaged something. It hurt so bad I started screaming and he yelled shutup. Shutup or you'll have the hotel detective knocking on our door. Then he left me alone and I thought good, he's not going to do it anymore. But he didn't stop. When I showed him how hard I was bleeding he just laughed and said I was dumb, that that's what happens the first time you break a cherry. And look what he did to my nipple.–

She pulled up her blouse. The entire area was bruised and swollen.

–That bastard.–

–What am I going to do Julia?–

–I'll tell you one thing you're not going to do. You're not going back to him.–

–Where will I go?–

–You have sisters. You could go to Marian's.–

–I can't tell my sisters. I'd die first. Besides they love him. They'd never believe it.–

–Tell them and then see how far that love goes.–

–I can't. It would be too humiliating.–

–Humiliating! Is that what you're worried about. Being humiliated. The man is a maniac.–

–Maybe he's right. Maybe some women bleed heavily.–

–What are you nuts? Comeon, let's go to the doctor.–

Annie Finds Cleo 1994

The ring of the phone startles me. Before I can climb over Mallory's treasure mountain I hear, –This is Mallory. I can't pick up now. Actually I won't be able to pick up later either. Where I'm going there aren't any telephones or computers that say have a nice day. Where I'm going we are all angels peeing on the dopes below. So when you hear it thunder don't run under a tree. There'll be peeing from heaven. It's me... me... me.–

–Mallory, it's Annie. I know you can't hear me but I wish you could so I could tell you how funny that message is. Julia, if you're there pick up. I found Cleo.–

–Really! Where?–

–Where are all the Greek restaurants?–

–In Greece?–

–In Astoria, Julia. She owns a Greek restaurant in Astoria.–

–With that miserable husband of hers?–

–That miserable husband died ten years ago.–

–Really! So what did she say? Was she surprised to hear from you?–

–It's been twenty seven years. What do you think?–

–Did you tell her about Mallory?–

–She was shocked, really shocked.–

–The first one of us to die.–

–What's happening with you Julia? Have you gone out with Richard yet?–

–Why are you asking me such a dumb question?–

–What's dumb about it? You're obviously smitten by him.–

–Smitten. What kind of a word is smitten?–

–Would you prefer enamored?–

–I told you he was Mallory's lover.–

–It's not like you're taking him from her. I'll bet he's called. Go out with him. Have some fun.–

–Will you shutup about him Annie?–

–Loosen up Julia before you burst a blood vessel.–

–If you don't mind my changing the subject I would like to have dinner at Cleo's.–

–I don't know if that's such a good idea.–

–Why not? Say yes Annie. Loosen up. Have some fun.–

–You're about as subtle as rotting fish.–

–For old times sake. Because we were such good friends.–

–Were we? I always thought we hung out together because we lived near one another.–

–There were other girls who lived there. Why weren't they in our club?–

–Chance darling, pure chance. Think about it. What did we have in common. I don't even remember how I became a member.–

–We had a lot in common.–

–Two by two you mean. Me and Claire, you and Mallory, Lynn and Cynthia, Cleo and Margaret. All but our star Bettina. I never figured how she got in.–

–Well I loved seeing you Annie. It took me back.–

–To what? We came from dysfunctional homes and we didn't even know it. And how about poverty? Spaghetti with ketchup, day old bread. I had to pretend we had a dog so I could get soup bones for free. Do you think Cynthia with her maid shared those memories? Or Lynn or Cleo? Certainly not Mallory who always dressed like a princess. You can keep the good old days. I think you should. Write about them. It might give you an entirely new perspective.–

–That's ridiculous. We were all lower middle class except for Bettina and Cynthia.–

–Lower middle class would have been an upwardly mobile step for my family.–

–Listen Annie, as far as I'm concerned you and Claire were the lucky ones. At least your parents were happy together.–

–That must mean poor people are destined for happiness.–

–Your families weren't happy?–

–That didn't keep Claire's mother from dying. She might have been happy but she was also rundown and overworked. And to live in back of a laundry with pipes hanging from the ceiling. Honestly Julia.—

–I'm talking about love Annie.—

–Well I'm talking about being poor. Write about that. I promise to read that one.—

But I don't write. I am alone I tell the glass figurines, the fancy ladies in 18th century hooped skirts, the men in vests and knickers, their glass hair tied in pony tails. The dogs, the cats, the whimsical figurines, the leprechauns. I have nobody I say. I am no longer a part of anything. I am emptier than the emptiest box. If I were to die tomorrow what change would that make in anyone's life?

Stop complaining, the limoges answer. We've been collecting dust for years and you don't hear us complain. Rudolph Valentino looks at me from his poster. Is he laughing at me? I sit on top of the three layered carpet and cry.

THE ELEANOR ROOSEVELT GIRLS ARE INVADED 1952

It's no longer us. It's become them as well. Them being the men who are connected to us. A disaster. Arnie, who is loathed by all, women and men alike, takes over our meetings. The Eleanor Roosevelt Girls sit gritting their teeth giving each other looks while he tells dirty jokes, racist jokes, sexist jokes, any joke that ridicules the other. He burps, he nose picks. We are silent only because of Claire. Our meetings bore Arnie. According to him we lack imagination. We need to put some zip into our meetings. His latest idea of zip is going to what he calls a *queer bar*. So we can see how the other half lives. Don't you want to see how the other half lives he asks.

–I work with the other half,– Lynn says.

–Pardon me for living.—

–I'm not going,–Tim says.

–Why not Timmy? Is it against your religious beliefs?–

–Please don't call me Timmy. I am not a three year old. My name is Timothy.–

–I beg your pardon. Timothy. Tell me Timothy, do I detect a note of fear? Is it true that priests are secret queers?–

–That's not funny Arnie,– Cynthia says.

–And don't call me a priest. I am not a priest.–

–Maybe a queer bar appeals to you. Maybe you secretly want some guys dingaling up your ass. Hey it's ok Timothy. I understand.–

–Shutup Arnie,– Lynn says.

–No female tells me to shutup.–

–You've got a mouth like a sewer Arnie,– I say

–Kiss my ass Julia.–

–I've got a better idea. You go to the queer bar and have some man kiss your ass so you can prove to yourself you're not a homosexual.–

–Me!– Arnie says. –Me! Ask my wife about that.–

–Any guy who does what you do to Claire is either a homosexual or a maniac.–

Claire looks at me in disbelief. There is the start of tears. Five pair of eyes move in unison all landing on Arnie.

–What the hell are you talking about? Do you know what you're talking about?– He shoots a tight faced look at Claire.

Claire's words quiver along her mouth. –I don't think there's anything wrong with going to a queer club.–

Annie turns to me. –Julia. Really Julia.– Her laugh is having problems leaving her throat. –What have you conjured up this time? Arnie, if you knew Julia the way we girls do you'd know what a wild imagination she has. Remember Julia is the writer.–

Fury is stamped on Arnie's face. Fear is etched on Claire's. I want to tell everyone what Arnie now knows I know. I want to call the police and have him arrested. Instead I say, –Admit it Arnie, you're a sex machine. Claire says you don't let her sleep.–

Arnie's laugh is menacing. He's not buying it. Everybody laughs except for Annie who looks at Claire who looks at me. And Bettina who lives in her own little world.

GAYLANDS 1952

We call one another and decide not to go. Then Claire calls Annie and Annie calls me. I call Lynn who calls Cynthia who calls Bettina. Cynthia is in a play. Bettina's daughter is sick. Six of us go. Arnie, Claire, me, Lynn, Annie and Tim. We're going because Claire has made it clear that if we don't go Arnie will take it out on her.

It's hard to breathe, the smoke is that thick. Hard to talk, the noise is deafening, hard to get a drink. The bar is layered with people. A woman, very fat, very butch, a cigarette dangling from her mouth eyes Claire. —Enjoying yourself?—

Claire looks to Arnie for her cue. —I'm talking to you sweetheart, not him. So are you?—

Claire nods dumbly.

The woman calls to the bartender. —Give my friend a glass of cold white wine. You look like the white wine type. So, are you slumming or what?—

Arnie eyes her up and down. —Forget the or what. We're married.—

—So are my parents.—

—Sa zeech his own.—

She ignores him, takes Claire onto the crowded dance floor. Claire looks back at Arnie who nods his approval. We all look in amazement. Arnie turns to a man at the bar. —How about dancing?—

—How about it,— he answers and walks off.

Arnie's laugh is loud. —Pardon me for living.—

Within minutes Tim is being looked over by a man at the end of the bar. He points at Tim, at himself, at the dance floor, making dancing steps with his fingers. Timothy shakes his head. Arnie who's been watching says, –Don't be a spoil sport. Dance with the fagala. Have some fun.– He goes over to the man, brings him to Tim.

While Tim dances awkwardly on the dance floor and Claire is somewhere out of sight the rest of us stand clutching our drinks pretending we belong.

Claire is now dancing with another woman who is very striking. Her hair is blue black and very short. She looks like she was poured into her jeans. Her jersey blouse clings to her breasts, showing her nipples. Claire is talking to her, the woman is rubbing her hands up and down Claire's back, rubbing her body against Claire's, cupping her behind. I look over at Arnie. His expression is bull like. Claire is the red flag and the red flag is laughing. Never have I seen her laugh like that, so free. I turn to Annie. –Do you see what I see?–

–I can't believe she's doing that. She must be crazy. Lynn?–

–I'm not blind. Somebody's got to do something. Look at Arnie.–

We head for the Ladies Room, go into a stall. A woman in line says, –I'd love to know what's going on in there.– The other waiting women laugh.

–Listen, we've got to get Claire out of here.–

–Lynn Lynn. Always dramatic.–

–He beats the shit out of her and you think I'm being dramatic.–

–Since when does he beat her?–

–You're the one who let Arnie know that we know and you ask when?–

–Did you know Annie?–

–Of course she knows. We all know. Wake up Julia.–

–Well I didn't know. How come?–

–Oh cute. Now we're going to focus on you. We're only here because she was so scared. You knew that.–

–Yes but...–

–Shutup Julia and listen. I think the best solution is that you take her to your place.–

–Me? What makes you think she'll go with me?–

–Well Annie obviously can't because that's the first place he'd look.–

–Then you take her home Lynn.–

There's banging on our stall. –Hey would you knock it off in there. There are only three toilets and some of us have to pee. What the hell are you doing in there anyhow?–

–We'll be right out.–

–Can't you have your discussion outside?–

–In a minute. Julia, I would gladly have her stay with me but I go into rehearsal tomorrow.–

–You think I don't work.–

–You don't work the hours I do. Besides, he'd never think she was staying with you. You're not even close to one another. Well look this is silly. Either you'll do it or you won't. If you won't I'll be more than happy to have her.–

–Ok, she can stay with me.–

–And don't let that bastard in no matter what he says.–

–But you said he'd never suspect.–

–Jesus, if you're sucking each other off find some other place will you.–

We come out of the stall just as Claire opens the door to enter. Her eyes shine. –Hello Eleanor Roosevelt Girls.–

I plunge in before she can say another word. –You're coming home with me.–

–What for?–

–I know all about it Claire.–

–First of all I wouldn't go home with you because I don't trust you anymore. I confided in you Julia and you as much as told Arnie.–

–It just slipped out and anyhow I wasn't talking about his striking you.–

The women in line are all watching. One shakes her head. –The straight world is slumming again. Listen and learn.–

Lynn glares at her. –Would you mind butting out?–

–Arnie's ok. He's just got a bad temper and anyhow most of the time it's my fault.–

–What did you do. Burn his toast?– a woman says.

–Claire, you don't have to go with Julia. You can come home with me but you're not going home with that bastard.–

–I am going home with him.–

–Why? So he can beat you up some more?–

–He beats you?– a woman says.

–Point that shit out,– another says. –We'll take care of him.–

–Knock it off,– Lynn says. –You're not helping.–

A voice from a stall. –Kill the bastard.–

Claire's eyes fill with tears. –Stop it all of you. You don't know him. You don't know how terrible he feels afterward. I'm telling you, it's my fault.–

The woman in the stall comes out. –Are you the woman who's being beat on? Yeah, I can tell it's you. Didn't your mother teach you that nobody deserves to get beat? You want my advice. Go while the going is good.–

She leaves just as the woman who was dancing with Claire enters.

–Claire, I'm so glad you haven't left...What's the matter? Why are you crying?–

–Ze plot thickens.–

Claire, forever the polite one, introduces her to us. A woman in line says, –Dina. Dina. Hey Claire, if you don't want her I'll take her.–

Another woman. –Leave the shithead. Go with Dina.–

RICHARD 1994

We're at a concert at Avery Fisher Hall. During intermission I ask, Did you love Mallory? Yes he says. Yes I did.

Do you want to go to bed with me Richard?

I haven't thought about it. Do you with me?

Only to know what Mallory felt when she had sex with you.

But you're not Mallory.

I know that. Don't you think I know that? Did you go to Mallory's place or yours?

Mine. She said hers was a mess and she didn't like people there.

The chimes tell us that intermission is over. Richard looks at me warmly. He thinks he's beginning to know me better. He isn't. He couldn't. He doesn't even know about this conversation.

It's my dream. Not his.

I wake up. Make myself a drink, watch TV. The images blur. They become Mallory and Richard. This is so sick. Why am I doing this?

The doorbell rings. It's Richard. Why are you here I ask.

Julia, I knew you were home. I waited by the fountain but you never came. He smiles at me. Great legs Julia.

I feel my breath coming in short spurts. Don't let him notice. Don't let him have the upper hand.

How are your legs Richard?

Not bad. He begins removing his pants.

What the hell do you think you're doing?

I'm showing you my legs.

Christ, who's going to make the first move, him or me. Who's going to mention the condom first?

You worry too much he says reading into my head. I'm clean.

How do I know?

I give my blood every month. They wouldn't take it if I wasn't clean.

I don't do it without a condom.

Ok he says. I hate the damned things but ok.

I watch him take off his underpants. I watch him put on the condom. I'm soaked. If he ever comes inside me he'll slip right out. He takes his shirt off, grabs me, unbuttons my top, kisses my body. I'm going to pass out. Before we're on the bed, before anything happens I've had an orgasm. They're coming one after the other. He's touching me, sucking me. Never has it been like this.

They say more people die of heart attacks during intercourse. My heart is pumping a hundred miles a minute. It's pumping out of my chest. I'll be the first person to die before intercourse. I'm going to make medical history. They'll write *she died of anticipation.* He's about to enter when the phone rings.

Don't answer he says.

I have to. It could be Richard.

He laughs. Richard! I'm Richard.

I wake up. My bed is soaked. It smells of sex and there's nobody there but me.

MALLORY BREAKS THE SILENCE 1952

Mallory calls. As if nothing's happened. No, I've missed you. No, how have you been? No nothing. Julia she says, how about coming over for lunch tomorrow? My no is ignored. How about dinner or if you prefer we can meet here and go out for dinner? I leave it to you. Of course it's on me.

Like I can't afford my own meals. Like I wouldn't dare say no to her.

Her apartment is lush. Beautiful furniture, beautiful paintings, beautiful plants, beautiful view. I focus on the superficial. The hole in my heart is open.

—My maid is off for the night,– she says.

—Mine's not,– I answer sarcastically.

–Julia, you could always make me laugh.– But she isn't laughing. Neither am I.

–I assume Irving is off for the night too.–

Now she is laughing. –You look good Julia. What's happening in your life? Martini?– she asks before I can answer her question.

–I'd prefer rye and ginger ale.–

Her 'oh' is disapproving.

–A Sunnyside drink Mallory. I haven't graduated to the Park Avenue martini yet.– She lets that one go.

–Are you still writing?–

–Yes, I'm still writing.–

–Good. I'm glad. Who do you write for?–

–For me. I write for me.–

–How do you support yourself?–

–I'm a receptionist in a beauty salon. Your kind of place Mallory. I've actually thought you might come in one day.–

–What's the name of the place?–

–Jacques.–

–The one on Fifth Avenue?–

–Yes.–

–I almost did go there once.–

–What would you have said if you saw me at the desk?–

–Hello Julia. I've missed you.–

Finally.

–That's interesting, considering you've made no effort to contact me in four years. Did you know I'm married?–

–Yes. Lynn told me.–

–I didn't know you saw Lynn.–

–I've seen her a few times.–

–When the mood hits you?–

There it is, the opening for my speech, my get even speech. Typed out, rehearsed before a mirror.

–It has nothing to do with a mood Julia.–

–Everything depends on moods Mallory. You think you look

beautiful because you feel good. You think you look awful because you're in a bad mood. You fall in love because you're in the mood for love. As the song says, 'I'm in the mood for love.' You dream of love, your body softens, your vagina tingles...—

—What is this, a monologue from one of your plays?—

—Can I finish?—

—I don't believe this.—

—That feeling, that mood can change every cell in your body. You meet someone. Well you're bound to. You're sending off signals. So you meet and you think I'm in love. Of course you're not really in love. It's the mood. He could be anybody, an ape, a gorilla, a chimpanzee. So you desert your best friend all because he came along when you were ripe and in the mood. So, how is Irving?—

Both our eyes hold tears. I ask for the bathroom. Twenty images of me swim in the bathroom mirror, my full face, my profile, a quarter of my face, the back of my head. All those years of hurt, longing for the day when we'd be friends again. Remembering the insults, the slights one running into the other. Not being invited to her wedding. Four years of silence rotting inside me.

In the living room I drink my rye and ginger ale, ask for another. Neither of us speak. Finally Mallory asks if my husband is nice.

—Nice! That's a rather insipid word wouldn't you say?—

—Alright. Then is he interesting or is that another taboo word? How about intelligent, charming, handsome, strong, sensual, over-bearing, boring...—

Boring comes out of my mouth before I can stop it. The two of us laugh til tears roll down our eyes. I hear Irving's voice before I see him.

—What's so funny? Let me in on the joke.—

—I thought you'd gone,— Mallory says. Cold, like a thousand year glacier.

—I'm taking you girls out for dinner.—

—We don't need you to take us out Irving. We're perfectly capable of taking ourselves out.—

—Just a suggestion Mallory. How are you Julia?—

—Alright,— I say, not looking at him.

—See you later Mallory.—

I wait for the door to close. —What's happening Mallory? Why was I invited here? I mean, you haven't shown the slightest interest in me all these years and suddenly it's come over, have lunch, have dinner, whatever you want.—

—I haven't shown any interest! You could have called me.—

—Why would I call you after what you did?—

—Me! You told. I trusted you.—

—Mallory, I never told anyone. You can believe it or not. I don't care.—

—Ok, so I'm wrong. I'm a skunk, a rat, the worst disappointment in your life. It's all my fault.—

—The worst disappointment! Do you think I've spent the last four years thinking about you? What an ego!—

—Ok, then you haven't. But I have. I've thought of you every single day. Julia, can't we let the past drop? You're the best friend I ever had.—

—You know what I think. I think something's gone wrong in your life and that's why you called. But I've got news for you Mallory. You can't just call me when it suits you. That's not friendship Mallory. Friendship could be 50-50, it could be 60-40. It could even be 80-20 but it can't be just one way.—

—I was your friend and you know it.—

—Sure. Until you were put in the advanced class and went to a better high school than me. You were too smart for me.—

—I never thought of myself as brighter than you. You're the one who always talked about it.—

—Smarter and prettier and luckier.—

—In what way was I luckier? You had a mother and father.—

—My parents were lousy parents.—

—Well for your information lousy parents are better than no parents.—

—Poor Mallory. She gets everything and in the end she thinks she's been cheated.—

—Do you know that Millie went out with Irving after I married him?—

—Your aunt Millie?—

—Not that she liked him. She did it because she hates me.—

—In other words she's to blame, not Irving.—

—If she wasn't so willing...—

—Mallory, your husband is rotten to the core. Any man who fools around with his daughter...—

—That's a lie. You know it is.—

—Why did you marry him?—

Mallory pours herself another martini. —Why did you marry Julia?—

—To get out of my house.—

—Ditto sweetheart.—

—But you were the envy of the Eleanor Roosevelt Girls. Your aunts were great.—

—You didn't live there.—

—Is that why you invited me here, to tell me the sad story of your life?—

—I invited you hoping we could be friends again. Tell me what I need to do to regain your friendship? I need you Julia.—

—You need me so I'm supposed to forgive you. Forget it.—

She bursts out crying. —It won't be the same. I wanted to call you Julia I swear but I thought you'd hang up on me. I did call a couple of times and then I'd hear your voice and think, she doesn't want to hear from me. Please, can't you forgive me?—

—I don't know.—

—We were good friends, you know we were.—

—I'm not the same.—

—I can see that but I still love you. I always will.—

—And I love you but Mallory I'm not ever going to allow you to hurt me the way you did.—

–I won't.–

–And I refuse to discuss Irving. That's not my idea of friendship, discussing men.–

–Can I talk about him for just five minutes?–

–Why?–

–Because it's important.–

–Ok. Five minutes but that's it.–

–Last year Irving's brother died. We flew to Chicago for the funeral. Then a couple of months later his widow called. Irving invited her to stay with us. It was supposed to be for a week...–

–And?–

–She's still here.–

–Well, get rid of her.–

–They're lovers.–

–Lovers! Why do you stay?–

–I did leave.–

–But you're still here. Why?–

–I have no money, no job.–

–I thought you designed clothes for Marko. Design for someone else.–

–I haven't worked since we got married. Besides my lawyer says I have to stay. If I leave he can claim desertion and I'd get nothing. Julia, we're going to take that bastard for everything he's got.–

–We, Mallory? We?–

My Mother Says I Look Nice 1994

She opens the door and smiles. –You look nice Julia.–

You look nice is one of her best compliments. It means I look normal, not the way I usually look with my wild hair, my makeupless face, my artsy clothes and sneakers. You look nice means I have the Madison Avenue clone look, the way the other side of the family looks. Where did you get that gorgeous coat she asks.

—From Mallory.—

—Oh and how is Mallory?—

She hears my silence, says nothing. She removes vodka from her freezer, creamed herring from her refrigerator, black bread from the sideboard. I put out the food and dishes. My mother pours the vodka. —To health,— she says. Since she turned eighty all her toasts are to health. We drink. She pours more.

—Did you have another one of your fights?—

I gulp down the icy vodka. —Worse.—

—What could be worse?— she asks, waiting for a funny story. I'm good at funny stories.

—She's dead.—

My mother stops breathing. Her beautiful skin sprouts wrinkles. Her eyes waver as if they're about to lose their gel. —How,— she asks weakly.

—She drowned.—

—Was it an accident?—

—No.—

—Oh my god. When?—

—A week ago.—

—Was she depressed?—

My mother knows about depression. Everyone in my family knows about it. It's sewn into our genes before we're womb free.

—I didn't think so.—

—How could you not think so? You were her friend. You must have seen something.—

—I didn't.—

—Or you refused to see because you didn't want to.—

She's not talking about Mallory. She's talking about herself. See, let that be a lesson Julia. I'm depressed. Did you know that?

—How could you not know? Julia, I'm talking to you.—

—She said she was happy. I was depressed but she was happy. Get it mom? Do you get it?—

–Don't holler. I'm not deaf.–

–Of course you're deaf. When you want to be deaf you make yourself deaf.–

Her face drops to her chin. Her unsaid words hang in the air. I'm on the verge of tears but nothing will come from my eyes until I'm far away. In my family tears bring on disdain and hostility. She taps on the table with her finger nails. I'm going out of my skin. –Don't you hear that?–

–Yes,– she says sarcastically. –I hear it,– and stops tapping. –How could she take her life? She had everything.–

–You mean she lost everything.–

–What are you talking about? She had her health, that gorgeous apartment, those beautiful clothes, a daughter. What more could she want?–

–She worked, she had a purpose in life. When that's taken away what reason do you have for getting up in the morning? She wanted to work.–

–Leave me alone Julia. I have my own problems.–

–What problems? Are you sick?–

–No, I am not sick. What do you want from me?–

–Why are you so angry with me?–

–I am not angry with you.– Her mouth holds clenched teeth.

–Mom, do you want more herring?–

–I've had enough.–

I put my arms around her. –I knew I shouldn't tell you.–

–How could you not tell me?–

–You can't imagine how I feel. It's almost as if she took half of me with her.–

–What nonsense you talk. Wait til you get to be my age. Every day another friend dies.–

–So you've told me.–

–Good. So I'm telling you again. I can't imagine? I can't imagine? It's getting so I dread when the phone rings. This one died and that one died but you get over it. You have to. Do you hear me

Julia? You have to.–

We have dinner in a local restaurant. Our conversation is light, pleasant. Nothing painful. How's the Caesar salad she asks? Fine I say. It's awful, made with vaseline. I can barely swallow but I do. This is my mother's favorite restaurant.

ARIES AND SCORPIO

When Sandy was fourteen Mallory confessed she didn't like her. It happens she said. She explained that Aries and Scorpio didn't get along, couldn't get along. Scorpios are devious. Deviousness is completely alien to an Aries.

You never know what's going on in a Scorpio head she said. You think they're charming and sincere but inside there lurks a boiling nature.

Isn't your mother Scorpio Julia? Well then...

Our cross to bear.

FOUR ELEANOR ROOSEVELT GIRLS PLAN A CRIMINAL ACT 1952

Irving sang another tune but it was different from the one Mallory had in mind. He found a trio who sang in perfect harmony. About their liaison with Mallory. Then there was the soloist, ex–Mrs. Marko who wrote a song especially for the occasion. The judge cocked his head when Irving sang his aria.

Those in the courtroom were awestruck by Mallory's beauty. It was easily understood why any man would want to bed with her. Mallory's claim that Irving Marko, now paunchy, jowly and half bald was playing around with his sister-in-law evoked titters. Millicent Marko was pretty if you liked a pinched ass face but what man in his right mind would choose a woman close to fifty over twenty two year old Mallory.

Mallory was awarded nothing but her clothing, her two fur coats, the jewelry Irving gave her, a set of crystal glasses, two abstract paintings and the English bone china which was a wedding gift from 'the girls.'

She stormed out of the courtroom with me. We took a cab to Toots Shor's. Toots himself greeted us, asked for Irving. Working hard as usual he asked. Mallory nodded. She then ordered the most expensive food on the menu. Wine. Champagne. Put it on my tab she said. Outside she jabbed me with her elbow. Would I love to see Irving's face when he gets this bill? We then went to every expensive store and charged everything to Irving.

Mallory moved to a walkup apartment on the lower eastside. It was bare except for the belongings awarded her plus a mattress, two pillows, bedclothes and lamps she bought. She wasn't about to charge furniture to Irving. Mallory had other plans.

Over champagne and Beluga caviar (Mallory hadn't any intention of changing her lifestyle) she told us her plan. She would crack open Irving's safe. I was to be her assistant. Cynthia would help us get the loot to the car. Lynn would drive the getaway car. The thought of getting even with Irving Marko made our hearts leap.

—When?— I asked.

—The opening night of the Metropolitan Opera. Irving never misses opening night. It's a ritual with him. Close your mouth Julia. You'll catch flies.—

—How will we get in the apartment?—

She waved a key at me.

—Suppose he changed the lock?— Lynn asked.

—He wouldn't. I know Irving Marko. Julia, we're going to clean out that safe. Now Cynthia you're to stay in the car with Lynn. Give us fifteen minutes, then take the elevator to the apartment. Ring three times so we'll know it's you.—

—How about the doorman?—

–You're his daughter.–

–But I've never been to his apartment.–

–Tell the doorman you just came in from California where you live.–

–Without luggage?–

–People do visit without luggage. But you will have luggage. We can't carry the stuff out in our hands. You'll have two large suitcases.–

–What if he offers to carry them?–

–You won't let him.–

–But if he does?–

–We'll stuff them with paper.–

–Mallory, the doorman knows you're divorced. Won't he be suspicious?–

–Did Toots know?–

–That was ages ago. I'm sure he knows now. I'm sure everybody in the building knows. Isn't that woman living with him?–

–Alright Lynn, let's assume the whole world knows. So what? What's the doorman going to do? Call the police? Call Irving at the Met? And say what? Your ex–wife is in your apartment. Believe me, he won't.–

We sat in Mallory's eastside walkup and like professional thieves plotted the entire caper down to the last detail. Mallory opened another bottle of champagne.

–The Eleanor Roosevelt Girls strike again.–

Again! When was the last time?

THE ELEANOR ROOSEVELT GIRLS STRIKE 1952

Mallory greets the doorman with a smile and a handshake. In her palm is a twenty dollar bill. I follow her into the building. So far so good. We take the elevator. A couple gets on with us. Mallory looks at the elevator door. They get off. We stay to the top.

—Did they know you?—

—Probably.—

—They were staring at you.—

—I saw.—

—I'll bet they know you're divorced.—

She puts the key in the lock. Hello she says. Anybody home? We hear nothing. Mallory is cleaning out the safe when we hear the doorbell ring. I gasp.

—It's Cynthia, Julia. Cynthia.—

—No it's not. It hasn't been fifteen minutes and whoever it was rang once. Our signal was three rings, remember?—

Mallory moves cautiously to the door. —Yes,— she says.

—Open up Mallory. It's me.—

Cynthia enters with her suitcases.

—You were supposed to ring three times.—

—Are you sure?—

—I hope you didn't park the car in Canarsie.—

Cynthia looks past Mallory. —This is some apartment.—

—Cynthia, where is the car?—

—In front as planned. Can I help?—

Mallory goes back to the safe. A bubble of laughter leaves her throat. —My god, my good sweet god. I thank you, I thank you and thank you.—

She throws the contents of the safe into the suitcase. Then like a drill sergeant points here and there as we pick up valuables. Money, jewelry, silverware, first edition books, antiques, a Renoir, a Leger, a gold candelabra, a small Arp sculpture. In less than twenty minutes we're out. We stagger under the weight.

We exit out of the building tall and straight as if we're carrying air. Lynn jumps out of the car colliding with the doorman who is reaching for a suitcase. Mallory blocks his way handing her suitcase to Lynn who winces. Mallory smiles. —Girls are so independent nowadays,— she says charmingly handing him another bill. A couple stand at the entrance. He greets them, opens the door. Lynn and Cynthia put the suitcases in the trunk. Lynn hisses as she gets behind the wheel of the car. –What the hell did you put in those bags, cement? My back is killing me. I'd better not have an injury.–

Two blocks away, Mallory lets out a whoop that doesn't stop. Shutup Cynthia says or you'll have the entire police force after us. What's with you?

–We're rich. We are rich.–

–We!– Cynthia says.

–Yes we. My beautiful friends and me.–

In Mallory's apartment we count over $50,000 in cash. This is 1952. For $10,000 you can buy a house. There is jewelry worth a fortune. The collection is worth thousands and thousands of dollars. –Pay attention Eleanor Roosevelt Girls. Lesson number one. Money is not just money. It's things and the things we have are worth far more than the $50,000. Believe me.–

Was it Irving Marko's things that started Mallory off on her collection? Did it stay in her head for over thirty years festering bubbling boiling coming out with a vengeance as she combed every corner of New York trying to recapture her youth, her strength, her courage, her power.

As Mallory predicted Irving Marko couldn't do a damned thing. He was cheating on his income tax, cheating the government and he knew that she knew. She also knew how to get rid of the booty. There was no way to trace her to anything. The cash was deposited to my account. Because I trust you more than god she said.

I LEAVE HOWARD 1952

The townhouse she bought was paid in cash. In my name. Eventually I would turn it over to Mallory. When Irving cooled down, even though she doubted he would do anything. I now spent more time with Mallory than I did with Howard. I was working as a publicist during the day and at night when Howard was in school I was with Mallory. Move in she said. Your husband is not a nice man.

—Wrong. He may not be fascinating but he is nice.—

—He ignores you.—

—He does not.—

—He ignores you Julia. He never hears a word you say. He isn't interested in your work, your writing or your life. He's interested in Howard. Period.—

—You don't know what you're talking about. Everyone says he can't take his eyes off me.—

—Because you're lovely. Admit it Julia. You married the man to escape your family. You accomplished your mission. You escaped. Now leave him. I'm offering you your life. You'll have a room to write in. Just like Virginia Woolf. What you have now is half a bed, half a bathroom, half a life. If that's enough for you ok. Forget I said anything. Far be it from me to force you into a situation.—

Howard. We're in our cramped apartment. He's studying. I'm writing. He's finished studying. I'm not finished writing.

—Let's go to bed,— he says. —I'm tired.—

Translated that means I want sex now.

—I'm not finished writing.—

—Finish tomorrow.—

—Howard, you're interrupting my flow.—

—How about my flow?— His hands are on my breasts, his fingers circle my nipple.

—Howard, I'm writing.—

His hands are undoing my bra. His mouth is sucking my nipple.

—Knock it off Howard.—

He stops. Cold air hits my wet hard nipple. I pull my sweater down. Thanks for nothing he says and storms out of the room. I return to the typewriter. Nothing comes out. I type a bunch of unconnected letters so he'll think I'm writing. Tears fall from my eyes.

I'm in bed next to him staring at the ceiling. He pulls me toward him. I lie there limp. It excites him. He handles me roughly, whacks my behind before he enters. –Comeon baby, give. Give.– He plunges inside with a fury. The sound of his slapping hand breaks into the silent room. He has his orgasm. Within seconds he's asleep. I lie there, my eyes open to the dark. His snoring is loud and ugly.

I spend my lunch hour the next day packing my clothing. I move in with Mallory.

WHERE I'M GOING ANGELS PEE ON THE DOPES BELOW 1994

The phone rings four times. Then the message.

'This is Mallory...'

I wait for her song to finish and hear laughter after the beep.

–Julia, if you're there pick up. Cleo invited us to have dinner at her restaurant. Do you want to go, yes or no? If you're there pick up. If not call, that is if you get this message.–

–I'm here.–

–You sound depressed.–

–Because I am depressed.–

–Julia, it isn't healthy to stay at Mallory's.–

I say nothing.

–Well, do you or don't you want to have dinner at Cleo's?–

–Sure.–

–You don't sound very enthusiastic.–

–Because I'm not enthusiastic.–

–How about tomorrow night?–

–Fine.–

–Where should I pick you up?–

–At my place. Is Tommie coming?–

–Why would she come? She had nothing to do with our club.–

–I'm never going to meet her, right?–

–Wrong. I'll see you at seven, tomorrow night.

CLEO 1994

She's standing by a table talking to diners when she spots us. Her face lights up. She rushes toward us, a large summer mountain squashing us in her embrace.

–You both look so good. Imagine living in the same city and losing track. Well what the hell. Here we are.–

She leads us to a table, sits down with us.

–How are you Cleo?–

–I'm doing ok for an old lady.–

–Old lady!– Annie says, –we're not old.–

–Sixty four isn't young. Well what the hell. Did you ever have any kids Julia?–

–I have a son,– I say.

Annie shoots me a look.

–I can't believe you have three boys Annie. I have the same kids I had when I last saw you, two boys and twin girls. My girls have six kids between them. One is more adorable than the other. But I've given up on my sons.–

–I have five grandchildren.–

–Do you? Isn't it great Annie? Do you have any Julia?–

–None.–

–Well I hope you're both starved because I've prepared a feast for us, food fit for Greek gods. Wine, ouzo. You'll stagger out of here thinking you just left heaven.–

She walks through the swinging doors to the kitchen.

–Annie, if you whisk out photographs I'm going to leave.–

–One son Julia?–

–Annie, my life isn't just my kids.–

–Neither is mine sweetie... Try to be pleasant Julia even if it kills you.–

We sit in silence. Cleo returns with ouzo. A waitress puts a huge platter of assorted appetizers on our table.

–That looks great Cleo,– Annie says.

Ouzo is poured. We toast each other. I taste the taramousalada.

–Cleo, this is unbelievable. Fabulous. Isn't it Annie?–

–That's our Julia. Give her good food and she turns into an angel.–

–It's amazing she stays so thin.–

–Give me the choice of a great meal or great sex and the meal will win out every time. Then again, there's probably nothing like a good orgasm, right Cleo?–

–I wouldn't know. I don't think I've ever had one.–

–Never?– we say in unison.

–I hear it's overrated.–

–Don't believe it,– Annie says.

–Oh well. Does anybody hear from Lynn? She was always so highly sexed, don't you think. I wonder if she ever married.–

–She didn't.–

–I'll bet she has plenty of lovers old as she is.–

–And orgasms,– I add.

Annie gives me a dirty look.

–Sorry but it is more interesting than discussing children and grandchildren.–

–Haven't you been with anyone since Paniotti died?– Annie asks.

–My sons would have a fit if I brought a man around.–

–Don't tell them.–

–My sons live with me.–

–Still! You're joking!–

–No Julia, I'm not joking.–

–They must be in their forties.–

–Julia, it's none of your business.–

–Oh let her Annie. She always did like to interfere.–

–When did I ever interfere?–

–Are you telling me you had nothing to do with the breakup of Claire's marriage?–

–Her husband was battering her. Don't you remember?–

—As I recall you practically pushed her into that woman's arms.—

—I don't know why you're saying that Cleo. We all had a part in that and as I recall so did you.—

—Annie, I never approved of that woman.—

—She didn't leave Arnie because of a woman. She left because he was hurting her.—

—And what about her daughters Annie? Do you think that's a healthy atmosphere for children?—

—It's a hell of a lot healthier than seeing your mother get beat up by your father.—

—I'm really surprised to hear you talk like that Annie. I can't believe you actually approve of homosexuality. I suppose her daughters are lesbians too.—

—Why would they be? I'm living with a woman and my kids are straight.—

—What do you mean living?—

—I mean we're friends, mates. Lovers.—

—No answer for that one Cleo,— I say.

—If it were you I'd understand. Frankly I always thought you and Mallory were...you know.—

—Well we weren't you know. Maybe we should have been you know but we weren't. I hope you're not too disappointed.—

—Julia, whatever anyone does is ok with me.—

—Oh sure. That's obvious.—

The waitress puts platters of food on the table. Annie looks uncomfortably around the room. I expect her to get up and leave. Instead she says, —You really went all out Cleo.— I add a grudging thank you.

Cleo: Annie told me you're a vegetarian so it's vegetables and
          fish.
Annie: This is delicious. Are you the chef?
Cleo: No. I have a wonderful chef who's been with me for years.
          I wouldn't know what to do without him.

Me:	Isn't it amazing. We're the cooks of the world but men are the chefs.
Cleo:	There are women chefs.
Me:	A few Cleo.
Cleo:	Like it or not, it still is a man's world.
Me:	Because we allow it.
Cleo:	Because it's nature.
Annie:	Conditioning.
Cleo:	Whatever it is we certainly have it better than our mothers. Look at me with my own restaurant.
Me:	Only because your husband left you money and a bad colon.
Cleo:	What's the difference how I got it? The point is I have a restaurant and children and grandchildren, a good life. And you Julia, what have you got to complain about? You're a published author and playwright.
Me:	As long as one woman is not free, no woman is free.
Cleo:	Julia, not everyone is a woman's libber. Like it or not girls are different.
Me:	Girls? Are we still girls?
Cleo:	I like being called a girl.
Me:	Well I don't.
Cleo:	I know. I've read your books.
Me:	You've actually read my books. Annie didn't even know I wrote books.

—How could you not know? Julia wrote from the time we were little kids. She wrote. Mallory designed clothes. Lynn danced. Cynthia acted and Margaret...— Her face crumples. —Margaret has cancer. It happened so suddenly. It scares me to think of it. Life collapses around you minute by minute. All you have to do is turn around and someone you love is gone.— She raises her glass, her eyes watery. —Let's drink to the Eleanor Roosevelt Girls. Long may the rest of us live.— She clamps her hand over her mouth. —I'm sorry Julia. I forgot.—

–It's ok.–

–No it's not. It was thoughtless. Was she sick Julia? They never said.–

–No. She just didn't want to live anymore.–

–How could she not want to live? I used to see her on television. She had so much life in her.–

–Maybe because life is shit when you get older.–

–It isn't to me.–

–Then you're the exception.–

–It isn't to me either.–

–Because you've got Tommie. Suppose you didn't have her?–

–It would be different but I wouldn't kill myself.–

–How do you know?–

–I know myself.–

–You can't know unless you're confronted with a situation.–

–Funny, I always envied your having Tim for a husband. Of all our husbands he was the most sensitive.–

–Cleo, I'm a lesbian.–

–But you weren't when we were kids. How could it happen?–

–I probably always was. I had a terrible crush on Claire. I was very jealous when she went off with Dina.–

–That's not true, is it?–

–It is.–

–Has anyone heard from Claire?–

–I'm trying to find her.–

–She could be with a man again.–

–I doubt it.–

–I'm convinced if they let us alone we'd all be bisexual but we're so socialized we can't even admit it. Besides love is love. What's the difference who you love? Just to love is great.–

–That's ridiculous Julia. I could never love a woman. I'm not even attracted to them.–

–Them? You're one of them. Haven't you ever wondered why women get their emotional needs met by other women and their sex from men? It doesn't make sense. If we need someone to talk to we go to a woman but we end up in bed with a man.–

–Because that's the way it's meant to be.–

–You mean that's the way religion set it up to keep us in our place. But animals who don't have any religion can be straight or gay and nobody cares.–

–Really Julia! How many gay animals do you know?–

–I once had a lesbian dog. We tried to mate her a number of times but she just wouldn't go for it. And look at harems. What do you think women are doing there? Or convents where women marry god but ...–

–Enough Julia.–

–Isn't it true Annie?–

–How the hell do you know. When was the last time you lived in a convent?–

–I'll get the dessert.– Cleo goes through the swinging doors.

–That was pleasant.–

–I was sure you were going to walk out.–

–Did you have to? You only made things worse with your snide remarks. Why couldn't you just let it go Julia?–

–Let's drink to the good old days. For christsake, she couldn't burp in the good old days without her father's permission.–

–Cut it out Julia.–

–She abhors your life, but you're not mad at her, you're mad at me.–

–Cleo is what she is, what she always was. I knew that before we came. You were the one that was gung ho about seeing her.–

–That's the way it's meant to be, it's a man's world. Another cliché and I would have barfed.–

–Julia, she's gone out of her way for us. The least you can do is control yourself. She is the way she is and all your insults aren't going to change one thing. It's one fucking night. We'll be leaving soon and we never have to see her again.–

Cleo sits with us. Her watery eyes spill over. Annie, the good, takes her hand. –I wanted everything to be perfect. I wanted us to be close the way we were.–

–It was a perfect meal Cleo. Superb.–

–Oh the meal. Sure the meal. You're being nice the way you always were and Julia hates me.–

–I don't hate you.–

–You don't think I like women but I do.–

–Cleo look around you. The world has changed since we were kids.–

–Maybe your world has but mine hasn't.–

–Julia, we are in Cleo's wonderful restaurant, three old friends eating a lovely meal, drinking ouzo and wine. Can't you shutup for a minute so we can have our dessert in peace?–

–Right. Keep your mouth shut like we did in the good old days. Don't make anyone uncomfortable no matter what. Talk against the Jews, the Blacks, the Gays, the Lesbians. Big deal. Who cares? What's one more injustice? What year is this anyhow?–

We leave the way we came, with hugs and kisses only these are obligatory without feeling. And we all know it. I look out the car window at the river, the New York skyline. How many times did I drive over the Queensboro Bridge? I look over at Annie. –Why did you say we were old friends?–

–Because we were. But things change. We're not kids anymore.–

–The best is over.–

–You keep romanticizing the past. Was it that great?–

–No but it was all before us, the hopes the dreams. And nothing turned out the way I thought it would. Nothing. Not a damned thing.–

–Your writing turned out the way you wanted, didn't it?–

–So what. Nobody reads anymore. They're all glued to the TV. It's all gone. Mallory's gone. I've got nothing.–

–When you're dead you have nothing.–

–But I am dead.–

–Then you're the most argumentative dead person I ever met.–

–I always liked you Annie. You were hurt when Claire went off with Dina but I was hurt when you became Claire's friend and not mine. I don't think you liked me much then and I don't think you like me much now.–

–It had nothing to do with like. I had a crush on Claire, not you. Listen Julia if Cleo was a stranger I would have walked out. I don't like women like Cleo. I didn't even like Cleo when she was in our club. But so what. I'm never going to see her again and neither are you so let's forget it.–

SHIRLEY, I'M TALKING TO YOU 1994

The voice is loud, the banging frantic. I open the door. A man yells we're being evacuated. I run past him to the sea wall where white capped pyramids collapse and rise. Stars lay on their side in the blackened sky. The man catches up. Lady, are you nuts! He grabs my arm, pulling me away, just as I see Mallory riding on top of a wave. My god he says, what is that?

Mallory, I knew you'd turn up.

Julia she sings above the roar of the sea.

I sit on the sand unable to move. Birds frantically try to fly, their bodies heavy with the weight of the swelling sea. And who is that walking on the water? Why it's Jonathon! He kneels at my feet blessing me, placing a cross around my neck.

Mother he says. Mother.

Now I'm running through the streets caught in a maze of buildings. What is this place? Ilya appears.

It's your place Julia, your theater, your play.

My play! I stopped writing them years ago. Too many people involved.

Involved is what it's all about.

How would you know Ilya? All you're good for is shrimp and salad. Taxi.

We drive through a forest. The driver is agitated. How am I supposed to take you where you're going if you don't know where that is? I need a direction.

You need a direction. How about me?

You! You're your own problem, not mine.

I fight to wake up. Something hard is next to me. I open my eyes. Shirley Temple, cute, dimpled looks at me.

—What are you looking at Shirley?—

Her doll eyes close.

—Open your eyes Shirley, this isn't the movies you know. This is life. I'm talking to you Shirley. At least have the decency to look at me.—

I hit her on the side of her head. —And don't act so superior. You're not a star anymore. You got old just like the rest of us. You got fat. Don't deny it Shirley. I've seen pictures of you. You're old and fat.—

I hit her again. —Old and fat Shirley.—

Her doll face is crestfallen.

—Cheer up Shirley. We were all young once. Did I tell you that when I was twenty two I moved in with Mallory. That's right. Twenty two. Well, we were all twenty two once, right Shirley? I was a manager for a beauty salon. On my lunch hour I wrote. Mallory said we shouldn't connect with any man unless he could further our careers. She said Virginia Woolf had Leonard. Marie Curie had Pierre. Even Margaret Mead. Do you think they would have let her go into the jungle if she wasn't married to all those anthropologists?

—Mallory always knew who buttered our bread. So what did she do? She spent her lunch hour hanging around the office of Barry Nave, the publisher of *Coutier*. Within weeks they were having this hot and heavy affair. Naturally Barry was married so where do they have the affair? In our place. Naturally.—

I pour wine into my glass. I offer some to Shirley. It runs out the sides of her mouth. –What a slob you are Shirley. Anyhow every night I wrote to the accompaniment of moans and groans. And every night after Barry left Mallory would come into my room and complain that he was a lousy lover, masturbating as she spoke until she reached orgasm. Then she would scream for real. Must you do that I'd yell, wet running down my legs. How would you like it if I did that in front of you? Guess what she answered Shirley?–

I pull her hair. –Shirley, I'm talking to you...She said, I don't know. I might. And every night I'd rush into the bathroom and masturbate in private. It was humiliating.

–Well Shirley, Mallory's lousy sex life paid off. One month later she was assistant to Margo Sanders, the editor-in-chief of *Coutier*. Margo was furious. She threatened to quit.

–I decided I needed my own mentor and chose Amos Andors who'd been Helen Lilianthal's mentor. I'll bet you know her Shirley. I bet you know everyone.– I pour more wine into her dainty painted mouth. –Swallow for christsake, didn't anyone ever teach you manners?–

I bang her on the back. The wine comes shooting out. –Shirley, I've been meaning to ask you, did you ever meet an actress named Bettina Lacy?

–Where was I Shirley? Oh yes, on Wednesday nights I took a writing class with Amos Andors. Me and fifteen others.–

Shirley's eyes blink. Half her lashes are missing.

–God, you're a mess Shirley.–

JUST HAVE THE ENVELOPE READY 1953

I sit at the feet of Amos Andors, the famous Amos Andors. Well, not literally at his feet. We are at his favorite watering hole. Tonight in class he read a short story of mine out loud. –Talented lady don't you think,– he told the class. They looked over at me, no love in those eyes. –But,– he continued, –not a commercial bone in the lady's body. Too bad.– The class laughed. Glee lived in that laughter.

Amos is ordering his usual double martini telling me stories of his life. I have to pee so badly I can hardly sit in the chair but I can't get up for fear of falling on my face or maybe Andors, the name everyone calls him, will sneak out of the place while I'm gone realizing I'm just another kid with a little talent. As he talks he has that amused look that great talents have when confronted by cute girl worshippers. But he's talking about me. No way I'll leave now.

–No doubt about the talent but you are not a short story writer.–

–Well I think...–

–Let me finish before you talk. Your stories are too short and they're not stories. They are character studies. Why don't you try a play?–

He orders two more doubles. I am going to stagger out trailing a quart of pee. I hold my legs together as I make my way to the Ladies Room. When I return he is miraculously there, a fresh drink in his hand.

–Why a play?– I ask like I never left the table.

–Because your strength lies in character and dialogue.–

A man with steely grey hair is at our table. –Andors. Good to see you.–

–Josh, meet June, a very talented young writer.–

–Julia.–

–Pardon me. I'm sure you know Josh Billings.–

I don't but I nod.

–Plays I hope,– Josh says.

Before I can answer Andors tells him I'll have my play finished before the season is over.

–Well when you do be sure to contact my office. I'd like to see it. Good to see you Andors.–

Andors winks at me. –Now that you have a producer the rest is simple.–

–Just like that I'll write a play and just like that he'll produce it.–
–He might but in all probability he won't. Give yourself time.
You're just beginning.–
  –I've been writing sixteen years.–
  –Is that so! How the hell old are you?–
  –Twenty three.–
  –That old. My!–
  –If I'm not old enough blame my mother, not me.–
  He touches my cheek. –You are a cute little thing.– He motions
the waiter to bring another round.
  –I can't drink anymore.–
  –Of course you can. You're a mature woman. Besides, I never
drink alone in a public place. It's bad for my reputation. You know I
was just about your age when I sold my first story. I sent the damned
thing to every magazine. I would get it back, put it in the next enve-
lope, wait for the next rejection and send it out again. The third time
round the first magazine accepted it.–
  –Didn't the rejections bother you?–
  –June...–
  –Julia.–
  –Julia, any writer worth his weight in words can't be bothered
by rejections. If it bothers you you have no right being a writer. Just
have the envelope ready and you're in business.–
  –Do you think Josh Billings will read it?–
  –Just write the damned play June. First things first.–
  –But...–
  –You're very talented. I said that didn't I? The problem is your
stories are too short. You should put them on greeting cards. Don't
look so downhearted. You're young, you're talented, the world is
yours...–
  –Is it?–
  –What a question. Of course it is. At your age you should have
spirit, hope and above all ego. That's the gift of youth. Ego. Grab it
kiddo. It leaves you soon enough.– His smile is warm and boozy.

–Are you hungry?–
　–Yes. Very.–
　–Then we'll eat. The food here is very good.–
　–Thanks for saying what you did to Josh Billings.–
　–Why? What did I say?–
　–That I was very talented.–
　–Why shouldn't I say it. You are. I expect a lot from you Julia.–
Finally he got my name right.

So Julia, Are You Going to Sleep With Him? 1953

She takes a sip of wine. –So Julia, are you going to sleep with him?–
　–No.–
　–Why not?–
　–Why should I?–
　–Helen Lilianthal did and look what happened to her.–
　–They were in love with one another.–
　–Well they're not in love now. I hear she's living with a much younger man.–
　–Good for her.–
　–Julia, this is your big opportunity. It may never come again.–
I pick up the newspaper and pretend I'm reading.
　–Well maybe you're right. The man is a lush.–
　–The man for your information is a great writer.–
　–Was a great writer.–
　–You don't know what you're talking about.–
　–He's a has-been Julia. He hasn't written a thing in years.–
　–And as a lush and a has-been he wouldn't know a talented writer if he fell over her.–
　–I never said that. Julia, he can open doors for you. What's wrong with having doors opened? Look at me. Do you think I

would have become assistant to Margo Sanders if it hadn't been for Barry? That's how it's done Julia.—

—That's your opinion.—

—It's not my opinion. It's the way it is. He has connections. You don't. Use him. He'll love you for it. To have a young beautiful girl in your bed...—

—Did you love Irving?—

—What's that got to do with anything?—

—I'm just trying to figure out if you loved him for him or loved him for you.—

—Love is ephemeral.—

—For you.—

—I loved my parents but they died just the same.—

—That's different.—

—No it's not. People die or leave you. Irving loved his wife and then he loved me and then he loved someone else. All love is fragile. One sentence can blow any love off the face of the earth. The best is to love yourself.—

—Are you saying our friendship could end just like that?—

—I wasn't talking about us.—

—You said any love.—

—Julia, don't you know I love you. We're never going to stop being friends no matter what happens. You're never going to get rid of me. Wherever you go I go.—

We sit on the sofa, our arms around one another. —Without you I'd have the biggest hole in my heart.—

—Me too Mal.—

—So, is he as dashing as his photos?—

—He's fantastic looking.—

—Think how it will look in your autobiography when you're old and famous. I had an affair with Amos Andors. Do it. Think of the future.—

—You're impossible.—

—I'll bet he's great in bed.—

–He's over sixty.–

–So? Did he make a pass at you?–

–No.–

–How could he not.–

–All he said was, you're a cute little thing.–

–There you go. That's a start.–

–He was teasing me.–

–Tease him back. Julia, you'd be crazy to pass this one up.–

WE VISIT TWO ELEANOR ROOSEVELT GIRLS IN THE HOSPITAL 1954

Cleo has colitis. The collision route of her colon, the battleground of her intestines, the rotting and the gutting are invisible to us. Only her doctors view her diseased insides. We visit a pale Cleo who smiles weakly struggling to assure us she's fine. We know better.

Claire's wounds are bright neon lights. Her face is a puffy blue green, her eyes blackened, her nose broken. When she talks there's a gap where a front tooth used to be. Her broken ribs can be heard as groans when we try to make her laugh. She insists she fell down the stairs. –I'm so accident prone,– she tells us. The last time she slipped in the tub. The time before that she tripped on her daughter's toys. There's no end to her accidents.

Cleo and Claire, in the same hospital, visit each other, limping from floor to floor. They've tried to convince the hospital staff to move one to the others room but they refuse. Cleo is in Gastroenterology, Claire in Trauma. One ailment has nothing to do with the other they say. But we know better. They have everything in common. Two shitty husbands. We also know that Arnie has threatened to kill Claire if she even thinks about pressing charges. She won't. Why would the police believe her when her own family doesn't? They love Arnie. Everybody loves Arnie except for us. Annie, who gives us this information tells us that Claire is convinced she is to blame. She provokes him and afterwards he couldn't be sweeter. It's like a honeymoon with flowers and candy, anything Claire wants.

Lynn: You're the closest to her. Can't you convince her to leave?
Annie: She won't leave because of her daughter.
Mallory: Her daughter! I can't think of a better reason to leave.
Annie: But what if the court takes her from Claire?
Me: Don't be silly Annie. Why would they?
Annie: They could.
Lynn: Nobody in their right mind would award Arnie the child. Besides they always give the child to the mother.
Annie: Not always Cynthia. They could agree she provoked him. Irregardless of what you think...
Lynn: There is no such word. It's regardless. Without regard is regardless.
Me: Listen Annie, there is no provocation that warrants a beating.
Cynthia: I'd love to know what Claire did to provoke him.
Annie: She's having an affair.
Cynthia: No wonder, with Arnie for a husband.
Bettina: Who is he?
Mallory: What difference does it make?
Bettina: Adultery is grounds for divorce.
Mallory: But not for beating up your wife.
Annie: It's all that person's fault. That person doesn't leave Claire alone.
Cynthia: Why do you keep saying that person?
Lynn: I get it. It's not a man, am I right Annie?
Annie: It's that lesbian she met at Gayland. She hounds Claire.
Bettina: How disgusting.
Mallory: What's disgusting is that Arnie is literally getting away with murder and nobody is doing anything about it. Don't tell me the hospital falls for that accident prone crap? And what about the police?

Cynthia: The police won't get involved in family matters.

Mallory: And her neighbors? Are they all deaf? It's obvious we're going to have to take matters in our own hands.

Bettina: You can't take the law into your own hands.

Lynn: No. What should we do Bettina? Let that bastard kill her? Because that's what will happen if we ignore what's happening.

Mallory: I think we should relieve Arnie of his balls.

Lynn: I'd go for the main organ.

Cynthia: I'm with you.

Bettina: You're sick. You're all sick.

Bettina, the actress makes a very ungraceful exit, tripping over her own feet. What a klutz, Mallory says.

We confront Claire who tells us Arnie has promised to change. This time is different she says, her smile showing the gap in her mouth. What's different about it we ask? I'm pregnant she says.

Pregnant we yelp. No joy in those yelps.

We brought Claire an enormous teddy bear the day she left the hospital. I kept thinking that poor unborn baby. If she knew she would stay in the womb forever. We watched Claire being wheeled out of her room, a solicitous Arnie at her side, flowers in hand. I wanted to punch him between the legs the way Mallory taught me.

Later Mallory and I visited a chalk faced Cleo. —Poor Claire,— she said fighting tears.

—Poor Claire. How about you?—

—I'm getting better.—

—I'm talking about your husband. Are you going to stay with him?—

—Yes.—

—Don't tell me you love him? I know you don't.—

—Leave me alone Julia.—

Mallory jumped in. —Why are you staying Cleo?—

—I have children. I've never worked. How will I support them?—

–You'd get a job.–

–Doing what?–

–We'll think of something.–

–It's easy for you to talk. You don't have children. Who would watch them assuming I did get a job? You think it's Paniotti's fault but it isn't. He gets very upset when I'm sick.–

–Naturally,– Mallory says. –He loses his servant.–

–No he doesn't. Cleo's mother replaces her. That bastard's got it made.–

–Neither one of you know him.–

–I don't need to know him Cleo. All I know is you were healthy before he got off the boat.–

–Did you ever think that maybe he doesn't love me either, that he's as stuck as I am, even more so. At least I'm in my own country.–

–We're not concerned with him. It's you we're worried about. Cleo, you have to do what's best for you.–

–I'm not brave like you Mallory.–

–So what are you going to do?– I ask.

–I'm going to stay. I'm going to make the best of it.–

TIME 1994

Time. It's all mixed up in my head. Outside Mallory's apartment dead leaves drop to the ground. How often have I watched green leaves turn red orange rust, more beautiful in death? How often have I listened to the ocean breathe, looked at a horizon long as time? How often have I swallowed words before they were said?

Aries people are free Mallory said. And are you free now Mallory?

There's a photo album at Mallory's. Inside is a photo of the Eleanor Roosevelt Girls. We are sixteen. We are laughing. Claire's face is bruise free, her smile lights up her face. Cleo looks marvelous, red cheeked and healthy. Even in black and white you can see it. Mallory's energy practically leaps off the page. Where did all that energy go? Was it circumstances that changed her or some circular something that altered everything while I wasn't looking.

I sit on Mallory's bed and cry. Why must I remember? Why can't I just go on with my life?

If You Come Back Limping Should I Shoot You 1993

Remembering. It was winter. We'd driven to Bear Mountain. Mallory was laughing, calling me unbelievable. Where does all your negativity come from Julia? Julia, we're alive. Look at this glorious sunset. Big deal I said. Big fucking deal. A sunset doesn't make your life. Maybe not she said but I wouldn't give up one minute of my life if it meant missing this sunset.

We strolled around the half frozen lake. Changing colors danced on the mountain. Winter colors. Crisp. Sharp. Mallory was ecstatic. She breathed in the cold air.

–Look at my mother Mallory. Remember how she danced and danced, all that energy. She went out all hours and I'm talking just a few years ago. Now look at her. She's always in pain. She says her best friend is her bed. That's what we have to look forward to. The bed. They should shoot us like horses.–

–You're really a bore Julia. Can't you shutup for one minute and enjoy the night?–

–Well I would Mallory if you walked faster. Speaking of getting older, you walk like you're a hundred.–

–I like strolling.–

–So stroll Mallory. Stroll. I'm going to jog around the lake.–

–It's icy Julia. Be careful.–

Her voice followed my running legs. –If you come back limping should I shoot you?– I could hear her laughter fade as I moved out of sight and sound.

Fuck you Mallory. Fuck your joy spreading lies. Your death was planned. Plotted. Arranged down to the last detail. Did you plan it while I jogged around the lake? Is that what your laughter was all about?

I sit in her apartment. Tears stick in my throat. Why Mallory? I was the one collecting pills. I was the one who thought death.

You stole my suicide.

HELLO ARNIE 1956

Four of us meet for dinner once every month. The single ones. Lynn, Cynthia, Mallory and me. Annie joins us once in a while. Cleo has just given birth to twins, nobody's heard from Bettina since she stormed out of the hospital. And none of us care. Margaret is with the Little Sisters of the Poor in Phoenix.

We always talk about Claire. Where is she? Is she alright? Or did Arnie succeed in beating her to death? There is no way we can reach her. Her phone's been disconnected. We've called information for all the boroughs, all the outlying districts, New Jersey and Connecticut. There is no Arnold Schuster listed. We call her sisters. They haven't any idea of where she is. Claire has vanished.

We're all angry at ourselves. Why didn't we take care of Arnie when we had the chance.

I sit at a bar waiting for Mallory when suddenly I see him. He's sitting next to a young woman. He talks. She nods. He laughs. She laughs. He leans over and kisses her lips. She smiles. He leans over and touches her face.

I move next to them. He doesn't notice. —Hello Arnie.—

He turns. —Julia! Long time no see.—

—How are you Arnie?—

Bastard.

–Great. And you?–

–Good. I'm good.– I look at the woman and smile. –I'm Julia.–

Her smile is strained. She looks at Arnie. He answers for her.

–This is Virginia.–

–Hello,– I say. She nods uncertainly.

–Is Howard meeting you here?–

–I hope not. We're divorced.–

–That's too bad.–

–And you?–

–I work in the neighborhood,– he says like he doesn't know what I'm asking. I see Mallory enter. Her hand waves as she sees me. She's standing next to me, unaware that Arnie is on the other side.

–Sorry I'm late.–

–Look who's here Mallory, our old friend Arnie Schuster.–

–Arnie,– she says, her voice going up an octave. –Arnie, is it really you? So how the hell are you Arnie?–

–Fine. I'm fine.–

–I'm so glad. Aren't you glad Julia?–

–Oh yes.–

Mallory takes a long sip of my martini and orders a double for herself. –And who is this gorgeous creature?–

–Virginia,– I say.

Mallory swallows her drink, orders another. –Virginia. What a lovely name. You're a model, am I right?–

Virginia warms up. –Well I'm trying to be.–

–With your looks! You shouldn't have any problem.–

–Mallory is the senior editor of *Coutier*.–

–Really!– Her face is suddenly alive. –*Coutier*. I read it all the time.–

Mallory hands her a card. –Do call me Virginia. There's a possibility I'll have something for you.–

Virginia's smile is broad. Ours is simpy. –Thanks Mrs...–

–Mallory. Everyone calls me Mallory.–

Nobody talks. Everybody holds a drink in their hand. Arnie

breathes in half the bar air. He motions to the bartender, takes money out of his wallet. –Well, it's been great seeing the two of you.–

Virginia looks bewildered. –Aren't we having dinner here?–

–We have reservations at the Russian Tea Room. Don't you remember?–

–We do?–

Arnie rises. Mallory gives him a big bear hug, then deliberately plants her lips on his. I see her tongue move in his mouth. I don't know who's more shocked, Arnie or me. She grabs his behind. –I always did have a crush on you Arnie. You are one sexy man, isn't he Virginia?–

Virginia looks from Arnie to Mallory.

–Call me, beautiful Virginia. I have something in mind.–

Virginia looks back at us bewilderedly as Arnie leads her out.

–How could you do that Mallory?–

–Tell me if they're gone.–

–Mallory, what the hell is happening?–

–Are they gone, yes or no.–

–Yes.–

–Then let's get the hell out. Joe, put it on my tab.–

Mallory is pulling me out, hailing a cab. –Sardi's,– she says. –I feel like Sardi's. How about you Julia?–

–What's going on Mallory?–

She pulls a wallet out of her purse, takes out a driver's license. –Well what do you know. Scarsdale. They live in Scarsdale.–

–How did you manage to get his wallet?–

–Do you think I'd french kiss that bastard and squeeze his fat behind for fun? Do you know how difficult it was to control myself? I wanted to vomit... What do we have here?– She pulls cards out of his wallet. –A credit card, assorted business cards, a laundry ticket, a commuter ticket. Oh great. A photo of a toddler and a three year old or is it four. That must be Kita. She's really getting big. Look how cute Julia. She looks just like Claire. Notice there isn't one picture of Claire...And look. A windfall. Three hundred and fourteen dollars. Not bad.–

—Oh god, he'll know you took it.—

—Not necessarily.—

—You told him where you work.—

—No, you told him where I work.—

—Didn't you give his girlfriend your card?—

—What's the difference? We're going to see Claire and find out what is going on in that household.—

She calls me at ten in the morning. —Meet me at Toots. Eight o'clock.—

—What's up?—

—Guess who called? You bitch he said. You took my wallet. I what? I what? Took my wallet. Why would I do that Arnie? You know damned well why. Arnie I said, Arnie calm down. Why don't you retrace your steps? You must have dropped it somewhere. Did you call the bar? I distinctly remember seeing it when you paid the bartender before you and Virginia went to the Russian Tea Room. Maybe you left it there. Did you leave it there?—

I groan. —Why'd you say that? Why did you say you saw it at the bar? Now he knows that you saw him putting it in his back pocket. That was dumb Mallory.—

—The next thing I know Virginia calls. Mallory she says sweetly. I think I'm going to take you up on your offer. I was hoping you would I say. I didn't make her an offer did I?—

—He put her up to it.—

—Who cares.—

—Do you think she knows about Claire?—

—Of course she knows. Didn't you see the way she looked at us?—

—You're not actually going to use her as a model.—

—I haven't made up my mind. Julia, call Cynthia and Lynn and ask them to join us. Toots. Eight o'clock. Tell them it's about Claire. Toots.—

—I heard you. Eight o'clock.—

CLAIRE 1956

I leave my car at the train station and walk to Claire's house. It's on a cul de sac. Pine trees stand next to one another, green sentries. Tall. Straight. Preventing onlookers from seeing in. A locked fence keeps intruders out. A growling dog lets whoever is inside know that someone is out there. I walk around the trees looking for an opening. The dog growls. I push my body through the trees. The dog snarls.

–Hi cutie,– I say, my voice reaching high C. –Oh aren't you adorable.–

Please don't let me smell. Dogs can spot a fear smell a mile away. He looks at me suspiciously. I hold out my palm. I know the whole hand is an invitation to bite. I don't look him in the eyes. Eye contact means attack. –Come here sweetie,– I say. –It's me. Julia.– Like he'd know, like he gives a damn what my name is. He's studying me. I take an unfinished muffin out of my bag talking all the time. –Wait til you see what I have for you.– He sniffs. –I hope you like corn muffins.–

I hold the muffin out, a peace offering. The dog takes it. I saunter nonchalantly toward the house feeling anything but nonchalant. He follows me. I don't dare turn. For all I know he's got foam hanging from the sides of his mouth.

I knock on the door. Nobody answers but I know she's there. I feel it. Now the dog is jumping wildly on me, his tail wagging insanely. I pet the dog with one hand, knock with the other.

–Claire, I know you're there. Claire,– I yell. The tail stops wagging. –It's ok boy.– I bang on the door. The dog barks. –Claire, if you don't open up I'm getting the police. I'm not joking Claire.–

I walk away, the dog jumping all over my rear. When I get to the gate she opens the door. I run back, the dog leaping and running with me. We stand on both sides of the door. The dog is looking from one to the other. Like me he's waiting for something to happen. Claire's face holds no expression. Her skin is discolored, grey, purple, a sickening yellow. One eye is partially closed, her nose has lost its shape. That can't be Claire. My heart explodes through my eyes. —My god Claire.— My arms go around her, her hands stay rigidly at her side.

—Go away.—

She closes the door but not before I push my way into her living room, planting myself in a chair. —Claire, listen to me. You can't stay here any longer, do you understand. Claire I'm talking to you.—

—Why have you come?—

—Claire, I've come to take you and your daughters away. You can't stay here.—

—I'm not going with you.—

—Where are your children?—

Her voice dull. —I don't want you here.—

—Claire, if you refuse to come with me the minute I leave I'm calling the police.—

—The police!— A gush of air comes from her closed mouth.

Is that her laugh?

—Leave me alone.—

—We've been trying to find you. We've been worried sick.—

—I don't need you. I don't need anybody. I have Arnie. I have my children. That's all I need.— Her eyes dart around the room as if she heard something.

—Is somebody here Claire?—

—You have to go.—

—Where are your children Claire?—

—Why don't you go?—

—Can I use your bathroom first?—

—No.—

—For christsake Claire, I have to pee.—

She shows me to the bathroom. I close the door. The other door opens into a bedroom. On the night table there's a phone. I copy the number, flush the unused toilet.

—What shall I tell everyone?—

—That I'm fine. Fine.—

–Claire, can't I see your children before I leave?–
–They're not here.–
–Where are they Claire?–
–You know.–
–I don't. Where?–
At the door she says, –You weren't here, were you?–
–What?–
–You weren't here.–
–No, I wasn't.–
And then from nowhere a cry of pain. –Don't tell Annie.
Promise you won't tell Annie.–
I walk to the gate. The dog accompanies me. He's not jumping.
He's not leaping. Neither am I. When I get to the entrance I turn.
Claire is watching me.

FINDING A SAFE PLACE FOR CLAIRE 1956

There has to be a safe place for Claire and her daughters. But
where? There are shelters for animals but for women and children?
Nothing. Mallory is willing to rent an apartment and pay all expenses
until Claire gets on her feet but what does getting on your feet mean
when you've sustained physical abuse for so many years?

Annie of a thousand fears, afraid of her shadow, of breaking the
law, of saying the wrong thing but devoted to Claire is determined to
find a safe place away from New York and Arnie. Afraid she might
not be successful she says nothing to us.

We meet at Mallory's to finalize our plans. Before Mallory can
tell us about the apartment she found, Annie tells us about a
Woman's Collective in Vermont. Where Dina lives, she says. –Can
you imagine! I left a message for her at Gaylands never thinking I'd
hear from her. Was I lucky! She said she rarely comes to New York
anymore and just happened to be there the day after I left the

message. You can't believe how happy she was to see me. She said she'd lost contact with Claire two years ago. They were supposed to meet for dinner but Claire didn't show so Dina called to find out what happened. Instead of Claire she got a recorded message that said the phone had been disconnected. She said she was frantic. She called every hospital. Then she went to the police station because she knew the violence had escalated but the police just ignored her. She went to the apartment. It was empty and none of the neighbors knew anything. She called Claire's sisters but they refused to talk to her. Claire had just vanished. Isn't that fantastic! A Woman's Collective in Vermont.—

Mallory Acts Out Her Conversation with Virginia 1956

It's a two character play and Mallory is playing both parts. When she plays herself her voice is husky and sophisticated. Virginia lisps in a high squeaky voice.

Virginia: Arnie is so wonderful, the best thing that ever happened to me.

Mallory: What a dope that woman is.

Virginia: Mallory, tell the truth, do you think I'm awful seeing him?

Mallory: Don't ask me Virginia. I'm the one who married a married man.

Lynn: (dancing around Mallory) And so Virginia's eyes light up. She has found a kindred spirit. A pal. None other than our Mallory.

Mallory: This is my play Lynn.

Lynn: Sorry.

Virginia: I know you know Arnie's wife. What is she like?

Mallory: Don't worry that beautiful head. They should have divorced years ago.

Virginia: Oh Mallory. Mallory. You are so fantastic.

Mallory: Then I hand her tickets to the play and say, you must promise not to tell Arnie I gave you the tickets. He must think they come from you.

Virginia: I don't get it but ok if you insist.

Annie: What if she tells?

Mallory: She's dumb but not that dumb.

Lynn: It must be great to have such power. How does our Mallory do it?

Me: She must be suspicious. I'd be suspicious.

Mallory: The woman's got half a brain but even if she were, you can be sure that her ambition would outweigh her suspicion.

Annie: Still she could tell Arnie, couldn't she? She could tell him and you wouldn't know.

Mallory: Then she tells. We don't have any guarantees in life. If it doesn't work I have an alternate plan.

Annie: What?

Mallory: Can we worry about the whats and ifs and buts when the time comes? Now let's work out exactly what each of us will do.

I'M IN SPAIN 1994

There's a new message on my machine. —Sorry I can't come to the phone. I'm in Spain. I'll call when I get back.—

I take nothing but the clothes on my back, money, my checkbook, bank cards and move to Mallory's. I only leave her apartment to get food or eat at the corner restaurant.

I read through reams of paper. A journal. My name crops up a lot. Sometimes her phone rings. I keep saying I'll remove her message but I don't. Actually I've gotten to like it. I even sing along. —So when you hear it thunder don't run under a tree. There'll be peeing from heaven. It's me...me...me.–

Her calls are from people who don't know she died, solicitors who want to know if she wants the *New York Times* delivered to her door, if she wants a free trip to Florida to look over some retirement property, one obscene phone call and a woman who keeps saying in a Spanish accent Maria Maria Maria. I don't pick up.

My messages are from Annie. Where the hell are you? And David. What do you mean you're in Spain? Where in Spain? How could you do this to Grandma? Then a pause. This message is silly unless you're picking up your messages in Spain which I doubt. If you do, call us. I know you're in pain mom, believe me I know but you have to accept that Mallory is dead and get on with your own life.

Ah life I say to the Giacometti woman on the wall. Life.

Richard calls. I thought we had a date. I waited in the restaurant for over an hour. Please call. I'm worried about you.

From my mother. I'm eighty four years old. How could you do this to me? Don't you ever think about anyone but yourself? I can't tell you how upset I am. Oh what's the use. You've always done what you wanted.

Annie. Julia, I called you at Mallory's. My cop's intuition says you're in your place or Mallory's. Are you actually in Spain? Barcelona, Madrid, Alicante? Stop playing games and call.

Cynthia. Julia, I just got your number from Lynn. How wonderful to be in touch again. Please call me in San Fran. The number is..... I'm going to be in New York the beginning of next month and am dying to see you. God, it's been a long time. How the hell are you? I was very sorry to hear about Mallory. I can imagine how upset you were. Maybe Spain is a good idea. It's always a good idea to get away. Hope you're back when I arrive so we can get together. Love you Julia. Did I leave my number? It's......

Lynn. I just spoke with Cyn who's flying in next month. I hear from Annie that Mallory wants us to celebrate her life with a party. It sounds just like her. I'm sorry you're in Spain now. I'm in New York for a couple of days but there will be other times. Meanwhile I'm definitely planning to be there when Cyn is. The Eleanor Roosevelt Girls. When was that? A hundred years ago. Oh yes, Annie says you look great.

Lynn again. Julia, I forgot to leave my number in Philly. It's..... See you soon I hope. I just know you're having a great time in Spain. Wish I were there with you.

Cleo. Julia, I'm just calling to tell you how much I enjoyed seeing you and Annie the other night. I started re-reading your first novel and I like it even better the second time. I probably sounded very archaic. Well what can you do? I'm still in the dark ages. You were always more adventurous, you and Mallory, Cynthia and Lynn. I called Margaret and told her I spoke with you. She's allowed phone calls. Would you call her? She'd love to hear from you. You know she always liked you a lot. Here's the number...... And please call me. I'll try to catch up with the times. Oh, I almost forgot. Margaret was very sad when I told her about Mallory but she did say that Mallory was now in God's hands and maybe that was better than here. I hope she's right. Sorry I left such a long message. Well, see you.

Richard. I was hoping you were back but I guess you're not since your message hasn't changed. I wanted to get tickets for *Standbye*. I hear it's a wonderful play. I think of you Julia. Call when you get back.

Joan. Julia, how can you take off like that without letting me know unless this is one of your short trips. I think I've got a publisher for your novel but I don't want to do anything without speaking to you first. Call as soon as you get this message.

Ronda. Julia, sorry I haven't called the past two weeks. I'm having a retrospective in May and just locating all my paintings is a job and a half. Would you loan me the painting you bought? Why do I ask? I know you will. Let's get together for dinner. Would love to see you. Hope you're enjoying Spain.

Sally. Julia, I just heard. How terrible. I was never good on the telephone especially these stupid message machines so I'll wait til

you come back. Call me anytime, day, night, four in the morning.
I'm there for you sweetie.

Ilya. Julia, I haven't called because I've been away and now
you're away. Let's get together when you get back.

THE ABDUCTION 1956

It was decided that while a disguised Cynthia and Lynn would
be in the theater three rows behind Virginia and Arnie, Mallory,
Annie and I would abduct Claire and her daughters. Cleo, at home,
was our connection to each other.

At 7:55 we called. Cleo's line was busy. We called again. Cleo
picked up, said she'd just spoken to Lynn, that Virginia and Arnie
were in their seats and the curtain was about to go up.

We drove to the house. We walked through the green trees, past
the growling dog who made a mad dash for us, teeth barred. –Hi
sweetie,– I said. –Hi nice dog. It's me. Julia.– Foam flopped out of
his growling mouth.

–Oh Jesus Mary and Joseph,– Annie said. The dog stopped in
mid leap and looked at Annie. It was love at first sight. While the dog
licked Annie, foam and all, Mallory and I made our way to the front
door. –Open up Claire,– I said.

Claire opened the door as if she'd been waiting for us. Within
minutes she packed a few belongings and woke her daughters. Annie
carried four year old Kita to the car. Claire carried Patricia, who was
a year and a half.

They clung to Claire during the long drive, finally falling asleep.
We tried talking to Claire but she just sat, her eyes fastened on the
dark shadowed trees. She didn't ask where we were going. The dog,
on Annie's lap, slobbered all over her. It took five hours to get to the
Collective.

Everyone got out of the car except Claire and her daughters.

The air was cold and clear. Silver stars were shining in the black sky, my arm around Mallory. –If only we could package the air. Heavenly,– Mallory said. Dina rushed out of the house, looked around. –Where is she?– We pointed to the car. Claire was huddled by the window, hugging her daughters. Dina opened the car door, sat next to Claire, said something and they all got out. Dina struggled to hide her shock. Kita held her little sister's hand. The girls suddenly wide awake were looking every which way. Dina smiled at them.They looked bewildered. She hugged them. Two of the women took them into the kitchen where they were given milk and cookies. Then Claire took them to their room. We could hear Claire singing, the girls giggling, then quiet.

The women in the Collective had eaten earlier but had prepared food for us. Claire joined the three of us and Dina but didn't eat. She drank herb tea, said she wasn't hungry. I don't think she weighed more than ninety pounds. She jumped suddenly from her chair and ran up the stairs. When she came down she told us the girls were sleeping quietly. She went out into the clear night. –So many stars,– she said. –I never knew there were so many stars.–

We stood outside. Dina handed Claire a sweater. –It's cold Claire.– Claire put on the sweater, moved into the wooded area. We started to follow. Dina motioned us to stop. We stood outside, the four of us. Then we heard it. A howling from some primeval animal. It went on and on. Annie began running toward the sound. Dina stopped her. –It's ok. It's ok.–

ARNIE THREATENS ANNIE 1956

Mallory left instructions in her office. Nobody but nobody would be allowed in without her knowledge. Calls were to be screened. Under no circumstances would she speak or see Arnold Schuster. If he called or appeared, she was out. If he made a fuss they were to call the police. She'd already informed them that Arnie had threatened her, not that she thought they would take action but at least it was on record. She advised me to do the same. She pleaded with Annie to protect herself.

—Wanna bet he comes after Annie?—

—It will be you Mallory if it's anyone. He knows you took his wallet.—

—Or it could have been you. How do you know he thinks it's me? After all we were together.—

—But you're the one who was practically on top of him.—

—Don't remind me.—

—So why will he bother Annie?—

—Because she's the most vulnerable, the kind of target a shit like Arnie can't resist.—

—But he hasn't the vaguest idea that she knows anything.—

—She was Claire's best friend. That's enough for Arnie.—

Annie calls hysterically. Arnie has been to her apartment. He threatened her. He said if she loves her children she'd better talk. He twisted her arm behind her back, almost broke it.

—You didn't tell him anything.—

—Mallory, how could you even ask that?—

—Have you told Tim?—

—No. You told me not to.—

—I think it's time you did. Tell him what Arnie did to Claire. Tell him how she looked and what we did. Just leave the Woman's Collective and Vermont out of it.—

—What if he goes after Arnie?—

—He won't.—

—He might.—

—Tell him to keep his hands off Arnie. That pleasure will be ours. And don't worry. We'll leave you out of this part. We won't involve you.—

—Involve me for christsake. Involve me.—

When I come home Mallory is sitting in the living room

drinking champagne. She tells me to sit, pours me a glass. —Was I right or was I right? That bastard went to Annie's children's school and scared them. Little kids. It's time to take care of him. I've already called Cynthia and Lynn. We are going to put that bastard out of commission for a very long time.—

THE NIGHT WE GOT ARNIE SCHUSTER 1957

It was agreed that Dina would come in from Vermont, ask Arnie to meet her at a friend's apartment so they could discuss Claire. We were to go there at a designated time unless Dina told us otherwise.

When we entered the apartment Arnie was on all fours, a bewildered overgrown dog, his balls shriveled and dangling, his handcuffed hands behind his back. —Arnie and I are playing Slave. You're my ugly slave, aren't you Arnie?—

Arnie said nothing. Not even a woof came from his mouth.

—How are you doing Arnie?— Mallory asked. —Everything copasetic?—

—Fucking broads. You don't scare me.—

—Then you must be stupid Arnie.—

I took out the gun I'd bought. Arnie's face was suddenly not his face. —Where should I aim broads? I think the balls first, then an arm or maybe a leg. Of course we could do the head first.—

—Not the head Julia. Arnie's been brain dead for years. You'd just be wasting a bullet.—

We all laughed. The color left Arnie's eyes.

—He looks so cute down there,— Cynthia said. —Look at those balls and that teeny weenie penis.—

—Adorable,— Lynn said.

Dina suddenly came from behind, playing with his balls, then manipulated his prick. We all stared unbelieving. —I always wanted to know how that worked. Oooo look. It gets big. Isn't that cute.

What should we do with it?–

A knife appeared in Cynthia's hand. –I think we should cut it off. Anybody for cutting it off?–

–Oh Jesus, don't hurt me. Please don't hurt me.–

–We don't want to hurt you Arnie. We want to kill you.–

–Why?–

–You prick,– Dina screamed. –How dare you ask why?–

–If you only understand the circumstances...–

–You mean the circumstances that lead up to using our friend as a punching bag?–

–It's not true. Claire would be the first to tell you.–

–You bastard liar.–

Cynthia cut his arm. Arnie's blood fell to the floor. I held the gun close to his head. –Ok Arnie, how about another lie. Comeon Arnie, we're all waiting.–

–I didn't mean to hurt her. I swear it.–

Dina grabbed the knife from Cynthia and cut his other arm. Arnie groaned. Cynthia took the knife back. –You hurt our friend. You almost killed her. You did kill her. You killed the Claire we knew. You bastard. What made you think you could get away with it? What made you think you could hurt her like that and just walk away?–

–I'll never touch her again. I swear it.–

Mallory pulled his hair. –We know you won't because we're going to make sure you won't. Another thing Arnie, we didn't appreciate your threatening Annie and we especially didn't like your threatening her children. Now apologize to Annie. Arnie, I'm talking to you. Apologize to Annie.–

–I'm sorry.–

–Now lick her boots like a good boy.–

–What?–

–I said lick her boots.–

He looked from Mallory to Annie to my hand holding the gun. Annie, her face almost as colorless as Arnie's, moved closer to him.

He licked her boots.

Cynthia pulled off her jeans. —Now kiss my ass. Go on prick-head, kiss my ass.— She grabbed his penis until he screamed.

—Jesus Cynthia, you'll have the whole building at the door.—

Lynn started to put a handkerchief in Arnie's mouth. He bit her hand. She went wild, kicking him hard while Mallory pinched his nose so he couldn't breath and I tied the handkerchief. Cynthia squatted. She spread her legs. —Take a good look you bastard. It's the last one you'll ever see.— We couldn't believe our eyes.

Lynn took the belt from her jeans and whacked his back. Now it was my turn. I hit him repeatedly on his head with the belt, then handed it over to Mallory. She struck his handcuffed arms. We handed the belt to Annie knowing she wouldn't do a thing. Besides what was left. Annie was very quiet. Then she said without any emotion. —Turn him over.—

—What?— Mallory asked.

—Turn him over.—

—But he'll only roll back if we do.—

—Then hold him down.—

We turned him over, held him while Annie whacked him over and over and over again. —That's for Claire,— she said. —And that's for Claire. And that's for Claire.— Tears ran down her cheeks. —And that's for scaring the shit out of my children.— It took three of us to move her away.

Lynn and Cynthia dragged a naked Arnie into the cold night air. Nobody was in sight. I helped put him in the garbage can. We couldn't tell if he was alive or dead. Dina spoke. —If you're still able to hear and if you survive you will keep your mouth shut about tonight because if you're stupid enough to talk about it we guarantee your death next time.—

—Because the gun Julia has is not a toy and you'd better believe she knows how to use it.—

Mallory added, —And if you dare go near Claire or try to communicate with her or her children in any way and that includes a post card we'll kill you. Got it Arnie. Do you get it?–

We made the headlines of every newspaper and there were lots of newspapers then. *The New York Times, The Herald Tribune, The New York World Telegram, The Journal-American, The New York Post, The Daily News, The Daily Mirror.*

They reported that on January 2nd, 1957 an unidentified man, approximately six foot three inches, 193 pounds, in his late twenties or early thirties was found by garbage collectors. His condition was critical.

The five of us met at Lynn's. We toasted in the New Year. We toasted Claire's new life. Then Lynn laughed. –Found by garbage collectors. I love it.–

–Well,– Cynthia said, –who else would find garbage but garbage collectors?–

Three days later Arnie was well enough to identify himself. In an interview before he left the hospital he told reporters that he was attacked by a gang of men.

Arnie never went near Claire again.

ANNIE TO THE RESCUE 1994

I sleep. I dream. The rub is Mallory comes and goes. Well why shouldn't she? It's her apartment. When I awaken I am surrounded by her collection. They watch me. Even in my sleep I feel their eyes on me. Somewhere a phone rings. Mallory's version of *Pennies From Heaven* plays through gauze. A doorbell rings. Someone is threatening to break the door down. The voice is angry. Is this another one of my dream people? The voice is joined by another voice.

I can't break the door down. It's against the law.

I am the law the voice says.

I sit up and listen.

Show me your warrant.

She could be dead.

Who could be dead? Is she talking about Mallory? She is dead I say but not loud enough to be heard.

–Julia, if you're in there open up. Do you hear me? Julia?–

I walk over the three layered carpet and listen at the door. Is it Annie?

–Julia, I'm leaving but I'll be back with a warrant.–

–Annie?– I open the door. –What's the matter?– The super walks away but not before he gives me a look of disdain.

Annie walks in, sniffs the air. –Jesus, this place stinks. Open a window. Get some air in here.– She opens the window, turns to me. –Look at you. Why are you doing this to yourself?–

–What?–

–Comeon. I'm taking you out.–

–Out? Where?–

–To Tommie's office.–

–Gee thanks. I'm not good enough to meet but she'll condescend to see me as a patient.–

–Look at yourself. Then tell me you don't need help.–

She goes to the bathroom, fills the tub, tells me to undress. –Well what are you waiting for? Get in.–

I sit in the tub and sulk. Annie frowns, takes a washcloth and scrubs me. –What are you, three? Should I get you a rubber duckie?– I say nothing. She shampoos my hair, rinses it, gets me up and out, towel dries me. She takes a suit from the closet. I refuse to put it on. She picks out something else.

–I don't want that either.–

–Fine. Then you choose something.–

I take a jade green silk dress and put it on. –Mallory looked stunning in this. So how much is this visit going to cost? It may surprise you but I haven't sold a book in years.– I don't tell her about my agent's call. –I am a soldier in the army of broke soldiers.–

–Don't worry soldier. It won't cost a penny.–

–How come?–

—Because we're old friends.—

—Are we? You said you had nothing in common with the Eleanor Roosevelt Girls.—

—You're such a baby.— She looks in Mallory's closet. —My god, there are enough clothes here for an entire country.—

—You should see the other closets.—

I ask Annie what Tommie knows about me.

—That you were close friends, that Mallory died, that you're not able to handle the loss.—

—Is that what you think?—

—I think a lot of things Julia but I'm not the analyst. Let's wait and see what Tommie has to say.—

—She could be wrong you know. They're often wrong. Mallory went for eleven years and look where she landed.—

TOMMIE 1994

Annie is right. She is beautiful. Well groomed, impeccably dressed, every hair in place. Too perfect if you ask me. Her long stockinged legs are artfully placed under her behind but not quite. Mallory would have loved her. She asks questions, jots something on a piece of paper. For all I know she's writing Annie Annie Annie or who cares who cares who cares. She studies me, is silent. So am I.

—Have you ever gone to an analyst before?—

—No. Mallory did for years and years and look what it did for her.—

Tommie smiles. —Perhaps you never needed to.—

—I didn't and I don't.—

—That's very possible. Still you might get something out of this.—

—I am mourning the loss of my friend, my best friend which I think is perfectly normal.—

–It is.–

–And I don't blame myself if that's what you're thinking.–

–Well good.–

–Good that I don't blame myself or good that I could tell what you're thinking. I am perceptive. Believe me I'm perceptive. You can't write the way I do without being perceptive.–

–I'll accept that.–

–Do you want me to tell you what I've observed about you?–

–Not especially.–

–You're conservative or maybe the word should be conventional. You like order. You behave like a straight, in manner and dress. Probably because you're professional and don't want your clients to know.–

–My clients are 80% lesbian, 10% homosexual and 10% like you, straight, bi or undecided.–

–Which one am I?–

–I don't know. You tell me.–

–I get it. You think I'm depressed because I loved her like you love Annie. Well of course. What else would a lesbian think.–

–I wasn't aware there was a collective lesbian thought.–

–I'm talking empirical.–

–Julia, don't waste this time showing me how clever you are. I know you're clever. This isn't a session about lesbianism unless it's a problem for you. It's about getting on with your life. You're a writer. You're not writing. You have an apartment. You don't live there. Your telephone message says you're in Spain but you're not in Spain. You're in Mallory's apartment. Mallory's dead but you've stopped living as well.–

–How could you know somebody all these years and not know her?–

–Maybe that's the way it is. Maybe we don't really know anybody.–

–Don't you know Annie?–

–I know Annie the way she is with me. I know our relationship.

I know how she is with others when I'm with her but I don't know her away from me. I only know what she tells me. And I can only know what she's feeling if she shares those feelings. Learning about someone is a process and sometimes that process gets stuck.–
   –I hate those words.–
   –What words?–
   –Sharing. Process. Overused establishment words.–
   –I see.–
   –Do you like my clothes?–
   –Is that important?–
   –Do you think I have good taste?–
   –Yes. Yes I do.–
   –Well surprise. They're Mallory's clothes. I never dress like this. I'm not what you see. That's what Mallory was. Not what I saw. Once when we lived together, you know we lived together for years, I commented on her taste, how she always had such great looking clothes even when we were kids. Great clothes she said. I had nothing. My talent was to make something of nothing. I used scarves and jewelry. You know what I had Julia? Two outfits, that was it, two outfits. I was poor. I never thought of her as poor. Of course after she married Irving she had money. She earned six figures but when she died she had nothing.–
   –Why is that?–
   –She was free with money. She was very generous. She always said spend it when you have it because you never know.–
   –How many years did you live together?–
   –Eleven.–
   –What years were they?–
   –I moved in when I was twenty two. We were both divorced. Actually Mallory was divorced. I was separated. She was so damned neat. She couldn't stand my habit of dropping things wherever I was. It drove her crazy if one thing was out of place. She always said that space was what life was all about. Clutter she said would kill us all in the end. Then she changed. She became a collector. When I look

back she was probably always a collector. First it was people, people who could further her career and then it was anybody and everybody. She wanted to know all about them, what made them tick and then when she found out she dropped them. They bored her. And lovers. Married, unmarried, short, tall, old, young but never fat. She couldn't stand fat. Fat turned her off. She loved them all until they loved her. I don't remember when she began collecting things. I think it was after her second divorce. Anyhow, if it wasn't nailed down she took it. I often wonder if her life wasn't hidden in that collection.–

–Would you like to explore that?–

–No.–

–Did you have the same friends?–

–Sometimes.–

–And when she dropped them did you drop them too?–

–If I didn't she'd chide me.–

–Did you have the same lovers?–

–The same lovers! I hated Mallory's lovers.–

–Hated?–

–Yes hated. She chose disgusting men. I will never forgive her for Ron.–

–Who was Ron?–

–Her second husband.–

–Why don't you tell me about it.–

–What for?–

–It might help.–

–How would you know?–

–I don't but I do know your reaction is rather strong.– She hands me a box of tissues, waits until I stop crying. –Julia, I'm here to help, not judge.–

–I know I should have moved out, I know that, but the three of us had such fun together and I knew it would all end once they married. I was stupid to stay so long.–

–Why did you?–

—We'd been living in the same house for eleven years. That's a long time.—

—You said you would never forgive her for Ron. What was that all about?—

—It was after their engagement party. I was in my room watching TV when Ron asked me to join them for a nightcap. It seemed perfectly natural. I was telling them one of my funny experiences and we were falling over laughing and he said god this is so great, the three of us together. Then he kissed Mallory. Now you kiss her Julia. I kissed her lightly on the mouth the way I always did. Not like that he said. Kiss her the way you do when I'm not around. I glared at him, then looked over at Mallory. She said I don't mind if you don't. I couldn't believe she said that. I kept looking at her not believing and she finally said well ok, if you don't want to we won't. And then the two of them began making love as if I weren't there.—

—Why didn't you leave?—

—My body was heavy like lead the way it is in dreams. I kept thinking this isn't happening, it's just another bad dream.—

—But it wasn't, was it?—

—No.—

—How did you feel?—

—Betrayed. I felt betrayed.—

—Why betrayed?—

—Because I knew she wanted something to happen between us and it made me sick.—

—Sick?—

—Alright angry. I was angry because he was there and I was turned on. She was moaning. He began screaming at me. Don't just lie there you stupid bitch. Do something. Can't you see she wants you. He pushed my head on her breasts. Suck her tits he said. Suck them. Then he pulled my nightgown up. What the hell do you think you're doing I said and he said if you don't Mallory will, won't you sweetheart. I screamed Mallory don't. Don't let him do this to us. Can't you see what he's doing? And she said I love you Julia, don't

you know that. I ran from the room and locked myself in the bathroom. She was on the other side telling me not to be like that and I was yelling fuck you Mallory. Fuck you. I went to Lynn's.–
–The dancer.–
–Yes and I wouldn't have seen Mallory if Lynn hadn't intervened.–
–Did you tell Lynn what happened?–
–She said she wasn't surprised. Mallory came over and apologized. She said she'd be heartsick if I wasn't her matron of honor. I told her she had a lousy nerve thinking I would after what happened. She said she was drunk and didn't know what she was doing. I called her a liar who didn't have the guts to acknowledge her own feelings. How dare you tell him you want me? If you want me say it to me. Look at the power you gave him. She denied she told him and in the end I gave in. I always did. When we broke up she blamed it on Bettina but we both knew it had to do with that night.–
–Did either of you ever confront Ron?–
–Confront him? I couldn't stand to be in the same room with him, much less talk to him.–
–Did you and Mallory ever discuss it again?–
–What for? She knew I was attracted to her. She was beautiful, she was bright. We were always so close but she loved playing these games with me. Once she grabbed me in the elevator and told me how she'd been attracted to me for years. And later when I made advances she said I was as bad as any man she'd ever been with. Why are you pressuring me she asked.–
–How did that make you feel?–
–How do you think? I was upset. I was confused. Why did she do that if she didn't expect a response?–
–That must be a very painful memory.–
–I should have forced the issue instead of dropping it.–
–Why didn't you?–
–I was afraid of losing her friendship. We touched each other under the stairs. We were little kids. It became such a big thing in my

life but it meant nothing to her. She'd start something, then drop it and leave me with a terrible longing. She's dead and look at me. I'm still longing. I hate her for that. I hate her.–

MALLORY, THE SECOND TIME AROUND 1963

I can't believe she's marrying him. I can't believe I agreed to be her matron of honor, that I'm standing at the chapel door waiting for the signal to enter, that Mallory's hand is in mine. Cynthia, Lynn, Cleo and Annie are the bridesmaids. Cynthia knows. I can see by the look on her face that Lynn told her. Annie is worried about Cleo. We all are. Cleo, who looks like she left her coffin for the occasion. Well at least Paniotti isn't here. Claire is in Vermont with Dina and her children. Margaret at the nunnery. Mallory decided we should wear red because it symbolizes health, vigor and strength. I haven't seen Ron yet. We're waiting when Bettina runs past us waving, opening the door where the guests wait.

–Who in hell invited her?–

–You must have Mallory.–

She stares at me, lets go of my hand. –Did you Julia?–

–Me!–

–She probably saw it in the newspaper,– Lynn says.

–Help! Is this a sign that all my weddings are doomed to fail?–

We're all laughing as the doors open to organ music. Ceil, who's giving Mallory away as if anybody could give her away, waits to escort her down the aisle. She's wearing a white tuxedo, Mallory's idea. Ron, who's lost weight for the occasion is wearing a pink tuxedo. Pig color. He winks at Mallory, then at me.

Is he out of his mind? I give this one three years.

The rabbi concludes. –I now pronounce you man and wife.–

–Husband and wife,– Mallory says, then turns to the congre-gants. –Husband and wife.– Ron's jaw looks like it's wired to his teeth. –Smile darling,– she says. He doesn't.

Drinks and canapés are passed around by tuxedoed waiters and waitresses. Lynn, Cynthia, Annie and I stay together. Cleo and Bettina are nowhere in sight. –I know where you'll find Bettina,– Lynn says. –Vomiting those delicious canapés down the toilet.–

–I can't believe she still does that.–

–She's so afraid of gaining a pound.–

–I'll never forget how sick I was at Mallory's first wedding.–

–I can't picture Annie drunk.–

–I wasn't drunk Lynn. It was from those stuffed whatever. They have them here but I'm not touching them.–

Cleo comes toward us. –Bettina is crying her eyes out. I can't get her to stop.–

Mallory joins us. –Is everybody enjoying themselves? The stuffed mushrooms are outstanding.–

–Bettina is in the Ladies Room crying.–

–Shit.–

–She says her marriage is unbearable. She needs a place to go.–

–I was having such a good time. I had to come over here.–

–She's an Eleanor Roosevelt Girl.–

–You could have fooled me.–

–Comeon Mallory, somebody has to help.–

–You mean take her in.–

–Yes,– Cleo says.

–Ok, then you take her.–

–I couldn't. Paniotti would have a conniption.–

–I'm going on a honeymoon so that leaves me out. Lynn?–

–She was never my friend. Cynthia?–

–I hate when you're cute Lynn. How about you Annie?–

–Well, I could ask Tim.–

–That bitch. I wondered why she came. She wants us to rescue her like we did Claire, not that she lifted a finger to help. Listen sweet Annie, what in hell did she ever do to help any of us other than to take Julia to sleepaway camp?–

—It was Lake Oscawana, Mal and you're not as cute as you think you are.—

—And think about this. Why weren't any of us invited to her wedding?—

—Because it was in a Catholic church and she didn't think Jews were allowed to go,— Cleo says.

—What bullshit! It's Catholics who aren't allowed to go to synagogues. Were you at her wedding Annie?— Annie looks at the floor. —And never wondered why the Jewish members weren't there. I suppose you were there Cleo. Well that's just lovely. No Jews allowed, is that it? That simplifies things doesn't it. The Jews will let the Christians provide Bettina with a sanctuary.—

—Mal, what you're saying is not true. I was at Cleo's wedding.—

—Yes? How odd that only Julia was invited,— Lynn says.

—My parents said I could only invite two friends so I invited Margaret and Julia because...well just because.—

—I think we weren't invited intentionally. Don't you think it odd that we invite them to our weddings but they don't invite us to theirs.—

—Our weddings! Funny I don't remember my wedding. Did I get married Cyn?—

—Not that I recall. Did I?—

—Nope.—

—That's a relief.—

—We were all at Annie's,— I say.

—I wasn't.—

—Because you dropped out of the club after you married Irving. This is silly Mal. The truth is none of us like Bettina and that's what this is all about.—

—No Julia, you hate Ron and that's what this is all about.—

—What difference does it make how I feel about your husband. You're the one who has to live with him.—

—Meaning what? Julia, I'm talking to you. Meaning...—

—Meaning somebody should go into the Ladies Room and talk to Bettina.—

—Good idea Julia. Me. I'm going to dance with Ron and I don't want a megilla made of this.—

—Megilla?—

—A Yiddish word Annie. Ask Julia.—

I stand alone with Cleo.

—We're the only ones who care. I feel terrible for her Julia.—

—I'll go in and talk to her.—

—Do you want me to come with you?—

—No. I'll be fine. Enjoy yourself.—

Bettina stares at herself in the mirror. Her face is swollen. Her eyes have little red veins in them.

What do I owe her?

—I hope you're not angry that I didn't see your play.—

What an opening.

—Don't be mad Julia.—

—I'm not.—

—My mother died. Did I tell you?—

—No Bettina. You didn't. We haven't spoken for a long time.—

—I called her on the phone. She didn't answer so I went over. I have a set of keys. I opened the door and there was this terrible smell. She was sitting up. The television was on and I stupidly thought she was watching. They say she'd been dead for a week.— Tears flooded her eyes. —I have nobody now but my daughter. I hate George. If it weren't for him I would be an actress and now I'm too old for anything.—

—What are you talking about? You're thirty three.—

—I've wasted my best years with a slob. He walks around in boxer shorts. Half the time his penis is exposed and my daughter sees that. She's thirteen. Julia, we were such good friends. Can't I stay with you, just for a while? Just until I get my life straightened out. Please Julia.—

—We sold the house Bettina. I don't have a place in the city anymore. My play's going into rehearsal at the Tyrone Guthrie. I'll be there.—

–Aren't you coming back?–

–Not for a while.–

–How about Lynn or Cynthia?–

–They can't Bettina.–

She was now crying bitterly. –There are six of you and not one will help me. None of you ever liked me. I was never good enough for you. I was just a hick from Indiana whose mother thought eating in a diner was special, who wasn't smart like the rest of you. I can't help the way my mother was. It wasn't me who said those awful things to you. I was your friend Julia.–

–I'll see what I can do.–

–Don't say it unless you mean it.–

Mallory enters the Ladies Room. Her –feeling better Bettina?– has a nasty ring to it. She motions for me to leave. Once outside she glares at me. –Are you planning to spend the evening in the Jane?–

–Mallory, why can't she stay at our place until the new owners take over?–

–Because I don't want her to.–

–But the house will be empty.–

–Julia, this is my wedding day. Why are you hocking me?–

–I know how you feel about her Mallory. Still...–

–You like her? You hypocrite. I know damned well you don't.–

–Mallory, she needs help. She's a woman who needs help. Please. I know what you're like under that hard exterior.–

–It's our place. You want her to stay, she can stay but Julia if anything goes wrong I am going to hold you responsible.–

–Thanks.–

–And would you mind making some small effort to be cordial to Ron.–

–I'm as cordial as I'm going to be.–

–He made a mistake Julia. We all make mistakes.–

–Right.–

–You are so stubborn.–

–Right again.–

—Ok tell Bettina. And for heavens sake try to cheer up Cleo. She's the one we should feel sorry for. Fuck Bettina.—

REMEMBERING 1994

What happens to all that energy? Where does it go? Do the dead know they're dead or do they whirl unknowingly through the Escape Speed parading their radiance. Shimmering sparklers raining down on the universe, the final flicker of light. Do the dead know that whatever was is now gone?

It's finished. Over. I'll never see her again, never breathe that lovely scent that was Mallory. Mallory no more, my mantra of death.

I look out her window. A tree bends and sways with the wind. Puffed up Galway clouds obscure the sun. Children walk holding their mother's hands. How careful parents have to be today. An ambulance screams through the street, that hated sound that Mallory will never hear again.

I walk her neighborhood. There's the Greek restaurant we loved, the mashed garlic potatoes, the wild mushrooms with celery chips, the pita we dipped in taroumusalata, the rare tuna steak with that wonderful ginger sauce, the bottle of retsina we shared.

I must call Margaret.

You have a life Tommie says, why are you living at Mallory's? Write she says but what can I write that will ease the loss. I pass a movie house. Whatever happened to that photo of Joel McCrea? I decide to go in. The ticket taker hands me my ticket. The actor on the screen reminds me of Richard. What am I going to do about Richard? Everything about me as dead as Mallory. Yet at night someone joins me in bed. Who is my bedmate, those teasing touches that jolt me into orgasms.

Years of feeding that powerful need. Going from lover to lover. Temporary people. Men who sailed through the night. They could have been apes, gorillas. I love you hovered in the air. Empty words, obligatory words. Not true. Sometimes there was love. Now there's AIDS, the chance of that nightmare sickness, the agonizing death. And nobody trusts anyone anymore in and out of bed.

Annie's mother was right. It was better then. People cared more, they smiled more, the cops on the street knew all the kids. We learned about money by going to the corner grocery store to buy things. And we could go alone without holding on to our mother's hand. There were poor then but you didn't see hoards of them on the street freezing in winter, standing in formation waiting for breakfast at God's Lighthouse. You didn't have the homeless coming at you from both ends of the subway. Maybe nothing's better, nothing's worse. It just is.

No. Hitler changed the face of the earth. He polluted it, gave those who followed permission to do anything. Any crime. Any murder. He knew before he died in his bunker that he'd done his work, that it would continue. Bosnia. Guatemala. Haiti. Murdered Indians. Chinese girl babies. Raped women. Boat people turned back the same as the trapped Jews. Go back where you came from. The list endless.

But it was different then. Then publishing houses were run by people who loved books, not the conglomerates of today who are setting new standards of mediocrity. Or the agents who bow low to the editors. And all are convinced that a good book is one that makes money. A good anything makes money. And mediocrity has become the new artform. Seen on the walls of art galleries, in chain bookstores. These merchants of crap, their green noses looking down on those who still have standards, have won the culture war. And soon we will be a nation of war mongers and idiots.

But since then was then and now is now why worry about anything. It's all chance anyhow. I could go to sleep on Mallory's bed and not see Rudolph Valentino in the morning or the ladies and gentlemen of the limoges in their dandy outfits or Shirley Temple who's now as invisible as me. Maybe what we're living now is the other side of life but we don't know it.

But if I'm going to die why don't I call my born again Christian son? What difference does it make what religion he is? But if I call he'll go through his religious rap trying to convince me that I too should be born again before I die. He'll do his deep breathing knowing it drives me insane, he'll say prayers before we eat, lengthening them, knowing I'm passing out from starvation.

Because it does matter that after six million died, one Jew, my son, has left on his own.

And if I'm going to die sooner than I know, why am I still worried about gaining weight or cholesterol when nobody has a weight problem or cholesterol problem wherever the dead go.

Why can't I go on with my life? Tommie is right. Mallory is dead but I'm not. And nothing I do will bring her back. We will never be lovers. It's too late now. I missed that chance like so many others. But then was then, gone like the dead. And now is now.

I call Richard. I call my mother. I call David but not Jonathon. I call Cynthia and Lynn. I call Annie and Cleo. I decide to take a stroll among the living.

RICHARD 1994

–I love garlic.–

–Me too.–

He tells the waiter to load the pasta with garlic. Is this so we'll both smell and not notice or is to keep us away from one another? We drink wine. He talks about his work, about the terrible conditions of his client's apartments, the leaking faucets, the holes in the walls, toilets that don't work, roaches, rats, peeling paint. And for this they pay too much rent. Then there are the battles with the welfare agencies to get money so tenants won't be out on the street. Nobody cares he says. I say the expected you do.

–Well I shouldn't say nobody. I should say not enough people.–
I can see he's a nice man.

He talks about a client. –She has three sons. One is in prison.
One is twelve. He drinks. The middle one, the good one has brain
cancer. incurable brain cancer. She can't work because he requires
constant care. Her landlord is charging $750 a month. Welfare won't
pay it. Where is she going to get the money? Which means I have to
convince the lord of the land to lower her rent. She's in her forties
and looks old enough to be your mother. Maybe all I'm doing is covering their wounds with band-aids or postponing the inevitable but
at least it's something.–

Has he told this story to Mallory?

–I think what you're doing is wonderful.–

He grins. –And I think what you do is wonderful. I read all your
books while you were in Spain.–

–Spain!– I say forgetting my lie.

–Yes Spain. Where were you by the way?–

I start to say Barcelona. Madrid comes out.

–I haven't been there for a while. I hear it's become the in city of
Spain. Was it fun?–

I nod. The food comes. –This is great. Speaking of garlic.
Wow!– He pours more wine into my glass. –What are you working
on now Julia?–

*My life. I'm working on my life, my old age, my sexless life. I'm
waiting for that big orgasm in the sky.*

–A novel.–

–I love the way you write but I knew I would. How long have
you been writing?–

–All my life. How long have you been a lawyer?–

–Five years.–

–What did you do before?–

–I painted.–

–And?–

–I didn't sell enough to pay my bills. I had a friend who was a tenant advocate. He convinced me to volunteer. I liked the idea of helping people so I decided to go to law school.–

He talks about his work, how most of his clients are women with children. The wine is getting to me. He's talking about important things, crucial things and all I can think is will we or won't we. My underpants are soaked. I excuse myself, go to the Ladies Room. I dry myself in the cubicle, start to masturbate. What am I crazy, what am I nuts! I turn on the faucet in the washroom, pour cold water on my red blotched face, desire blotches, ugly blotches, telltale blotches.

I sit at the table pushing food into my mouth, rehearsing how I'm going to tell him I don't want to go to the theater. I don't want to go anywhere with him. I have to go home comes out of my mouth. Why he asks. Tears salt my garlic pasta. His touch tender.

–Please come to the theater with me Julia.–

–I can't.–

–Why? Is it me?–

You I say laughing. Shades of Bettina. The bottle of wine finished I ask for champagne. Might as well get completely crocked. He orders a bottle. A glass I say angrily.

Why am I behaving like this?

–Ok– Richard says, –a glass.–

The play is good. Funny. The crisis has passed.

Afterward we sit at a bar drinking brandies. He's telling me his life story, about his brother in California, the terrible death of his mother, the father he doesn't talk to. I like being with you he says.

–Would you be with me if it weren't for Mallory?–

–I liked you the minute I saw you. I didn't know you and Mallory were friends.–

–What are we going to be Richard? Friends. Lovers. What?–

–What do you want Julia?–

–You're not getting off that easy. What do you want?–

–I'd like us to be both.–

–You were with Mallory. You were going on a trip. You cried.–

–Yes I cried. To think she was going through such terrible pain and I never knew. I failed her.–

–You said you loved her.–

–I never said that. Julia, I was lonely, she was lonely. I liked being with her but I didn't love her.–

–Did she know that?–

–I don't know. We never talked about love.–

–Well I want to talk about love. I don't love you but I want to have sex with you but...–

–But what?–

–You're young, you're good looking. I'm sure you have an active sex life. AIDS.–

–I don't have an active sex life.–

–How come?–

–I'm not attracted to many women.–

–Oh for the good old days when you just did it without this song and dance routine. I worry about AIDS.–

–I just gave my blood. I'm clean.–

–I'm squeaky clean. I've been a celibate for a long time.–

–Why?–

–I don't know. Have you ever been married?–

–Yes. Once. You?–

–Twice. Do you have any children?–

–I have an eighteen year old daughter.–

–You started young.–

–Do you have any kids?–

–David's my kid.–

He laughs. –Really! No wonder you seemed so familiar.–

–I have another son but I never talk about him. He's a born again Christian. I don't know how you could be a born again Christian if you never were in the first place.–

–Jesus.–

–Exactly.–

–Can we go to my place? Is that alright with you?–

–Will I see your paintings?–

—You can't miss them. They're all around.—

He puts his arm around my waist, hails a cab.

THE ELEANOR ROOSEVELT GIRLS 25TH ANNIVERSARY 1967

The minute I see her at my door posing, a stage entrance smile on her face I know something is wrong. —Julia,— she says, pecks me on the cheek, hands me a gallon jug, then moves past me posture perfect and plops herself like a dish of jello on my sofa. —Nice apartment. How are you Julia?—

—I'm fine Cynthia. And you?—

—Good.—

—So, what's it like living in tinsel town?—

—Alright.—

—Are you sure you're ok?—

—Yes Julia.—

—You don't seem ok.—

—How about breaking open the jug and pouring us Manhattans. Made them myself.—

I hand her a drink. She taps my glass. —To the reunion of the Eleanor Roosevelt Girls.—

—How's Hollywood treating you?—

—I'm getting work. What's happening with your new play?—

—It opens in the Fall.—

—That's exciting. Have they cast it?—

—Just the lead.—

—Is there a part for me?—

—I wish.—

—You wish? You're the playwright.—

—I don't have that kind of say Cynthia.—

—Right.—

—Maybe the next one.—

–Of course. The next one. Pour me another.– She gulps it down.
–Did you know that bad things have a way of hiding inside you so
quiet you don't even know they're there.–

–What's wrong Cynthia?–

–Nothing, not a damned thing.–

–You're in some mood.–

–What mood is that? Gloomy or could it be pensive. Everyone's
in some mood or other but you should know that. You're the writer.
I'm just the one with her head stuck in the thesaurus.–

–I thought that was Lynn.–

–No. Lynn is the one who sleeps with a dictionary in case she
dreams a word she doesn't know.–

–Remember when she told Margaret that pigeons were called
nuns. I'll never forget the look on Margaret's face.–

–What look? She only had one look.–

We're both laughing when the doorbell rings. Lynn and Annie
enter. –Cynthia,– Annie says, –what a surprise. I didn't know you
were going to be here.–

–The reunion was my idea.–

–You're getting fat Annie.–

–I'm not fat Lynn. I'm pregnant.–

–Again?–

–It's only my third.–

Cynthia lights up, forms an O with her mouth, swooping the
smoke in, passing it on to Lynn who inhales deeply. –That's good
stuff Cyn.–

–It should be. I grew it myself. California sunshine.–

–Is that marijuana?– Annie asks.

–It sure tastes like it. Julia?–

I take a deep drag and hand it to Annie who pushes it away.

–What were you laughing at? We could hear you all the way
down the hall.–

–Your pigeon definition.–

–I always thought penguins should be called nuns. Poor

Margaret. Our resident enigma. Do I see cocktails?–
–Cynthia made enough for the army. Anyone for Manhattans?–
Lynn twirls an imaginary mustache. –Anyone for the army? To
us. And to cocktails you drink.–
   Annie sips her drink. –What else would you do with a cocktail?–
–A cocktail is also a horse with a docked tail.–
   –A docked tail?–
   –Yes, a docked tail.– She kisses Annie on the cheek. –Have a
child for me sweetie. Have two. Now this is what I call a great
Manhattan. She moves to the window. –Nice view Julia.–
   –Is Claire coming?– Annie asks.
   –She can't make it.–
   –But she's ok.–
   –Yes. She sent a telegram.–
   –How about Cleo?–
   –Not coming.–
   –How disappointing. I was hoping she'd be here.–
   –Really Annie. I didn't even know you liked her.–
   –Julia, don't you know by now that Annie likes everyone.–
   –She isn't sick again, is she?– I ask.
   –Cleo is having an affair.–
   –Cleo,– we yell. –Not Cleo.–
   –I could be wrong but I don't think so. She came backstage
when I was with the Shirley Ross Company, the only one of you who
showed, thank you very much my loyal fans. I could see this male
lurking in the background not with her but with her if you know
what I mean and when I said who's your friend she turned purple and
said this is Marshall and before I could say another word she handed
me a bunch of flowers and whisked him off into the night air.–
   –He could be a friend.–
   –So why did she run off like that?–
   –What about Mallory?–
   Mallory pokes her head in the door. –What about her? I just love
open doors. You get all the gossip but I didn't get who whisked who

off. Anyone I know?– She hugs everyone while Lynn tells her that
Cleo is probably having an affair and she says, well good for her.

There's no hug for me, just a one note –Julia.–

She picks up her shopping bag and heads for the kitchen where
she ushers orders. –Champagne glasses Julia?–

–Don't have any.–

–Well then some decent glasses. Will somebody arrange the
caviar and black bread on a plate? What are you all drinking?–

–Cynthia made Manhattans. Want some?–

–I'll stick to champagne. Annie, you're getting fat.–

–I'm pregnant.–

Cleo sticks her head in the kitchen door. –Who's pregnant?–

–Me.–

–Congratulations. Don't you close your door Julia? I could have
robbed you deaf dumb and blind.–

Annie hugs Cleo. –Lynn said you weren't coming.–

–Isn't this our twenty fifth anniversary. Would I miss that?–

–I told them you were having an affair.–

–Honestly Lynn. It wasn't your right to say anything. Anyhow
it's not true, he's just a friend.–

–You're talking to an old pro. I know the signs.–

–What's the big deal?– I say. –Everyone is having affairs
today.–

–I love the word affair. It sounds so festive. Is yours festive
Cleo?–

–Shutup Lynn.–

Lynn grabs Cleo and bites her cheek. –You bit me.–

–A love bite sweetie. Didn't your mama ever give you a love
bite? Mine did.–

We're all laughing, including Cleo. We're all in the kitchen
enjoying each other. Over and over again somebody says how wonderful or I'd forgotten that. Cynthia is unusually quiet. Lynn who's
always been close to Cynthia now hovers over her, keeping a
watchful eye. Something is definitely wrong. We're all putting food

out, paté, shrimp, guacamole, cheese, fruit. I put the stuffed mushrooms in the oven. –This is lovely,– Lynn says. –Isn't this lovely Cyn? Thank you Julia.–

–A feast,– Mallory says looking at me, the start of a smile on her face. Is she trying to erase four years of silence? She pops the champagne, hands the first glass to Annie. –To our little mother. I do hope you're not going to make this a habit.–

We all toast Annie.

–When is Claire getting here?– Mallory asks.

–She can't make it.–

–What do you mean she can't make it? Didn't you tell her I'd pay her fare?–

–Yes, I told her.–

–If you'd given me her address like I asked I would have wired her the money. Honestly Cynthia.–

–It won't be the same without her,– Annie says.

–Our shining moment.–

–Vermont 1957.–

Mallory corrects me. –You're wrong Julia. It was 1956.–

–So, sue me for a year.–

–Is she still in Vermont?–

–No. California.–

–Where in California?–

–On an ashram.–

–What's that?– Annie asks.

–A yoga retreat.–

–Why have we lost touch? We're our childhood. Who knows us better?–

–Really Mal. I didn't know you were so sentimental.–

–Didn't you Julia? Well now you do.–

Annie raises her glass. –Let's toast Claire.–

Cynthia takes the telegram from her bag and hands it to Lynn who reads, –To my heroes, my knights in shining armor on our twenty fifth anniversary. There isn't a day that goes by that I don't think of you. I love you all. Claire.—

We're all in a circle. We're all crying, our arms around one another. Lynn looks at us. —What a bunch of sissies. This is an occasion for happiness. Let's drink to happiness, to Claire and to us, the fabulous Eleanor Roosevelt Girls from Sunnyside. One for all and all for one.—

—That's the Three Musketeers Lynn.—

—Oh shutup Julia.—

Three of us have children. Claire, Cleo and Annie. Two are still married to the same man. Cleo and Annie. Three are divorced. Me, Mallory and Claire. One has remarried. Mallory. Two never married. Cynthia and Lynn. One lives with a woman. Claire.

I write, Lynn dances, Mallory edits a fashion magazine, Cynthia acts. Claire works with children on an ashram. Cleo didn't become a pilot. Annie didn't become a teacher. Both are fulltime mothers. Cynthia now has a three year old sister. Sixty four year old Irving is a father once again.

—Imagine having a sister who could be your daughter.—

—Who are you to talk. Isn't your eldest eighteen?—

Annie lifts her glass. —Let's drink to Cynthia's sister and wish her a good life.—

Cynthia bursts out crying. Lynn puts her arms around her. —Tell them.—

—Tell us what?—

—Nothing.—

—I knew something was wrong the minute you walked in.—

—For heaven's sake Cynthia, tell them.—

—He's doing things to her.—

I gasp and without thinking blurt out, —What things?—

—Sexual things.—

—What do you mean, sexual things?— Cleo asks.

—What do you think she means?—

—That's ridiculous,— Cleo says. —He's her father. Besides what could he be doing to a three year old?—

Cynthia looks at no one, her voice toneless. –He masturbates her. he...–

–Stop,– Annie screams. –I'm going to vomit.–

–I don't believe it,– Cleo says.

–Did you confront Irving?–

–No Julia.–

–Didn't you do anything?–

–I told his wife.–

–And what did she say?–

–She said I had a sick mind.–

–Didn't you report it to the police?–

–The police! What good would that do Annie? Even Cleo doesn't believe it.–

–I wasn't being literal.–

–Anyhow, haven't we learned from personal experience how effective the police are?– Lynn says.

–Well if the police can't help and her mother's turned into an ostrich, then what?–

–We can pretend nothing is going on or we can take action.–

–What action Lynn?–

–I'm all for murdering the bastard.–

–Should I get my gun out?–

–Come off it Julia. You're not going to shoot anyone.–

–Well I'm sure as hell not going to let him get away with it.–

Mallory's annoyance is apparent. –Let's find out what Cynthia wants, ok Julia?–

–We have to get my sister away from that house.–

–How?–

–What do you mean how? We'll abduct her,– Lynn says.

–That's kidnapping.–

–We know that Cleo.–

–It's against the law.–

I look over at Cynthia who is openly staring at me. –Look, I need some coffee. Does anyone want coffee?–

–That's a brilliant solution Julia. Coffee.–

–I'm not solving anything Lynn. I'm just making coffee.–

Mallory follows me into the kitchen. –Does she know that you told me?–

–No.–

–You never told her I knew.–

–I said no.–

–You're not lying.–

–I don't lie Mal. Anyhow, why is it so important now? Get out the cups, will you?–

–I thought for sure you'd say something.–

–Me! How about you? You married Irving after I told you.–

–Don't lay it on me. You're the one who witnessed it and did nothing.–

–Because Ceil told me not to. Besides, I was only a kid.–

–But you're not a kid anymore, are you?–

She moves into the living room carrying a tray with cups and saucers. I pour coffee. Cleo says she never heard of a father harming his child 'in that way.' Annie feels it's wrong to take a child away from its mother, that we should make another attempt at talking to her. Cynthia says it would be pointless. Mallory and I say nothing.

Cleo persists. –I don't understand. Why would he do such a thing to his own child. Cynthia, did he ever touch you?– Cynthia is looking at me.

Is she waiting for me to say something?

–Cynthia...–

–No Cleo.–

–Do you have any idea of what they do to people who kidnap children?– Mallory says.

–And what about people who molest children?–

–You'll never get away with it.–

–What about Claire?–

–Claire was an entirely different matter.–

–Is that a no, Mallory?–

–I'll have to think about it.–

Lynn turns to me. –Julia?–

–I need to talk to Cynthia.–

–So talk.–

–Alone.–

We sit on the bed. I pull out a cigarette, offer her one. –Cynthia, I'm going to tell.–

–Tell what?–

–I know you've been waiting for me to say something.–

–I've been waiting? Your writer's imagination is really working overtime.–

–Have I been imagining those looks?–

–Apparently.–

–You never told Lynn. Close as you are, you never told her?–

–Whatever are you talking about?–

–When you were sick, when I brought you your homework. I saw and you know I saw.–

–Saw what?–

–Your father. Irving was fondling you.–

–You're nuts.–

–Cynthia, if I tell them I'm sure Annie will change her mind. I don't know about Cleo but I know Annie.–

–You know. What do you know Julia? You think because you're a writer you have greater insights than the rest of us.–

–Cynthia, are you saying I imagined it?–

–That is precisely what I'm saying. It's all in your head Julia but that's what makes you such a good writer.–

We sit not looking at one another. I fight the tears burning behind my eyes. –Cynthia, you know I would never do anything to hurt you.–

–I know that. I've always known that. Let's go inside.–

–You go. I'll be right in.–

–Julia, why are you crying? You have no reason to cry. Comeon, let's join the others.–

She puts her arm around my waist as we walk into the living room in time to see Mallory saying her goodbyes.

–Why are you leaving so soon?–

–Look, I'd like to help but I don't feel like spending my old age behind bars.–

–You weren't worried about our spending time in prison when we helped you.–

–That was quite different.–

–We committed a crime Mallory, for you.–

–Look, I don't want to know your plans because if I don't know I can't ever confess to anybody.– She goes around the room kissing everyone on the cheek.

–Confess to whom?–

–What?–

–Confess to whom?–

–Comeon Julia, it's very naive of you to think you can just pull off a kidnapping. Assuming you do get the child away from Irving, where will she go? She can't go to Cynthia's. That's the first place they'll look. Which of you will take her? You Annie? What about your own children? Cleo? What do you tell Paniotti? What do you tell your parents and your children? What about the photos they'll have plastered in every city and they will you know. It's a ridiculous scheme and it's impossible for me to believe you're all going to go along with it.–

I walk her to the door. She smiles as if nothing was said.

–Mallory...–

–Tell me Julia, have you cast the play yet?–

–I didn't think you knew.–

–Of course I know. It's my business to know. So, have you?–

–Janet Sullivan's got the lead.–

–Really! You can't do better than that. I think we ought to do a feature on you. The girl from Sunnyside. Who would have dreamed...–

–Thanks, thanks a lot.–

– I'm not talking about you. I'm talking about how little we had

going for us. So, is it alright with you if I set it up?–
 –A feature in *Coutier*. Who could refuse that?–
 –Good. I'll give you a call sometime tomorrow.–
 –Thanks Mal.–
 –Well goodbye.–
 –Don't go.–
 –I have to Julia. We're working on the layout for the December issue.–
 –I'm talking about Cynthia.–
 –Let it be Julia.–
 –She never walked out on you.–
 –Can't you let well enough alone?–
 –What happened to that tough girl from Sunnyside?–
 –She grew up.–
 –No Mallory, she lost her nerve.–
 –That's your opinion. Goodbye Julia.–
 –Just tell me this, is this magazine feature the end of a four year deep freeze or is this just a business decision?–
 –Why must you do this?–
 –I want to know if Ron is still pulling the strings?–
 –Nobody rules my life, not even my husband.–
 –You didn't answer my question.–
 –Put yourself in my position Julia.–
 –I can't because our friendship has always come first.–
 –I live with Ron, I don't live with you and I refuse to be put in the middle of your feud.–
 –My feud! You weren't there?–
 –You see there it is. It isn't enough that I make this overture. It isn't enough that I love you. No, you have to go on and on and on. You and your damned principles.–

 The minute I enter the living room Lynn confronts me. –What's going on between you and Mallory?–
 –Nothing.–

–Nothing? I felt like putting on my winter coat. Did you try to sway her?–

–Yes.–

–Don't bother giving us the answer. We all know it. Wake up Julia. This isn't the Mallory we knew.–

–How are we going to get away with kidnapping?–

–I have a better question Julia. How are we going to live with ourselves knowing a three year old child is being sexually molested? Do you have an answer for that one?–

–Look, I have to go home so here's my vote. We go to the authorities first.–

Lynn looks toward Cynthia. –Do you want to reconsider going to the authorities?–

–No because if we do and they do nothing and they won't, they'll definitely suspect me since I'm the logical one to report it.–

–Annie, are you still for telling the authorities?–

–Well wait a minute,– Annie says. –I have to think about what Cynthia just said.–

–You're pregnant Annie. How can you even consider...–

–Cleo, let her make up her own mind.–

–I still say we take a chance and tell the authorities,– Cleo says.

–Ok, two for abducting, one for authorities, one undecided. How about you Julia?–

–Say we kidnap her, what do we do with her?–

–I have some ideas.–

–But Mallory has a point. Her photograph will be everywhere.–

–So, what are you saying Julia? Yes for the authorities or yes for the kidnapping.–

–I don't know.–

–When will you know and how about you Annie?–

–Do we have to decide this minute?–

–Well my vote stands. I am positive that the best solution is talking to the authorities. And if you do decide on... I can't even say the word.–

–Kidnapping.–

–If you decide on that, count me out.–

We watch Cleo put on her coat.

–Come on Annie, let's go. We could share a cab.–

–I want to stay.–

–What for? They're not going to decide anything tonight. Even Julia's undecided.

–What if it were my child? How could I look my children in the eyes knowing I did nothing.–

–Annie, think of what would happen to your children if you go to prison,– Cleo says.

–But it's morally wrong to do nothing.–

–Annie, you don't have to. I'd understand.–

–Cynthia, I know in my heart that if it were me who needed help you'd all be there just as we've always been there for one another.–

–Except me.–

–Don't be silly Cleo.–

–Don't say anything more please. Margaret and I always knew we were the outsiders. Don't think we didn't.–

I go to her. –That's not true.–

–Oh yes it is. Whether you admit it or not, you all know it's true. We stopped being part of the club years ago because...– Tears pour down her cheeks. –Just so you'll feel better, I feel awful.–

She walks out the door. Lynn turns to Annie and me. –So, what's it going to be?–

One week later Cynthia's half sister is with Claire at the Ashram. The Eleanor Roosevelt Girls decide never to meet again.

MALLORY ONCE MORE 1978

If her death was accidental. If she had an incurable disease. If she was blind or deaf or missing a limb. Or had no friends or money. If she was invisible like most women her age. But there was Richard.

But if she loved him knowing he only liked her, then what? Or if her love was overpowering and his was mere transient pleasure, the humiliation of it, the anguish. But even if that were true, if she'd stopped for one moment to realize that now is the time, it's all the time, there is nothing else, she'd still be alive. Maybe when she swallowed that last swallow of sea all the ifs came together in one grand symphony and she knew. But then it was too late.

Mallory stopped talking to me one week after her wedding when she was forced to interrupt her honeymoon. She blamed me. Bettina had forgotten she'd run the bath water and fell asleep, her sleep interrupted when Mallory's townhouse became one large swimming pool. It was all my fault. I'd ruined her honeymoon, jeopardized her marriage, wrecked her lovely townhouse and totally destroyed twenty six years of friendship. Ours.

I called Mallory from Minneapolis. I wrote letters hoping she'd call back or write. But she didn't. The only time we saw each other was at the Eleanor Roosevelt Girls 25th anniversary party. She didn't come to my wedding. Well, I didn't invite her. I wasn't there when Sandy was born. Neither was she when I gave birth to David and Jonathon. She divorced Ron. The following year I divorced Norman. I lived in Spain. She lived in Italy. I lived in California. She lived in Chicago. I was active in the Woman's Movement in California. Mallory, back in New York, was active there. I was invited to Moscow with a group of writers. She was with magazine editors. Neither of us knew the other was there. One day in Red Square I turned and saw a woman who looked like Mallory. She was on one end of the square. I was on the other, too far away to be certain. I walked quickly toward her but she'd disappeared. Later on I discovered it was Mallory. It was the one time we were in the same place at the same time.

In 1978 I was in Stockholm at the Kulturhusset, reading from my works. My plan was to spend one week there with Britta Lindstrom who translated my books into Swedish and another in London with Raye Birkenshire. Then back to Los Angeles and my sons. At my

hotel there's a message. Call Olga. Emergency. I call. She tells me
Ceil Margolies phoned from New York, something about Mallory.
   Ceil doesn't have an answering machine. She's not in. None of
Mallory's aunts are in. I keep dialing. Finally Esther answers. She
tells me that Mallory just got out of surgery, that they can't know if
it's malignant until the biopsy is done. Can you come Julia? She's
been asking for you. It's been eleven years Esther. Yes I know but
coming out of the anesthesia she kept saying your name. Please Julia.
   I cancel my plans, call my kids and get the first flight to New York.
   Her hospital room looks like a greenhouse. The minute I enter
she smiles. –Oh Julia Julia. It was all worth it just to see that wonderful face again.–
   –You always would do anything to get attention but isn't this
carrying it a bit far Mal.–
   –Mal. The sound of it. Do you know aside from Ceil you're the
only one who ever called me Mal.–
   Ceil hugs me. Her look tells me the prognosis is bad. The rest of
her aunts are absent. At her side is a very young very good looking
man.
   –Come sit by me. Hold my hand and talk to me.–
   The man gives me his chair. I bend over and kiss her. Her lovely
scent is replaced by a strange smell.
   –Have some champagne Julia.–
   –I see you haven't changed.–
   –That's what you think.–
   –Tell her to stop drinking. She knows she's not supposed to.–
   –Ceil, you worry too much.–
   –Mal, you're on medication. You know you're not supposed to.–
   –The doctor says one glass in the early evening and one before I
go to sleep.–
   –That isn't what he told me.–
   Mallory sips her champagne. She's smiling, composed. Her
dressing gown a bright red, her hair short, beautifully coiffed, her
nails manicured.

–Do you realize it's been eleven years since we last saw each other? Eleven years ago Adam was a bar mitzvah boy, weren't you Adam? Julia, meet Adam Bergman, no relation to Ingmar or Ingrid. Adam, my best and oldest friend, Julia Jaffe.–

He shakes my hand. –I've heard a lot about you.–

–So Julia, tell me all about Sweden. Is it as lovely as they say?–

–It's breathtaking.–

–Were you working, having fun, what?–

–I was invited to give readings.–

–You didn't cancel anything on my account I hope.–

–I gave my last scheduled reading last night. I was going to spend a week with my translator and another with Ray Birkenshire in London...–

–Ray Birkenshire! Why would you want to spend time with her. All that phony charm. I hear she puts pins in dolls. It wouldn't surprise me. Don't tell me you like her novels.– She turns to Adam. –Her women are bitches unlike Julia's women who are strong and independent.– She smiles at me. –I always said you were the most talented Eleanor Roosevelt Girl, didn't I Ceil?–

–And you are the most famous.–

–Fame. What's that? All that fame will mean shit when I die but you, when you die they'll lionize you.–

–Adam, why don't we leave these two alone?–

Adam waves at the door. –See you.–

–Sure... Ceil, why don't you take a break tomorrow?–

–I don't want to.– She bends down, kisses Mallory. –Feel good ok? And please darling no more drinking tonight. The combination is deadly.–

–Hey, if the surgery didn't kill me I'm not going to die from a little champagne.–

The minute the door closes she whispers, –It's the end Julia.–

–Don't be silly.–

–Look at me. All dressed up with no place to go but the grave. They think I don't know but I know. I'm going to die. I'm forty eight years old and I'm going to die.–

–You are not going to die.–

–Julia, I have cancer.–

–I know.–

–Everybody's so afraid to say the word. Instead it's you look great and a bunch of stupid hospital dialogue. I'm lying here with cancer and everybody acts like I have a broken toe.–

–Mallory, breast cancer is curable.–

–Then why is nobody talking about it? How bad is it? Has it spread?–

–I don't know. Talk to your doctor.–

–Promise you'll be here when I talk to him.–

–I will.–

–I don't deserve your friendship. I never did. I'm a very selfish person.–

–You always were.–

She looks at me and laughs, then winces. –It was worth the pain of laughter just to hear that. Anyone else would have said no you're not but not you Julia. I could always trust you to tell the truth. Why did we fight over Bettina?–

–It wasn't about Bettina.–

–You're right. When they were wheeling me into the operating room I thought I'm going to die. I'm going to die in surgery. My heart is going to stop and I'll never be able to tell Julia how sorry I am. I've had such a hole in my heart all these years.–

–Me too.–

–I do such dumb things.–

–We all do Mal.–

–No. That's one contest I win, only this time I'm going to die because of it.–

–What are you talking about?–

–I wouldn't let them remove my breast even though I was told that a lumpectomy would diminish my chance for survival. But you know me. Vanity always wins out. After all, who wants a one breasted woman? A one breasted woman is a freak. So I chose the lumpectomy. And he's going to walk out on me anyhow, I can see it on his face. He's just hanging around until I leave the hospital. Maybe he'll wait a week, two weeks, maybe even a month but he'll leave. I must have been nuts. I don't even love him anymore. But he is gorgeous isn't he?–

–I didn't notice.–

–I lost Sandy because of him. Six months after he moved in with me I received papers from Ron's lawyer saying he wanted custody of our daughter. I am irresponsible. I don't take care of her. I'm either busy working or traveling or living with men young enough to be my sons. I am not the mother he wants for his child. That bastard, after what he pulled on the two of us. He won just like Irving but this time I was cheated out of my daughter. Adam said he'd marry me if it meant keeping Sandy but I didn't want to marry him. So there you have it. What the hell is the difference? They all walk out on me anyhow. Why does everybody end up leaving me?– She looks outside the darkened window. –I'd give anything to walk down a street, any street, to breathe the night air. I'll die when you leave.–

–I'm not leaving.–

–Of course you are. You'll go back to L.A.–

–Oh Mal.–

–Why do you live there? It's a nothing place. It isn't the country, it isn't the city. You go to sleep and when you wake up you're a little old lady.–

I spend the night in her hospital room. Every body turn leads to a moan. Through the night her eyes snap open. She looks around the room frightened, bewildered, not remembering where she is or why she's here. Then she sees me, whispers Julia and falls asleep. Adam comes and goes. Ceil comes and goes. 'The girls' telephone. Along with friends and business associates. Only I stay.

Mallory refuses to leave her bed. Her doctor wants her out and moving. I threaten to leave. She walks the corridor with me. She won't eat. The nurse's lips tighten, the doctor is losing his patience.

I feed her. She eats. Her moods clash one with the other. She threatens to jump out the window but is convinced she'll break every bone and end up an invalid with cancer. Her depression leaves. She sings a bawdy song trying unsuccessfully to stop the laughter forming in her throat. Her laughter gallops the hospital corridor disturbing other patients. The laughter gone she screams at her doctor, at the nurses, at the technicians who keep taking her blood.

I'm impossible she says gleefully. Good. Let them have cancer and see how cheerful they'll be. If they want entertainment they can go to a movie.

Mallory leaves the hospital. It's the staff who is now cheerful. A nurse says, give me a regular person any day. You can keep those celebrities.

FRIENDS AGAIN 1978

We're sitting at a bar drinking scotches. Mallory is three weeks into her radiation treatments. Adam has left as predicted. She looks at the bartender, pokes me with her elbow. –Cute huh. Look at that adorable behind. Men usually have flat asses. Ron's was flat and flabby. And their pee is so loud while ours comes out in whispered trickles.–

We laugh until our stomachs ache. The bartender is smiling.

–That's because we put toilet paper in the bowl to muffle the sound.–

–Julia, I don't believe you do that.–

–I do.–

–What's your secret for stopping a fart sound?–

Now we're choking on our laughter. The bartender is trying not to laugh. –He heard. You heard didn't you, you cute assed eavesdropper. What a funny word. Eavesdropper. You're the writer. What's the origin of that word?–

–I don't know.–

–Eaves dropper.–

–Mal, when did you start drinking?–

–I never started because I never stopped.–

–I'm taking you home.–

–Did y'hear that, bartender, whoever you are? I'm being taken home by my sweetheart. Isn't she beautiful? I know you think it.–

He turns away from us, a smirk on his face.

I hail a cab. –You're drunk Mal.–

–Damned right.–

–Why did you say that to him? What was the point?–

–We could have been but you didn't want to.–

–No we couldn't have.–

–Oh yes Julia. If you hadn't stopped, it could have ended up differently. But here we are. Ron left me and here we are. You'd love me even with one boob, wouldn't you? But not that round assed bartender. He would never love a one breasted woman, not that he even noticed me. The minute we walked in he started ogling you. Poor guy. And when I said we were sweethearts his heart sank. I could hear the damned thing go kerplop right down to his penis. That's where male hearts go, down to the penis.–

In her apartment we drink coffee. –Mallory, I want you to stop drinking.–

–You want!–

–You're going to kill yourself if you keep this up.–

–Drinking doesn't kill people. Life kills people. Did you know that drunkards never break their bones? They could fall from great heights and still not break anything. Did you ever fall from a great height? Nah, not you.–

–Mal, I'm moving here because of you. I'm bringing my kids here. I'm taking them out of school, away from their friends. I can't nurse an alcoholic on top of everything else.–

–I am not an alcoholic. I work every day Julia, every single day. Now you tell me how I can do that and be an alcoholic. I drink a lot,

I know that. Maybe if you had my life you'd understand why.—
  —Everybody has problems.—
  —Don't talk to me about everybody. I'm not interested in everybody.—
  —My kids are important to me.—
  —They should be. Love them but do yourself a favor. Don't get too attached because you never know. In one second everything can be taken from you. You blink an eye and suddenly someone is missing. My mother for example. She didn't have to die.—
  —She had cancer.—
  —You think I have cancer because she had cancer. Genetics, right. She never had cancer. The truth is my father's death was more significant to her than my life so she killed herself.—
  The day she came back to school, Mallory at her desk straight backed. I'm an orphan she said. My mother didn't love me.
  I watch her take a bottle of scotch from her cabinet and say nothing.
  —That's some fucking thing to live with Julia, your own mother committing suicide.—
  —Why did you wait til now to tell me?—
  —Because my cells are multiplying and I might never have another chance.—
  —Don't talk like that. You're going to get well. We both know it.—
  —We should have been lovers Julia. We really should have.—

We're seven. We're walking hand in hand to the five and dime. Our arms are swinging freely. We're eating broken pieces of chocolate. We're sitting in the movies. The matron in white walks the aisles eagle eyeing all the kids. A bunch of them throw spitballs but we don't notice. Mallory and I are transfixed. Ginger Rogers is turning in the arms of Fred Astaire, the hem of her gown swirls and swirls. Afterward we practice the steps. Mallory holds me while I twirl. Then I hold her and she turns and turns.

TIME 1994

Time is where I live, where I lived. In the spaces called life, in everyone who briefly stopped there. Don't kid yourself. It is brief. I am walking in Sunnyside. On Greenpoint Avenue. Taking in the ugliness of it. A voice calls. Julia. My heavens Julia. Where did you come from? She sees my puzzled look.

–Gerry from 48th Street. Don't you remember?–

–Gerry,– I say.

Who the hell is Gerry?

She's talking about how we haven't seen each other in over forty years. She's trying to catch up on time as if you ever could and even if you did, nobody's in the same time even at the same time. Some are living in the war zone of life while others, surrounded by enemy fire, remain observers. Family war zones, marital war zones and killing ones where millions of people vanish from the earth.

Jonathon, the vanished, insulting me with his deep breathing and pretty face. He's pissed, he's angry but he's still smiling. Not me. My words are attached to my fury. His lips are beginning to lose their smile. You're abusive he says. His words, my words. Years of caring, of wiping up piss, shit, pain, tears, all those meals, all that laundry and for what? Jonathon takes himself out of my life but not my mind. Gerry is talking but it's Jonathon I hear. She's saying something about suspected. Never suspected. What? What? But I don't ask because I don't really care. –You think you know somebody but you don't. Did you ever think of that Julia?–

Gerry. Gerry McLean.

–Of course I remember you. You went to St. Theresa's.–

–And now my grandchildren go there.–

–You mean you all live in Sunnyside. Amazing!–

–Aren't I lucky having them near me.– Photographs come out of her bag. –See. See.– She's bursting with pride. A young girl in a communion outfit grins into the sun.

Christ's bride.

The last time I saw Jonathon he came with Jesus. Jesus saved his life, made him see. A big cross hangs on his neck. Mother he says. Before I was ma or mom or Julia. Since he's found Jesus I'm mother. Jesus teaches us to love everyone. Love thine enemy he preaches.

Is he looking at me?

I'm a Jew, Jonathon. You're a Jew. Jesus was a Jew. Mary was a Jew. Joseph was a Jew. Jesus' disciples were Jewish. Jesus died a Jew. Remember Passover, renamed the Last Supper by the goyim.

The goyim! That's pretty hostile mother.

Do me a favor Jonathon. Don't give me lectures on Jesus. I know all about Jesus. Jesus is the reason the kids from St. Theresa's beat the Jewish kids up.

Jesus never taught violence.

Well something got screwed up somewhere because his followers leap with joy whenever they get the opportunity to kill one of us.

Won't you hear me out mother?

I'm not interested in hearing you out. Get it. Mother does not want to hear you out.

Jesus loves you.

Well good. Thank him for me.

The photographs back in her bag Gerry asks me if I ever see any of the girls from my club.

My club?

—You mean the Eleanor Roosevelt Girls? Don't tell me you remember them?—

—I could never forget them.—

—Why?—

—That was awful about Mallory. They never said what she died from.—

—She killed herself.—

—I don't believe it. Why would she do that? She was so famous. I used to read about her all the time. You know Julia, I was very hurt when I wasn't accepted in your club.—

–You wanted to be in our club?–

–Don't you remember? They said I was too young and I happen to know that Lynn was a year younger than me. I can't tell you how upset I was. I don't think I ever got over it.–

–Are you serious! It was only a club.–

–It was a big thing to me.–

–I can't imagine why.–

–Do you still write Julia?–

–No. I'm now a brain surgeon.–

She laughs. –I've forgotten how funny you can be. You're so lucky to have a career. I'd give anything to have one. Women of our generation. Well most of us but not the Eleanor Roosevelt Girls. You girls did alright for yourselves. Well maybe if you'd let me join.– She shrugs, says it was nice seeing me, then walks away holding her bag with the pictures inside. I watch her turn a corner.

Don't I remember. Oh I remember all right Gerry. You bet I remember.

Here in Sunnyside is my past. Behind locked doors, in movie houses that are no longer there. The past is your mother Gerry calling my mother a kike and you with your friends from St. Theresa's calling us Christ killers. The past is the dead, the misplaced and the living. The past is you Gerry asking me if I remember what you conveniently forgot.

THE NEXT FIVE YEARS WILL TELL 1978-1983

After six weeks of radiation there is no sign of cancer. The next five years will tell she's told. If after five years she's cancer free that will be a very good sign. Mallory knows that. She knows everything the oncologist tells her. She's read every book and article she can get her hands on. She's a breast cancer specialist. She also knows she's going to die on the last day of the fifth year, the way all guaranteed gadgets conk out on that last day. One of life's sick jokes. Like feeling lucky only to get hit by a car or lose your job, your mate, whatever is important to you.

Mallory reads about alternative medicine. She goes on a macrobiotic diet, gains twenty pounds. A guru teaches her to meditate, to silence her noisy mind. She sits in full lotus position freed from thought. Who wants to think? After weeks of meditation alien creatures decide to enter the empty spaces of her mind. She's disoriented, tells the guru. He explains the aliens are her own thoughts. Mallory knows better. She stops meditating. She drinks a quart of carrot juice a day. She drinks chlorophyll to cleanse her blood. She stops drinking booze. She joins AA. Her abstinence makes her a cranky evangelist. She gives up men. She's convinced they are the real aliens. They've ruined the earth and everything in it. She hates them, always has but never had the guts to admit it. She complains about everything: friends, relatives, political people, her staff. Life is shit. From the minute you're born it's shit. It's only when you're dying that you recognize the truth of it. As for happiness, what a crock that message is. Who's happy? Only idiots and they're so out of it they don't even know they're happy so what good is it.

Her rage is joined by bitterness.

The second year she teeters between negativity and hope. Negativity is clearly the winner. She starts drinking again. What's the point of abstaining now? Macrobiotic food is a bore. All those overcooked vegetables, all that brown rice, all those smiling waiters and waitresses. She's working hard to lose the twenty pounds she worked so hard to gain. She calls herself a walking time bomb. She works all hours of the day and night. AA is a joke. –I'm tripping over those twelve steps.– Her disdain for men includes women. She hates the entire human race except for those who have the guts to be different. Anger is healthy she says and Mallory is definitely angry.

The third year is Mallory's turning point. Life hangs in the balance and her life has never been better. She has cancer to thank. Cancer is a warning signal that all is not well in the world, that nobody is immortal. And when you know that, who gives a shit what people think. So what if you fuck up, so what if you're rejected? Do what you want and to hell with everyone. It's all in your attitude she tells me and Mallory's, according to Mallory, is great. If great means working all hours, buying everything in sight, spending money like it's going out of style, having five lovers at the same time, not in the same bed but at the same time then Mallory's attitude is great. Sex she says makes all cells happy. Cancer cells don't stand a chance in a sex happy body. I'm talking sex Julia. Not love. It's love that's the killer. People who love you know just what buttons to push. I'm going to beat this thing. If anyone can I can.

Julia, did you know it's the angry people who survive cancer? Passive ones go gently into that pie in the sky. You know the ones I'm talking about, the good ones, the ones that don't give anyone a hard time, the martyrs loved by all. Well I'm not going to make it easy for others and I'm not going gently into wherever it is cancer patients go. I'm going to scream my way back to health. Fuck you cancer. You're never going to lick me.

Her fourth year leads to nightmares and insomnia. She can actually feel her cancer cells roaming around her breast. They're holding meetings inside her body. They're planning field trips. No telling where they'll go next, those lousy bastards. And you know why they've returned? They returned because they knew about my negativity. It was as good as an invitation. You can fool everyone but not them. They know.

Her doctor prescribes sleeping pills, tells her to stop drinking alcoholic beverages and coffee. She takes the pills. Booze and coffee she will never give up. Til death do us part she says. Her laughter lacks sincerity. She brings strange men to her apartment. Overworked, underfed, overdrunk, underslept, oversexed, popping pills and drinking Mallory in five years has aged ten.

The frightened Mallory, the dying Mallory, drags me to her doctor's office for her five year checkup. We go in the examining room, wait for the doctor. A nurse enters, tells me the doctor wants to see Mallory alone. A bad sign.

Don't look at the waiting patients. Who knows what lurks in their bodies?

I close my eyes. When I open them, the room is crowded with naked bodies. An arm beckons. I am being propelled through a long tunnel. No I scream but no sound comes out. And it's all there, the maze of houses, the rubble, my looking frantically for my home not knowing the street or the number so even if I stop somebody for directions what will I ask? Somebody says Julia let's go.

Go? Where?

A dazed Mallory stands over me. We walk out into the bright sunlight. My eyes never leave her face. The news is bad. You can't miss it. —I can't talk now,— she says.

We go into a gourmet shop. She buys smoked salmon, white fish, Beluga caviar, black bread, bagels, cream cheese, apple pie.

Is this her last meal?

In her apartment she puts out the food, pops the champagne. —No toasts Julia. Please no toasts.—

—Mal, talk to me. No matter what, we'll see this through.—

—See this through?— She looks like she's about to cry. —There's nothing to see through. The cancer is gone.—

—Gone! That's great. Isn't that great?—

—If it's so great why am I depressed. When I had cancer I was alive. I lived. When I knew I was going to die I was happy. I want to be happy again.—

—So! Pretend you're going to die.—

—Do you have any idea of what the last five years were like? Do you know how many people I insulted, how many enemies I made, how many men I slept with, how much money I spent.—

—You always spent money.—

—Don't tell me what I've always done when you haven't any idea.—

—Ok. I won't say anything.—

—How was I supposed to know I'd live to pay my bills? My god, I owe a fortune.—

–Are you telling me you're broke?–

–I'm not exactly broke but I'm on the way.–

–Mal, you're alive.–

–Don't remind me.–

–Well, I'm going to drink to life even if you won't. L'chayim.–

She lifts her glass in the air.– Sure, l'chayim,– she mutters. And suddenly the two of us are laughing uncontrollably.

What Killed Mallory 1985

The limoges are packed and gone. All the 18th century men and women in their glass finery have left Mallory's for the local antique store. And the dishes and the glassware. But not the English bone china. Mallory's aunt Ruth has that.

Shirley Temple sits on my lap.

–Sorry I hit you so hard Shirley.–

She looks at me with her glass baby blues. I've washed and combed her hair so it's no longer matted. It's also no longer curly.

–I'm sorry to tell you this Shirley but you don't look good with straight hair. Actually you don't look like Shirley Temple anymore. Well none of us look like ourselves anymore.–

The tree outside Mallory's window. Bare. All the leaves gone except for one shriveled red hanging on a branch. Ceil didn't hang on. She fell quickly, was dead before the ambulance arrived. The car that lifted her into the air took off before she thudded to the ground. That's what the witness said, just took off like a bat out of hell.

At the funeral parlor Ruth talked nonstop about Ceil, how good she was, how she'd never been sick a day in her life except for minor colds. Imagine to die like that. Well at least she didn't suffer Esther said. A listening woman disagreed. That's not true. When you die that minute is like a year of your life. Time is very different. Ceil would tell you that if she could. A year she said. Tessie was furious.

A minute is a minute. Have it your own way the woman said walking away. Opinionated bitch, Millie said. No wonder Ceil couldn't stand her.

Mallory sat alone. Her eyes moved slowly around the room as if she couldn't take in what was happening. I went over to her, told her the service was about to start. She said she wasn't going.

–What should I tell the girls?–

–The girls! The girls. Why are you calling them the girls? We're none of us girls anymore.–

–But you're going to the cemetery.–

–No.–

–Mal, you loved Ceil.–

She rose quickly and left. Millie was suddenly next to me. –Where did Mallory go? We're ready to begin.–

–She isn't going to the funeral service.–

–What do you mean she isn't going? What kind of crap is that?–

–I don't think she's feeling well.–

–Oh! And I suppose we feel great.–

Ruth joined us. –Where's Mallory?–

–She left.–

–After all Ceil did for her. That's gratitude for you.–

Tessie and Esther came over. –Where's Mallory? They want to start the service.–

–She's gone.–

–If that isn't typical.–

At the cemetery I watched the lowering of the coffin, watched workers pile shovels of earth on Ceil's new home. That will be me one day. Someone will be watching while I'm dropped into a hole. From dust to what?

I took a cab to Mallory's. Her eyes were red and swollen. She talked about losses, her daughter, her off and on again relationship with Ilya, her failed marriages, her remaining aunts who never liked her. With Ceil gone what did she have? I wanted to say me but said nothing. She began crying, said she'd never appreciated Ceil, that she hadn't seen her in over a month.

—It's not as if she lived in another city. She lived right here in Sunnyside but I couldn't spare the time. She kept calling me, asking when I was coming over. I always said later. Well it's later now. Isn't it later?— She couldn't stop crying. —I'm no good. I never was. The girls are right about me. I'm a selfish bitch. Don't look at me like that. I am. You know I am. Poor Ceil. What kind of a life did she have. Stuck with a brat when she was twenty five. She gave plenty to me and what did I do. I robbed her of her life.—

She said she'd made a decision to leave the magazine, do something worthwhile with what was left of her life. When I asked what, she said write. Write I said not able to hide my surprise. Yes write she said.

Mallory went to her office but instead of giving notice she was given notice. My fate is sealed she told me. Two weeks later she left the country.

MALLORY — VENICE AND SPAIN 1986-87

In my closet there's a box of letters from Mallory. In 1985, letters from Venice about the mystery of the city, weaving in and out of canals, the magical winters when the tourists are gone, the opera, the heavenly food, taking the vaporato to Tortola. I'm writing she says and it's wonderful. Six months later.

Dearest Julia:

I made a mistake. Well we all make mistakes. I wrote Ilya. I blame you. You told me if I had trouble writing a good way to get started was to either write a journal or letters. I chose a letter. Would you believe, well of course you would, Ilya showed up two weeks later. No letter, no phone call, just an open door and standing there, Ilya all smiles. Naturally we ended up in bed. I know what you're thinking and I know you're right but Julia a lover who doesn't need a road map to find your clitoris isn't something to sneeze at. But Ilya is Ilya and the last week was fight bed fight bed fight bed. I couldn't write a word of my novel I was so upset. Not Ilya who pounded out his play on that damned noisy typewriter of his. A writer writes he said. It's as simple as that. He's ruined Venice for me. I can't stand the place. Nothing is the same. Where to go, how to stop this terrible feeling that every miserable thing that's ever happened to me is my own fault. Don't write me here. I'm leaving. Wait until you get a letter or phone call. I miss you terribly. I keep thinking if only Julia were here. If only Julia were here.

I love you - Mallory.

Dearest Julia:

Thanks for editing my novel. When I said be honest I wasn't asking you for a hatchet job. Your criticism makes me want to take the damned novel and set it on fire. It's my first attempt Julia and ok, maybe I didn't rewrite enough but you could have been kinder. I'm not you. I can't sit at my typewriter and knock out a novel every two years. I can't go to the typewriter the first thing in the morning and pant with joy at the thought of that blank page.

I remember when we lived together, the clicking of your typewriter through the night, all those words tumbling out with such ease. You were in your twenties Julia. I'm in my fifties. Do you get the difference?

Then think how hard all of this is for me. Leaving after Ceil died, the devastation, the guilt of knowing I hadn't seen her for so long and then to make this monumental decision to quit the magazine so I could fulfill my lifelong dream of writing only to come in to work and be told I'm no longer needed. Replaced after twenty years by a woman young enough to be my daughter. You say write what you know, you don't need to fabricate. Your life is enough. Do you know how frightening that is for me?

Love - Mallory

Dearest Julia:

The words are stored in my head ready to be released. When is the question? I've decided to relax and let whatever happens happen. You say write every day no matter what. Sorry. It doesn't work for me.

So this is my current life. I walk, I eat. I go to movies, I eat, I go to concerts, I eat, I go to the theater, I eat, I go to bullfights, I eat, I go shopping, I eat. There's the first breakfast, then the second which is usually churros and hot chocolate so thick I eat it with a spoon; then the three course lunch with wine; later the tapas and wine or cognac. At eleven there's dinner. I'm rounding out beautifully which suits my lover who thought I was too skinny for a woman. My clothes are falling apart at the seams. Well, why not? So am I.

In Madrid everybody my age is either married or dead. My lover is twenty five, thirty two years younger than me and painfully inexperienced. I fake my orgasms. He doesn't know the difference. Sound familiar?

I miss you. What's happening with your novel?

Love - Mallory

Dearest dearest sweet Julia:

Of course you were right. Now that I've settled down I am actually writing my life and what a life it's been. There I was with this unbelievable wealth of material. If it hadn't been for your cruel criticism. Cruel? You saved my life with your brutal honesty. I thankyou thankyou thankyou.

This is now *My Day*, not as inspiring as Eleanor Roosevelt's day but my day just the same. I wake up. Make coffee. I don't even dress or shower. I immediately sit at the typewriter and write. What can I tell you? It's as if somebody else were writing those words. They keep coming. Thank god this is Spain where dinner is very late. Mostly I leave the apartment around eleven and have dinner at a neighborhood restaurant. I'm unbelievably happy. God, what I've missed.

And you are right about lovers. They do sap your creative
energy. So I stay alone and love it but mostly
I love you love you love you - Mallory

IF YOU'RE SICK IT'S YOUR FAULT 1987

This is what the new experts say. And some old ones too. Your
health depends on you. Your body, once the property of doctors, is
no longer their responsibility. They oversee. They advise. They take
your checks and health insurance assignments but ultimately the
responsibility for your health is yours. So

If you've had a trauma or your thinking is not positive, if you've
been divorced or widowed or somebody close to you died or was
taken from you and still alive, a mate, a parent, a child, a friend, a
puppy, a cat, a parrot. Or if you lost your job, your pride, your
income, your home, you could get sick, very sick. But if you are positive and have faith in a higher power who knows better than you and
if you meditate or go to a house of worship, any one will do, or
belong to some support group, well then. You will be well.

Mallory's parents as you know died. Her father when she was
six, her mother when she was eight. But Mallory didn't get sick. Well
we all know that kids have great recuperative powers. At eighteen
she married Irving who screwed his first wife and ended up screwing
Mallory. Well once a screwer always a screwer. But Mallory's positive attitude plus a little hanky panky with the help of her friends
turned a painful rejection into a positive event. Namely a townhouse
and some valuable objects.

Eleven years later she married her second husband Ron who we
all know tried to screw her best friend. This too ended in divorce
which was ok because Mallory had Sandy, her six year old daughter
who she adored. But Mallory made the mistake of living with a man
twenty four years her junior which ego-upset her ex-husband. She

also had the nerve to take him into her bed while Sandra was there, well not in the room but there. Ron decided she was unfit to raise his daughter, now eight. Fathers who want to screw their child's mother's best friend while screwing the mother are alright but not mothers who do it with young men. The court took Sandra away from Mallory.

This was the trauma that did it.

Two years later, right on schedule Mallory developed breast cancer. Maybe if she'd gone to a synagogue or ashram or chanted away her losses. Or joined *Screwed Mothers Anonymous*. But she didn't.

Seven years later, in 1985, cancer free her beloved Ceil dies. Distraught beyond words but determined to change her life before it's too late she goes to *Eve* prepared to give notice. But before the words leave her mouth she's told she's been replaced as senior editor. Mallory could have been destroyed, should have been destroyed. But wasn't. No prayers, no chanting, no crystal floating above her fractured ego. Not our Mallory. Traveling with typewriter in hand she sets off for Venice to write her first novel. As planned.

The experts say it takes two years for the trauma to take hold, to attack your body, to move cells or multiply them, the list is endless. And remember Mallory had two major traumas this time. So right on schedule Mallory faced her second catastrophic disease.

In the middle of writing her a letter telling her how lucky she was to be in Spain, how the weather in New York was dreadful, how the homeless were multiplying like rabbits and how everyone blames them as if they were homeless for spite, how the subways have become one big smelly latrine, that radios the size of dog houses were screaming music wherever you go, in the middle of writing that letter, Esther calls.

–Julia, are you free for lunch?–

Esther has never asked me to lunch. –Is something wrong?–

–I'll talk to you when I see you. Can you?–

We're having lunch in my favorite Japanese restaurant. I'm trying to impress the waiter with the ten Japanese words I know. He

brings us sake. I look at Esther. How old is she? If Mallory is fifty
seven and Esther is ten years older that would make her sixty seven.
–You look great Esther.–
     –Thanks,– she says drinking her miso soup. Then, –Julia, I'll
get straight to the point. Ruth is certain she saw Mallory on Fifth
Avenue.–
     –She must have seen her double.–
     –She insists it was Mallory.–
     –Did she talk to her?–
     –She couldn't. She was on a moving bus.–
     –Esther, that's impossible. I just spoke with her a few days ago.–
     –You're not lying?–
     –Why would I lie?–
     –I called Madrid last night and this morning. There was no
answer.–
     –She was probably off somewhere.–
     –Do you think so?–
     –Yes. Ruth's got you all upset for nothing.–
     –I hope you're right.–
     –Esther, she's fine. She told me she's finishing her novel. She's
probably off somewhere celebrating. You know Mallory. She could
be in Italy or Morocco.–
     Esther sips her sake, sighs. –I hope you're right.–

     I receive an invitation to Jane Buzatel's one woman show at the
Brooklyn Museum. It's a gala opening, by invitation only. Jane,
whose life was overshadowed by her husband Harland Whitley,
famous painter, famous womanizer, famous boozer has finally come
into her own.
     It's a wonderful cold wintry night where you can actually see
stars. I walk up the stairs to the museum remembering the first time
I saw Jane at our Consciousness Raising group eighteen years ago.
As soon as I enter I see the CR group around her. One of our own
made it and at age eighty four. Vivid colors jump out of the canvases

on the walls.

Oh Jane, how fabulous.

I stand before each painting in absolute awe. How could she have been overshadowed by anyone? The force of the work, the vibrancy of the colors, her sense of space and movement. Well, come to think of it how could any of us been overshadowed. But we were.

Afterwards we have dinner together. Olivia Saldoni, the playwright who formed the CR group moves her chair next to mine.

–Mind if I sit here?–

–I'd love it. How are you Olivia?–

–Not bad considering. What are you up to?–

–I'm finishing yet another novel.–

–No more plays?–

–Too many people. I couldn't handle it.–

–I know what you mean.–

–How are the rehearsals going?–

–Come to the opening and you tell me.– Her expression changes. –Julia, you're a good friend of Mallory Grossman. Do you know what's wrong with her?–

–What do you mean?–

–She looks like hell.–

–When were you in Madrid?–

–Madrid! I saw her in New York.–

–You're sure it was Mallory?–

–Positive.–

–When?–

–Yesterday. She made me promise not to tell anyone, said she was flying back to Madrid today but when I went back to the hospital...–

–Hospital. What hospital?–

–Mt. Sinai. When I went back my sister–in–law told me she'd been taken to surgery this afternoon.–

–Why didn't you call me?–

–I thought you knew. I was really surprised to see you here tonight.–

—How could you think I knew? You just told me you promised her... Jesus, Olivia, one lousy phone call. That's all you had to do.—

—Julia, my play's in rehearsal, remember what that's like, my sister-in-law is very ill. I'm running back and forth between the theater and hospital... Look at you, you're hysterical.—

—I am not hysterical.—

—Yes you are.—

Suddenly the room is whirling above my head. Olivia is handing me a brandy. My friends surround me.

—I'm going to the hospital.—

—Julia, they won't let you in now. It's almost ten.—

—Wanna bet?—

—I'll go with you.—

—Olivia, I'll be just fine.—

—Julia, you almost passed out.—

—I didn't almost pass out. I was upset.—

Jane puts her arm around me, tells me not to worry, that it's probably nothing.

—No, it's something. She would never not call, never.—

While Olivia waits for the garage attendant to deliver her car my stomach goes into spasm. —What is it Julia?—

—My stomach is killing me.—

—I'm taking you to my place. In the morning we'll go to the hospital. Be reasonable Julia. They'll never let you in now.—

—I'll tell them I'm her sister, that I just flew in from California. Nothing will stop me from seeing her.—

AT MT. SINAI 1987

After sneaking in, climbing up the back stairs, after the yelling, refusing to leave her room, after the nurse in charge threatens to call the police, her doctor is on the phone giving me permission to stay the night. I sit in a chair watching a tube drip liquid into Mallory's veins. I throw white light into Mallory's body as if that will eradicate her cancer. I see her the way she was, beautiful, funny, bright, healthy. Not the woman on the bed with her drawn pasty face.

I watch the dawn come up. The view of Central Park is lovely. Maybe it will cheer her. I leave the room to get some coffee. When I return she's looking out the window. The nurse props her up, gives her a sip of water. I take her hand. –Mal.–

She looks up dazed. –Julia?–

She sleeps most of the day. Her doctor comes by, examines her, then motions for me to follow him out of the room. –She doesn't know so don't say anything.–

–Aren't you going to tell her?–

–In time. Meanwhile I think it advisable to contact the rest of the family. I understand she has a daughter.–

–Is she going to die?–

–Everybody is going to die.–

–I don't appreciate pat answers. How bad is it?–

–She has colon cancer. The prognosis is not good. However, some do survive. Let us hope she is one of the lucky ones.–

–I want to be there when you tell her.–

–That's fine with me. Tell me, does your sister suffer from depression?–

–Wouldn't you be depressed if you thought you had cancer?–

He pauses, tells me he'll arrange for a psychiatrist to visit her.

–A woman.–

–What's wrong with a male psychiatrist?–

–Too much testosterone.–

He laughs out loud. A snort follows the laugh. The nurses turn, look surprised. He goes behind the nurses station, marks something on her chart and grins at me. When he leaves one of the nurses says, –Well what do you know. He can actually laugh. We didn't know he had it in him.–

Ron invites me in. It's all very cordial. And cold. He says he's sorry Mallory is ill but he will not influence Sandra in any way. If she cares to visit Mallory that's fine with him but if she doesn't want to he will do nothing to convince her otherwise. Mallory he says has hardly been a mother to her, that because of Mallory Sandra has been undergoing therapy for years. He does not want to jeopardize her well being in any way. The woman was ill equipped to have a child.

–The woman. The woman. You asshole. The woman is lying in a hospital bed ridden with cancer.–

–Don't take that tone with me.–

Before I get a chance to answer an awkward Sandy enters the living room. There is nothing about her that even slightly resembles the fiery spirit of Mallory.–

–Sandra, I don't know if you remember Julia.–

–Hello Sandy.–

–She prefers the name Sandra.–

–It's good to see you Sandra.–

–Sandra, as you know, Julia wants you to visit Mallory in the hospital. The decision is strictly yours.–

–She's very ill and I know it would cheer her immensely to see you.–

–I was in the hospital but she didn't come to see me.–

–When was that?–

–When I was nine. They took out my appendix. I waited and waited but she never came.–

–Sandra, I don't know what happened. Maybe she was out of the country, maybe your father forgot to tell her.–

–I told her.–

A woman enters the room, takes Sandra's hand. –Hello Julia.–

–How are you Christine?–

–I'm fine. I was sorry to hear about Mallory.–

A vehement –I'm not going– bursts out of Sandy's mouth.

A spurt of spirit. Well, what do you know.

–You can see how it is,– Ron says smugly.

–I'll have you back here in an hour.–

–I'm not going. I made up my mind.–

–Sandra, she's your mother.–

–I've talked it over with daddy and we decided it was not a good idea.–

–I am not leaving without you.–

–You don't give orders here.–

–But you do.–

–Yes Julia, I do.–

I grab Sandy's arm. Ron moves toward me. –Don't come near me or I'll clobber you right in front of your women. Now you tell your daughter she has to see her mother or I'll tell her the truth about the ugly court battle you waged against Mallory so you could take Sandy away from her.–

–Fuck you.–

–Either you tell her she has to leave with me or I'll tell her about that other thing. You want me to tell her and Christine about that other thing. And don't bother pretending you don't know what I'm talking about.–

–Don't you threaten me.–

–Tell her.–

–You bitch.–

–Sandy, your mother has colon cancer. She has maybe six months.–

–Is there something wrong with your ears? She's not going.–

I reach out, sock him in the stomach. –You'd better believe she is.–

–Chrissie, call the police.–

Chrissie picks up the phone.

–Sandy, if you don't come with me you're going to regret it the rest of your life. All I'm asking is that you visit her.–

Christine puts down the phone. –Julia's right. You have to go.–

Sandra on the verge of tears looks into all the adult faces. –Daddy...–

He says nothing, glares at his wife. I turn to her. –Thanks Christine.–

She looks at me, then leaves the room with Sandy.

–Two of a kind. That's what you are, two of a kind.–

–Thanks for the compliment.–

–It wouldn't surprise me if you've been shacking up all these years.–

–And if we were we wouldn't need you to give us our cues.–

–Fuck you,– he says leaving me alone in the room.

SANDY AND MALLORY 1987

Mallory's eyes gradually open. She's unaware that Sandy is in the room. Her doctor is at the foot of her bed studying her chart.

–So, is it all over the damned place or contained. In other words am I going to have a shit bag attached to me the rest of my life?–

His stethoscope is on her heart. That done, his hand is on her stomach. –Does that hurt?–

–I asked you a question.–

–Yes it's contained and yes we removed it all and no you will not need the bag much longer. You are going to be fine.–

–For how long?–

–Mallory...–

–Because so far the little bugger has attacked my boobs and my colon. Where do you think it will head next? The brain, the bones, my uterus, my lungs. You know once it gets started it just gets carried away with itself.–

–I've explained to you that your breast cancer has nothing to do with this.–

–Bullshit.–

–You certainly are colorful Mallory.–

–Thanks Jack. If you're going to be sick you might as well be colorful.–

–Mallory, wouldn't you like to say hello to your daughter?–

She turns. –Oh my god. Sandy. When did you get here?–

Sandy moves cautiously to the bed. –Hello Mallory.–

–And flowers. How lovely.– Mallory's tears work their way around the bed. Only the doctor is dry eyed. –Let me look at you. You're beautiful. Isn't she beautiful?–

Sandy, stooped over, straightens up.

–This is amazing. I named you after my mother and what do you know, you look just like her and she was beautiful, wasn't she Esther?–

–Absolutely. Sylvia was the beauty of the family.–

–Sit by me Sandy. I want to hear all about you. How'd you find out I was here?–

–Julia told me.–

–I might have known. Tell me about yourself. Are you in school? What are you studying?–

The doctor stands at the door. –It looks like Julia found the perfect medicine. Mallory, I'll make you a bet and I'm not a betting man. You're going to beat this.–

–What's the bet?–

–If I lose I take Julia to dinner. If I win, Julia takes me to dinner. Is it a bet?–

Mallory laughs. –Some bet.– As he leaves she turns to me. –He's cute, lucky you.–

–A little young for me Mallory.–

–He's forty seven. What's ten years? So Sandy, what are you majoring in? Talk to me.–

I drive Sandy home. She talks incessantly. Do you think she likes me? Do I really look like my grandmother? Was she really beautiful or did Mallory just say it. I mean, I know I'm not pretty. Well anyhow, boys never look at me.

–Because you have the worst posture I've ever seen.–

–Do you think I'm pretty?–

–You can't miss. Everyone in that family is beautiful.–

–Why couldn't I live with Mallory? I wanted to, I told the judge

THE SEXIEST MAN IN AMERICA 1993

Once I had a friend I loved. Even when I hated her that love was there. Why do we love the people we love? Criminals are loved. And murderers. Some have fan clubs. Rapists are loved and child molesters and batterers, sometimes even by the battered. Thieves are loved and liars, especially those who look you straight in the eye. Sexists are loved often by seemingly strong independent women who should know better. But don't.

Mallory's latest lover was Russell Mitchell who directed and acted in movies that denigrated women. Her magazine devoted five pages to Mitchell claiming he was the sexiest man in America. A party was held in his honor. While Mallory mingled with her guests Russell eyeballed the women, holding them captive with his Hollywood stories, a boyish grin on his sixty year old face while photographer Mina Wormser shot photo after photo. Enough Mina he said loving every click of the camera. I walked away disgusted by the adoration he evoked, this man who used and abused women on and off screen. I was holding a glass of wine when I saw Russell next to me, his hooded eyes landing on my breasts.

–What are you looking at Russell?–

He held his ground, his hands cupped my breasts, a look of surprise on his face. –Well whadaya know.–

–Asshole,– I screamed. –Fucking asshole.–

His hands flew in the air landing at his sides. –Jesus, don't make such a big deal out of it.–

Mallory stood next to us. –What's happening?–

–She doesn't wear a bra. If that isn't fantastic for a woman her age.–

–Where the hell do you get off putting your hands on my breasts?–

Mallory wore a sick smile. –Honestly Russell.–

–That's it. That's all it warrants, an honestly Russell.– I grabbed my bag and headed for the door. Mallory blocked my way.

From a distance Russell watched.

–Let it go Julia.–

–Your boyfriend puts his hands on me and I'm supposed to let it go.–

–Julia, there are over a hundred people here. You're embarrassing me.–

–He gets away with it because there are a hundred people here!–

–Julia, they can hear you.–

–Then let them hear.–

–Julia, the party is for him. He's the guest of honor. Can't you chalk it up to his being drunk? Ok Julia, ok?–

–Are you saying when you're drunk you don't know what you're doing? Bullshit. When you're drunk you do what you want to do when you're sober but haven't the nerve. Now would you please move away from the door so I can leave.–

–Please don't. Julia, please.–

–Mal, I'm leaving.–

–Why are you putting me in this position?–

–The question should be why do you always side with the hims in your life and expect me to go along with it.–

–Do you have any idea of how bad you're making me feel? Are you aware of how embarrassing this is? Let it go Julia, for my sake.–

I pushed her away and went out the door.

The next day she sent me a huge bunch of flowers. Her note said, –Our love will outlive them all.– I never called to say thanks and she never called to see if I'd received them. A few days later she phoned. I said I was on another call and would call back. I didn't. She phoned a few times after that, once offering me her summer place to write.

We met in a restaurant. I was deliberately late. She looked up as I entered and rushed toward me. Julia she said warmly, her arm around my waist as we walked to the table. She toasted our friendship. I said nothing. She thought the two of us should take a trip together.

–Don't you think it unusual that with all our travels we've never gone anywhere together? How does Prague sound? You've never been to Prague have you?–

–You know I haven't.–

–Neither have I. So since both our father's families come from Prague don't you think it's a good idea? Finding our roots.–

–Can you leave just like that?–

–I'm the editor-in-chief, remember. If I can get tickets for next week would that be ok with you?–

–No Mallory, it wouldn't.–

–Why not?–

–Because I want to finish my novel.–

–How long will that take?–

–It depends on my characters.–

–I hate when you say that.–

–And I hate your pretending that nothing has happened between us.–

–Alright. Something happened.–

–But you don't want to discuss it.–

–What's the point of discussing it? You're always right.–

–No Mallory, it's you who are always right.–

She gulps down her wine, looks over at the people in the next table, then at me. Tears lay in her eyes. –Can you tell me what the novel is about or is that a secret?–

–It's about the Eleanor Roosevelt Girls.–

–Should I run for my life now or wait until I read it?–

–Don't worry. You won't recognize yourself. Nobody ever does.–

–I'm sure I will.–

–I doubt it.–

–And do we go sailing off into the sunset or does the sunset finish us off?– She lifts her glass. –To the Eleanor Roosevelt Girls.–

–To the Eleanor Roosevelt Girls.–

–I had to fight for that name. I thought that using her name would have a profound affect on our lives. One of her favorite sayings was, *What one has to do usually can be done.* When my life seemed unbearable I'd remember that saying. *What one has to do usually can be done.* Her mother also died when she was eight.–

–I know.–

–Remember when we saw her on Fifth Avenue. How old were we, thirteen? She was so pleased when we told her we'd named our club after her. Remember what she said?–

–Yes. The important thing in life is to do something useful and always have good will.–

–Then she turned her corner of good will and I turned the corner and bumped into Irving. I always managed to turn the wrong corner.–

–You didn't do too badly Mal.–

–Oh sure. I've really made an impact on other's lives. She dedicated her life to people, to every decent human cause. Wherever there was misery or something to be done you'd find Eleanor Roosevelt. What have I ever done that had a profound affect on anyone?–

–You've had some pretty profound articles in your magazines.–

–Please Julia, don't insult me by buttering me up. I know who I am and I know my shortcomings. I only hope the other members did better than me, that one of us lived up to her name.–

–How could we? She was a legend. We were poor girls from Queens.–

–Wouldn't it be great if you wrote a novel showing how naming our club after her changed our lives. Don't write us as we are but what we might have been.–

–Don't you think chance played a big part in her life? She did marry the President.–

–Yes but he became the President after he got polio, when she encouraged him to go on. *What one has to do usually can be done.* She became his legs, she did what he couldn't do himself. She reached people, she touched their hearts, she took action. She would have made her own path with or without him. Write it Julia, show how her name affected our choices, our lives. We'll have Claire run a Battered Woman's Center. Cynthia will empower women in her Drama Therapy classes. Lynn's dance company will celebrate the strengths and power of women's lives. Cleo will be a doctor who helps women with stress related diseases and Margaret, let's not forget Margaret, she will be the Mother Superior in some remote African village. And Annie finally goes to law school and fights for civil rights. There. Who needs reality when we can have this.—

—But we don't know the reality. We haven't seen them in years.—

—The reality is that nothing changes.—

—You've left me and Bettina out.—

—Forget Bettina and I didn't leave you out. The book I've suggested will win you the Pulitzer Prize.—

—Make it the Nobel. And you?—

—Just don't portray me as the woman I am. I'm not very happy with that woman.—

Without warning the two of us are crying. I decided to put my novel aside and go to Prague with her as soon as flight tickets were available. We were happy, we made plans. Then just before the coffee came we had one of those dry mouthed nausea in the pit of the stomach arguments, one of those arguments that seem to come from nowhere but never do. We parted with cold kisses and tight faces. She didn't call me afterward. Nor I her. Maybe it was about getting older, about losses. Maybe talking about Eleanor Roosevelt and remembering how it once was, how we used to be and the lost dreams was too painful.

PRAGUE 1993

One week later I flew to Prague. It was May, music month and Prague was filled with lovely sounds. I found a room in the Old Jewish Quarter, a room facing the Jewish Cemetery. Large black

crows screamed morning and night, calling to the twelve layers of
Jews, one on top of the other, their shrieks loud as if they were carrying centuries of dead Jews in their claws.

I walked around this ancient city with its pastel colored buildings holding winged stone chariots, gargoyles, etched drawings. I
walked down Parizka Street to the Old Town Square where musi-
cians popped up unexpectedly in outdoor cafes and restaurants. I
walked on narrow cobblestoned streets to Wenceslas Square to the
wide boulevard of Wenceslas with its restaurants, hotels and outdoor
cafes. In the museum gift shop I bought a crystal for Mallory and one
for me. Then back to Parizka and the ancient stone steps that lead to
the worn cobblestones of the Jewish ghetto.

City of Kafka, of Rabbi Loew and his clay golem turned man,
who defended the Jews of Prague against anti-Jewish gangsters; all
gone. I walked through the cemetery of dead Jews lying in their
overcrowded graves while gangs of German tourists took photos of
the enormous cemetery with its worn Hebrew writing on toppling
gravestones. I studied their expressionless faces as if they didn't
know it was their families or maybe them who wiped out this once
thriving community.

Life is so fragile. A Hitler comes along and seals the fate of a
people while others either go along or turn away.

There is a list of dead Czechoslovakian Jews, Holocaust Jews,
carved on the wall of the synagogue adjoining the cemetery. I see the
name Grossman but where is Jaffe? The list incomplete I'm told.
You turn one corner and you have one life; another corner means
another life. But sometimes there are no corners to turn. Kafka knew
that.

On Vocickova Street there's a wine cellar with long tables and
benches. I half expect to see Mallory sitting next to me. I walk
through the day on winding streets looking at wonderfully shaped
roofs on colorful buildings. Mallory would love it here. The ghosts
of our dead families would float above our heads.

At night Kafka walks with me across the Charles Bridge through

the fog on his way to the Castle. One of the religious statues on the bridge is of Jesus, a gold halo of Hebrew writing circling his head. Mallory stands in front of the statue, her arms outstretched as if she is the one being crucified. What are you doing here I ask. What am I doing here? Didn't we say we were going to Prague?
The birds are my alarm clock.

I constantly think of Mallory. She would love Prague, the beer cellars and wine cellars and the statue filled Charles Bridge with stairs that go down to the Vtlava River and outdoor cafes. But she wouldn't like Terezin anymore than I did, that model concentration camp, its horrors so cleverly hidden that even the International Red Cross was fooled. Primped and fixed with false cafe fronts and music and smiling Jews all dressed up for the occasion, afraid to open their mouths knowing a train was waiting to take them to Auschwitz-Birkenau sooner rather than later. She would cry as I did viewing the artwork. All that talent, all that life, all that vitality, all that hope, all those dreams murdered.

But she would love my animated journalist cousin who I found quite by accident, her wit and intelligence, her style, her cluttered apartment with its collection, artifacts that she shleps from country to country, this time from London back to the Czech Republic, called Czechoslovakia the last time she was here. But not her chain smoking boyfriend who sits silently, a comic book expression on his face.

MALLORY AGAIN 1993

I've barely landed in New York when I call Mallory. A voice tells me the number has been changed to an unlisted one. The operator tells me she cannot divulge the number at the customer's request. I ask for the supervisor who tells me in her computer voice that she's sorry and then, have a nice day. I call Mallory's office. The receptionist tells me she's no longer there.

No longer there?

I call Esther. Ruth answers. Esther had a stroke. After the shock I ask for Mallory's new number. Ruth says she wasn't aware that she'd changed her number and doesn't have it. I call Olivia. She knows nothing. I call others. Nothing. I grit my teeth and call Russell. He's not in. He's never in. I fall into a deep sleep, awaken, my body shaking. Where can she be? I call Russell.

–You've got some fucking nerve calling me...Jesus Christ, it's four in the morning.–

–I'm worried about Mallory. I can't reach her. I was hoping...–

–We're no longer an item. Don't you read the papers?– He slams the receiver down.

Bastard.

In the morning I call her summer home. Her machine message says she's not in. I rent a car and drive there. There's a 'For Sale' sign at the entrance to the house. In the flower garden Mallory is talking to people. She waves to me as if nothing happened, then motions me to come over. –Julia, meet the Kahns. They've just bought my house.–

We sit in the kitchen drinking coffee. –What have you been up to Julia? Did you finish your novel?–

I don't tell her I've been to Prague. I can't. –Why are you selling the house?–

–I'm simplifying my life. So, did you finish it?–

–I called your office.–

–Oh did you?–

–What are you going to do Mal?–

–Esther had a stroke.–

–I know. Why didn't you call?– I ask without thinking.

–What could you have done?–

–Be supportive I guess.–

Jesus, why am I lying?

–You were very angry with me, remember?–

–Mallory, why do we fight?–

–I don't know. We always did.–

–I don't understand why you left the magazine.–

–Left it, is that what they told you. I didn't leave it, I was let go, replaced by Nina Black, wife of the Evan Ladro. I committed the cardinal sin. I got old. They claimed I was out of touch, that's what they say when they want to get rid of you. You're out of touch. And don't kid yourself. Everyone older is considered out of touch. As for new horizons they tell me I'm overqualified which is another way of saying, too old. But why should I complain. Look at poor Esther. She can't talk, can't move, can't anything. She just lies there staring. Why do they let us linger? Why can't they just let us die? I'm alone. I might as well face it. I had a mother, a father, I had husbands, a daughter. I had Ceil. I had Esther and now nobody.–

–You have me. You'll always have me.–

–Do I? We've drifted apart Julia. Let's not kid ourselves.–

–That's not true.–

–Don't lie. You never did. Look, I've been aware of it for some time. I'm actually afraid to talk to you. You're so judgmental. I know you don't approve of my life, well you never did, did you and maybe you were right but it is my life Julia, not yours and I have the right to do with it whatever I choose if there is such a thing as choice. I'm beginning to doubt that along with everything else.–

–I'm sorry you feel that way about me.–

–Don't be sorry. It happens. People drift apart. Sometimes for no reason at all. But I want you to know that my feelings for you have never changed. I loved you the day I met you and I still do but it's not the same, is it?–

–You sound like we're never going to see each other again.–

–We will. We're glued together Julia. I don't know why but we are.–

THE LAST CHAPTER 1994

We are shaped before we're a dot on a dot.

If your parent's sex was good during conception you will be one happy embryo. And if the sex continues to be enjoyable particularly during the third trimester you're going to be a very ecstatic fetus. And if your mother is content and she's bound to be with all that great sex you will be swimming happily in that amniotic sac. So the experts say. In other words your parent's sex life at that crucial time is directly responsible for your happiness.

Finally an explanation for my negativity. Thank you experts for finding our scapegoats. However would we find them without your help?

And those of us who overnight became old wouldn't be searching for wisdom and patience if experts didn't assure us it's part of the Old Age Package.

Mine must be lost in the Post Office.

One thing they don't have to tell me. All humans are afraid to die unless religion has sold them their heavenly reward, that pie in the sky.

Make mine lemon meringue.

Mallory may have run out of life but she didn't run out of money. Half went to Sandy, the other half to me. Now I won't be able to join the homeless on a street corner.

I didn't make Mallory the party she wanted. Having friends and enemies in the same place at the same time is not my idea of fun. What I did was rent a house in Montauk and invite the Eleanor Roosevelt Girls to join me.

I arrive a day early. The air is cool and salty, the kind of day both Mallory and I loved. Autumn. Our favorite season. Walking along the beach I am lulled by the gentle movement of the sea. Seagulls soar to the heavens. Winged dancers. I watch the sunset, the orange and red afterglow that never fails to excite me. I drink a glass of champagne, then another, my glass raised to the first star, the one that always shines the brightest. Mallory's star. Someday someone will be looking up saying Julia's star.

I sit on the sand and wonder about the rest of my life. What to do about Richard. Should I come riding in on a white horse and carry Richard off with me? He is definitely the fairest of them all, sweet and loving and there aren't too many of those around. Then maybe I'm meant to be alone. I've finally reached the age where you're supposed to know everything only to discover I know nothing. Maybe this isn't all there is, maybe there is something somewhere else, later or in a different place. But I'm not taking that chance just now.

I stand by the sea. Waves come in, enormous foaming white mouths. I feed them my pills, the death pills I've been collecting for years, long before Mallory's walk into the ocean. How many times have I counted them, held them in my hand, my mouth open like the foaming waves. Only to be stopped by the ringing of the phone or seeing my mother, my sons, my friends at my graveside knowing I caused them pain.

Maybe I am only a dot on a dot on a dot but this dot along with other dots reached out to one another in love and friendship, supported one another, fought abusive husbands and cheating husbands and one who incestuously abused his daughters. Like Rabbi Loew's golem we were way ahead of our time. And didn't even know it.

The next day I sit on the beach feeling a wave of joy, something I haven't felt in years. And suddenly I see them coming toward me kicking the sand. Laughing. Cynthia, Lynn, Annie, Claire and Cleo looking as they did all those years ago. My friends, my comrades, my heroes. The fabulous Eleanor Roosevelt Girls.

About the Author

Bonnie Bluh is an author, playwright, singer, and award winning actress. Her first play, a musical, *Toe Toe Lee Lo*, was written when she she was 7 years old and performed at PS 150.

She is a New Dramatist Alumna. She has lived throughout the United States, in Spain, and in Israel and presently makes her home in New York City.

This is her fourth book.

	DATE DUE		
MAY 1 8 1999			
JUL 1 7 1999			
AUG 1 7 1999			
BUR			
NOV 0 9 2001			
AUG 1 4 2004			
MAY 1 7 2007			
AUG 0 9 2007			
MAR 0 8 2008			